ENCHANTING THE DRAGON LORD

Kingdoms of Lore Book Three

ALISHA KLAPHEKE

PROLOGUE

Dorin

D orin woke shivering and blinking. The expected warmth of a hearth fire and the usual hearty scents of fresh country bread, ham, and boiled eggs were absent. Dorin's head was heavy, and he struggled to think through a thick fog. Why was it so dark? It was as cold as the underworld...

He felt for the bedcovers and found only stone. His heart ticked faster. Where was he? Panic clawed through the fog of his thoughts. His hand brushed his leg. He was naked. And what? Lying in a cave? What in the name of Rigel and Ursae was happening? His eyes adjusted to the scant light coming from one end of the dark space. He held up a hand, and his fingers stuck together with some disgusting material. He sniffed.

The scent of blood had him on his feet in a breath.

"Hello! Anyone here?"

His voice echoed off the stone walls as he hurried to the cave's entrance. He had no memory of leaving the castle, of taking to the trails or...or anything. At the opening, the mountains stretched wide beneath the rising sun. This was no ordinary cave. He stood on Spike Peak, the highest point in the Balaur Mountains, a place no elf or man could reach, and he was covered in blood.

CHAPTER 1

BRIELLE

Brielle tossed her crown onto the nightstand and waved her maids from the chambers. "Thank you, thank you, all. I am finished with princessing for the night. See you bright and early, I'm sure."

She shut the door and immediately began scrounging through her armoire for her hidden pair of trousers. Thank the stars her older brother, Etienne, had been a slender youth two years back when she'd nicked these. Tugging the trousers on under her skirts, she fell onto her bed. Once they were belted, she rolled and leaned over the side to grab the muddy boots she'd stolen from her horse's groom. She laced them up and—oh, no. Her toes jammed right through the end.

Slamming a fist on the bed, she gritted her teeth. She had to get out of the castle. The whole place was the wrong fit for her and always had been. She was dirt and legends. The life she had been born to was silk and dark agendas. "Where can I get boots?" she muttered.

Ah. Etienne.

Her brother would still be in the great hall, feasting and rubbing elbows with Wylfenden's nobles, flirting with that pretty, golden-haired young lady from the lowlands. He'd be busy for hours yet. Perfect. Etienne insisted on grooming his own horses fairly regularly, so, unlike most princes, he had muck boots. Stall-mucking boots were much better suited to searching the foothills for dragon artifacts than any fine riding footwear.

Brielle stood up and smoothed her skirts over the trousers. "There." Leaning against the door, she listened for her guards. "Hmm." Still there, right outside the door. Sometimes, if King Raoul—her father and the worst of the worst—wasn't paying attention to her, which was often, he called them down to the main doors. But not tonight, it seemed. How to get them to let her leave... hmm. Confidence could do a lot.

She pushed her doors wide and smiled at her guards. "Good evening!"

Sputtering, they bowed hurriedly and glanced at one another, eyes bunching in confusion.

"I have to visit Etienne's chambers. I don't need an escort."

"Yes, my lady," George said, his heavy jaw working. "You'll return shortly?"

"Oh, yes. I'll only be a moment."

Javier gave George a shrug. She took off at a quick walk down the hallway before they could stop her.

Etienne's apartments were dark and beautiful. Carved wooden falcons and snarling bears glared from the door, and his guards' uniforms were embellished with Etienne's personal symbol. On each of their shoulders, gold-threaded embroidery showed a lynx rampant on a field of white.

"I have a gift for my brother." She sidled past the men and turned the bronze doorknob.

They didn't say a word but remained at the open doors, watching her like those falcons on the door. She moved through Etienne's sitting room and into his bedroom, where the guards most likely wouldn't follow.

"Where do you keep your footwear these days, Brother?" Not in the armoire. Not under the bed like a normal person.

"Princess? Do you need assistance?" Etienne's guards seemed to be growing impatient. They were probably thinking back to when she was little and she had slathered his pillow with honey and loosed a particularly industrious marmot inside his chambers.

"No, no. Just fine." The boots were in the chest, and she had them in hand. A fine bottle of coastal red sat on Etienne's desk. Nabbing that as well, she hurried past the guards and went back to her own rooms.

When she arrived, George and Javier gave her inquisitive looks. It was so tiring having people watching her all day, every day. She held up Etienne's boots. "Promised I'd clean them myself." They frowned, unbelieving. "I lost a bet," she added.

"Ohhhh." They chuckled and nodded.

She set the bottle of wine on the table outside her doors. "I certainly don't need that. If it went missing, well, I can't say I'd even notice." Throwing George a smile, she left them.

That should do it. The doors creaked as she swung

them closed. Her desk chair served nicely to keep the handles from turning. One never worked right anyway. She'd broken the left during a challenging night arguing the tightness of braids with her lovely, old nursemaid, Celeste, ages ago.

Boots and short cloak on, she leaned against the door and listened. "Go on," she whispered to herself. "The coastal red isn't going to drink itself."

"It's about time we get extra for trying to keep up with the Fire of Wylfenden," Javier said quietly. George laughed.

Oh, they were so hilarious, using her nickname. Heat built in Brielle's chest, anger making her temples pound. Father called her the Fire of Wylfenden. The name was a twist on what he did to those with magic—burned them alive—and her exuberant personality. He thought she was going to be the next leader of his Broyeurs.

She would rather die.

Yes, she enjoyed hunting—ancient artifacts, not people. She swallowed a bitter taste on the back of her tongue as she took her long, braided rope from its spot under the loose stone by her hearth. Slowly, quietly, she opened the window to her courtyard, slung her bag over her shoulder, and climbed out of her window.

The flat stone of the courtyard hit Etienne's boots hard, and she exhaled, landing safely. She hated leaving the rope hanging, but she hadn't come up with a solution to that problem yet. So far, she'd been lucky with her escapades. She pulled up her hood, hurried to the secret tunnel's fake tile opening near the fountain, then started down the ladder, making sure to secure the entrance after she was inside.

It was utter and complete darkness down here, but she'd been through the tunnel—originally built so royals could flee from revolutions or enemy attacks—so many times that she knew the way and had no need for seeing. The walls were damp against her palms, the passage only wide enough for one person to pass through at a time. Right now, she was under Father's throne room. She flicked her fingers upward, wishing she had the guts to do that to his face.

Moonlight shone from the tunnel's exit, and she pushed the stiff-hinged, iron door open to find the foothills of the Ecailles Mountains. The tang of new grasses, blooming maples, and spring mud filled her nose as she stepped over a snow drift that hadn't quite given up yet.

Picking her way over silvery boulders, she found the path to her somewhat secret cabin. Etienne had helped her build it two years ago along with help from Celeste and a few men paid to keep their mouths shut. If Father learned about her tramping about in the mountains, she'd be locked in her chambers for eternity. If he discovered most of the things she dug up had an element of magic to them, well, she'd be bound for burning at the stake like all the water mages and witches.

She let out a breath. The cabin was as she'd left it—a small bed near a nightstand in the corner, moonlight painting the coverlet gray, and a spare chest for extra clothing and blankets. She always worried Father would find the cabin and tear it apart.

Once she'd shed her skirts and all the ridiculous garb required of a woman, she donned a man's shirt, tucked it into her trousers, and headed into the night.

She'd worn a path to a new dig site up an incline near Fire Veil Falls, where the sunrise lit the water and made it look like flames. The spot was amazing for artifacts. So far, she'd discovered an engraved bowl with minimal damage, four polished jade stones wrapped in silver and gold wire, and dragon teeth that had been drilled so that loops of gold could pass through, like charms of a sort. She kept them on a chain around her neck but only wore the grim necklace at the cabin.

If anyone saw her with dragon teeth charms, she probably wouldn't survive the day. Plain dragon teeth would be fine. They held no power, and, in fact, Father had employed a dragon and the man who trained the creature in the last war. The incredibly short-sighted and belligerent King of Wylfenden didn't think of dragons as magical because he didn't believe they used to shift into a human form like the old stories of Lore claimed. He just saw them as animals. And they were now. But with the gold loops, Father's Broyeurs would see the teeth as a totem, a magical item, and punish her for possessing them. She knew the teeth and gold loops didn't have any magical properties, but maybe in the next layer of dirt and stone, she'd find something that did.

With her spade and brush, she got down to business, the moon lighting her way. The night was chilly and lovely, the feel of it energizing her as she worked. The mud under her manicured nails made her grin.

A rounded shape appeared in the dirt, its edges smooth and its top side cut here and there.

Were those runes?

She used her brush to shift the clods of mud away from

the object but quickly grew impatient and began digging it out with her fingers.

It was a stone, smooth and dark, and she couldn't quite tell in the moonlight, but yes, those did look like runes. She held it carefully, palms cupping its oval shape.

A humming rose in her ears. But was it her imagination? Was she hoping so hard for magic that she was hearing things? She listened again. No, it was there. Incredibly slight and subtle, but the hum was definitely there.

She packed up, then headed back to the cabin to wash the stone at the spring beside the path. She lit a lantern and brought it to the spring as well so she could see the scratching more clearly. The dirt came away from the cuts and curves.

"Oh, they are runes!" she whispered to herself, her voice too loud in the night.

She had no idea how to read them. Of course, there were no scrolls or books in the castle library about magical topics. Rubbing them clean, she spoke over the runes, whispering to them like they could hear her.

"What do you mean? Can you tell me your purpose? I could use some help."

The spring breeze tousled her hair and sent a shiver down her back. Was that the hum of magic again?

An owl called out, and she jumped. She laughed at herself for being a fool, then dried the stone on her trousers and readied to sneak back to the castle. Because of the visiting nobles, she'd be called for breakfast shortly after dawn, so she had to get back to bed before Celeste came to wake her.

As risky as it was, she slept with the stone under her pillow. It was just too fantastic to hide away. She'd bury it with her other findings, hiding it from Father's Broyeurs, but not yet.

That night, she dreamed of dragons.

CHAPTER 2

DORIN

The wind whispered, go, go, go. He stretched his wings and soared away from the peaks and toward the place where the humans lived. He could feel the destination in his bones, could sense the exact spot where he was meant to land, to see who needed his help. Why would someone summon him? Flying toward the castle, he tried to remember his name, but it was as if he had never been more than this—scales, wings, teeth, and hunger. How could he help one of these humans? He had no knowledge of their doings.

He tried to turn, tipping his wings and changing his direction on the wind currents, but the whispers, the pull, the urge to find the one who had somehow called him steered him back toward the castle. He wanted to see this human who had beckoned him, for it had to be one of them. There were no dragons here. How dare this person drag him from his nightly hunting?

The night was nearly gone, and he would lose himself

even further soon, just as he did every dawn, and now he had to waste hunting time to seek this person out. His lip curled, and he tasted the spark of his dragonfire deep in his throat.

The tug of whatever strange magic this was drew him into a closed courtyard. How did he know what this was? He landed, shaking his head and wishing he could shed the strange fog that hung on his every thought. Where was this human who called for help? Why did he care so much?

A pinch in his chest pulled him toward a set of windows. The curtains hadn't been pulled, and he could make out the shape of a human female sleeping in a bed, a fire dancing in the hearth on the other side of the room.

He set one talon against the glass gently. *Wake, human. I am here. What pulls me from my hunting?* he thought in her direction.

He'd never tried to communicate with humans. Would she understand?

The glass under his talon cracked. The female sat up, then turned to face him. Her hair was like fire itself, red as flame, and her eyes widened in wonder. She slowly stood and came to the window.

Dawn broke across the sky, and he fell backward, the terrible sickness that always took him at sunrise somehow catching him by surprise once again.

CHAPTER 3
BRIELLE

A clicking sound woke Brielle, and she instinctively grabbed for the rune stone. She rolled over to see a shape at her windows. Rubbing sleep-blurred eyes, she sat up.

Glittering, slitted eyes. Shining scales. Wings.

Dragon.

Her heart leapt as she forced a scream back down her throat and crawled slowly out of bed, pocketing the stone in her nightdress. If she screamed, Father's men would have the dragon tracked, hunted, enslaved.

The animal cocked its head like it was studying her, and she tried very hard not to be afraid. Her hand trembled as she set her fingers against the jagged crack in the window, directly opposite the dragon's talon. Its quick gaze touched her hair, then her face, and the tightness of the scales around the eyes showed a question almost or a longing. But for what? Why was this creature here in her private courtyard?

The sun's first rays crawled over the walls, and the dragon exhaled, breath steaming the windows. Then it toppled backward. She pressed her face against the glass to see the dragon lying in the courtyard, shaking, eyes shut. Sparks of pale light flashed around its body, and the dragon threw its head back like it was in pain. The light grew brighter and filled her vision, blocking the creature from view. When the sparking flashes stopped, in place of a dragon was a man.

Brielle stepped back, hands bunching in her nightdress. Magic.

If the guards spotted this man, he was as good as dead. They'd hand him over to the Broyeurs and he'd be doomed, his pyre readied, his life taken.

But could they burn a dragon? How was he also a dragon? Was this like the ancient stories?

First things first. Brielle had to get him out of the castle. She donned her trousers—with the runed artifact in her pocket—shirt, and boots again. Next, she grabbed a plain, black cloak and a pair of too-large trousers she'd nicked from a stable boy last moon. She'd hoped the trousers would fit, but alas. She'd only kept them in hopes of altering them at some point for an extra pair. Everything tucked into her bag, she climbed down the rope to the courtyard.

There was no time for this. Celeste would be in her room in moments to give her breakfast. The sun had risen, bathing the courtyard in pink light. Anyone passing the windows of the corridor that led to her chambers and beyond would be able to look outside and see the naked man lying unconscious in her courtyard. And soon, the guards would do their morning rounds, taking the door to the courtyard—which was a stone's throw from the door to her chambers—to inspect the area.

"Not good. Not good." Jumping from the rope, she landed hard, then ran to the man. "Wake up," she hissed, noticing blood on his hands and down his neck. She swallowed, hoping it wasn't human blood. Regardless, he was certainly helpless now and needed aid. "Please. I'll help you, but you must wake up. I can't carry your big self, magic man."

She moved the sheet of his golden hair away from his face. The point of his ear caught her eye first.

An elf.

"Also not good." She took just a second to appreciate his strong features, wide shoulders, and, well, the rest of him, then she looped her arm around one of his. "Wake," she said in the elven Balaur tongue.

No one but Celeste knew she could speak the enemy's language. She'd learned it from old scrolls in the library and one of the kitchen women who had, in her youth, worked for a rural Balaur goat farmer near the border.

The man—oh, elf—opened his eyes and looked directly at her. The look hit her like an arrow to the chest, and she nearly let go of his arm.

"Where am I?" he asked in the elven tongue.

"The worst place you could possibly be. Now, get up and put this on quickly."

She helped him stand, then put a cloak and a pair of trousers into his hands. He swayed, and she kept him upright by putting her back to his until he seemed steady.

"At any moment," she said, watching the door, "my

guards will make their rounds and catch you here. They will kill you." She turned and set a serious look on him, willing him to understand.

"I still cannot fathom how I ended up here." Finally able to stand on his own, he pulled the trousers on and buttoned them up. With a practiced movement and a bit of a flourish, he threw the cloak on. He didn't move like a farmer or a servant. He seemed accustomed to fine cloaks.

"Who are you, anyway?" She grabbed his hand and dragged him toward the secret tunnel. When he didn't answer, she glanced over her shoulder to see his full lips pulled into a straight line, his golden hair falling over one cheek. The Source and all the goddesses save her—he was gorgeous. "Fine. Don't tell me. I'm only saving your life here."

She led him through the tunnel, and he didn't utter a word as they maneuvered through the dark passage. Voices carried from the courtyard and bounced off the tunnel walls.

"What is this?" the voice of George boomed down the passageway.

"She's climbed out!" It was Celeste.

Brielle walked faster. "Curse it. They found my rope. You just ruined my life, you know, handsome dragon elf."

"I'm sorry, what? And why were those people speaking Wylfen?"

The way he said the name made it sound like a curse. Maybe it was a curse in his language. "Because that is Wylfen Castle," she said, "and if you don't hurry up, it'll be the last place you see."

"Wylfen Castle..."

The words came out of him like the darkest spell, the sounds stretched and lowered like the name of her birthplace bore the weight of every war his people had fought against hers. He had to hate her kingdom. He surely hated her right along with it.

Brielle pushed through the tunnel's iron door and hurried along her usual route. Between a stand of pines, the cabin came into view. "That's my place. We'll be safe there. No one knows about it except my brother, who has likely forgotten, and Celeste, who would die before she outed my proclivity toward unchaperoned mountain excursions."

The elf rubbed his head as he followed her inside.

"Sit there." She pointed to the bed. "Let's get the blood off of you, then you can tell me—"

"Did you say *dragon?*"

"Well, yes, you dolt. Of course I did. How did I not know that dragon magic still exists? Are there a lot of you?" She dipped a cloth into a bucket of stale spring water, then wiped his filthy fingers.

He looked at her like he had no idea what was going on. It seemed his hatred of her and her people was momentarily forgotten. "It's my brother who can speak to the creatures," he snapped, his face bunching in confusion and anger. "I have no dragon magic."

"Oh, no? Then explain to me why you tapped on my window as a dragon, then changed into an elf as soon as dawn came. I'd say that's pretty magical. And if you didn't already know, magic is punishable by death here in Wylfen."

He shot to his feet, and she stumbled back, catching herself on the side of the bed. "I...I was a dragon..."

"You were." She stepped closer, moving very slowly. He looked about ready to explode, like one of Etienne's firesnaps.

Spinning to look out the cabin window, he ran both hands through his thick hair. His bare arms showed where the cloak pulled away. Thick muscles shifted under his smooth skin. Dragon elves were apparently very strong. She swallowed. She hadn't seen a male this well-built since she'd last laid eyes on Fae Prince Werian of the Agate Court. Her friend Zahra would have so much fun hearing about this adventure. If Brielle lived to tell it.

He was pacing now, his long strides covering the length of the cabin in five steps before he had to turn to walk back again. "I've been living in the mountains for a month now." Speaking more to himself than to her, his words were quiet and disjointed. "Every night, I lose myself and have no idea what happened overnight. I wake naked, and oftentimes, I have blood on my face and hands." He whirled on her, eyes blazing. "Not that I should even be speaking to you, Wylfen."

She ignored the venom in his address. "Hunting," she explained instead.

"What?"

"I would assume dragons need to eat a good bit considering their size," she added. "I bet you hunt at night when you're a dragon. Can you believe this? You are a dragon!"

His lip curled, showing one sharp, elven incisor. "It's not a happy circumstance."

"I didn't say I was pleased about it."

"Your face did." He raised one thick, blond eyebrow.

She spread her hands wide. "All right, it's fascinating. I'm sorry. I can't imagine how bizarre this is. I'm guessing from your response that you had no idea people could shift into dragons anymore either?"

His sneer said he didn't want to discuss this—or anything else—with her. "Definitely not. The last recorded dragon with human or elf shifting abilities was the goddess Nix, right?"

"Her mate, I believe," Brielle said. "I can't remember his name. Speaking of names, what's yours?"

"I'd rather not say."

"I see. Well, I'd rather not have my evil father discover the rope I use to escape my room at night, but you've ruined that for me, so spill it. I have earned that much, to know whom I'm saving and why I'm risking my neck."

"Wait." His gaze slid from her face down her body, then back up again. "You live in the castle. In Wylfen. Who are *you?*" The question was a sharpened sword.

"Since you seem a bit cloudy upstairs," she said, pointing to his head, "I'll explain what you'll figure out eventually. I'm Brielle, Princess of Wylfen."

His eyes flashed. A bit of the dragon seemed to peer out, and a thrill of fear and delight shot through her. Fascinating.

"My enemy." His deep voice rumbled like a storm coming over the peaks.

She shook herself. "Oh, right. Enemy. Except for the saving your life thing." What a piece of work this elf was.

"I'm Prince Dorin of Balaur."

The spark of righteous indignation went out of her, and she shivered. The eldest prince of the elves. The one who would be king, and soon, if the scouts were right about King Mihai's worsening cough. Dorin had led armies against her people and would do so again when the time called for violence. Did she hate him though? Her country was such a horrible place sometimes, burning those with magic, enforcing so many rules about what freedoms the people could and could not have. And the way her country's army treated the scar wolves... Horrible.

"I should take you as my hostage and hold you for a peace treaty agreement with your father. But since you saved me, maybe..." he said quietly, studying his fingers and the dried blood she hadn't yet cleaned from his left hand. A hundred emotions washed over his handsome features. The poor thing looked like he was about to explode from feelings. "If what you say about me is true or even partially so, you need to run far, far away from me."

It was as if his political mind and his heart were in an argument over how to handle her. If he weren't so dangerous, the dark but confused look on his face would've made her laugh.

"Believe me or not, I—" The light caught on his cheek, gold flecks along the bone and temple. She reached up a hand to touch it. "You have scales, Dorin. Dragon scales."

A shout outside broke through the dawn's peaceful birdsong. "Princess! We know you are inside. Be calm, and no one will get hurt."

Guards surrounded the cabin, swords drawn. How had they found this place? She hoped Celeste hadn't been questioned. Most likely, one of Father's many spies had trailed Brielle here at some point and tattled. "Hurry," she hissed at Dorin. She opened the closet and shoved him in.

"I don't think they know about you. I really believe no one saw you. As soon as I leave with them, you go."

She shut the door on his scowling face and hurried outside where George, Javier, and several more castle guards stood with swords ready.

"Where is he?" Javier asked, his voice too tremulous to be frightening.

"Who? Yes, you found me." Why did they have their swords drawn? Was she mistaken? Had someone spotted Dorin? "Let's go home, then." She forced a yawn. "I'm tired. Last I checked, it's not a crime to take a walk in the woods."

She sauntered toward the open tunnel door, the finger that had touched Dorin's dragon scales still tingling. It was so wild that he had this arcane power. The Broyeurs couldn't be allowed to kill him. Dorin was a rarity, a piece of the past, an artifact come to life. *Please follow me, George and Javier. Please.*

A figure appeared in the dark of the tunnel, and Brielle's hopes fizzled.

"Good morning, Princess." The head of the Broyeurs, Captain D'Aboville, had the eyes of a mind-twisted scar wolf and the lean look of one of the tortured animals, all sinew and bone. He always looked hungry, but not for food. For pain, specifically the agony of anyone he could control.

Brielle's stomach turned, and she fiddled with the rune stone still hidden in her trouser pocket. "Why are you here? I would have thought you'd be spending this beautiful spring morning sharpening things in a dungeon somewhere."

He strode over, stopping only inches away. If he so

much as touched her with one awful finger, he was going to eat a fist.

His sudden and disgusting smile sliced at her bravado. "Because we have a witness who says you are housing a witch. I find it doubtful, of course, Princess, but I was the one on duty when it was reported, and so I must do my job."

A witch? Whoever had seen Dorin must have only stuck around for the sparks of light and missed the fully naked male section of the adventure. "Nope. Sorry to disappoint you. It's just me. I was playing with a few of Etienne's firesnaps." She stepped away, holding up her hands. "Yes, I know. Very dangerous. I'll lock myself in my chambers for a full day. It'll be such a hardship to miss Father's breakfast with the coastal nobles. I'll probably never recover from my grief."

D'Aboville glanced at Javier, who shrugged. D'Aboville's jaw muscle worked. "Search the cabin."

Suffering stones. "Fine. Take your time. It's my monthly cycle, so watch out for feminine materials scattered about the place." She pretended to enter the tunnel but instead sidestepped the entrance and hid behind a knot of middling saplings and low bushes, keeping an eye on the men.

None of them rushed into the cabin. Instead, the men looked to George, who grimaced and began to turn away, his lips parting to speak to D'Aboville.

"Go on, George." D'Aboville breathed out of his nose and started forward. "Search that cabin or find a new position outside the castle."

The men closed in on the cabin. Javier opened the door.

What could she do? They couldn't go inside. They would definitely find Dorin. She searched the pockets of her stolen trousers, and besides the rune stone, she came up with one folding knife, a rock, and a dried up old scorchpepper.

"Way to be prepared, me," she whispered, furious with herself for not keeping a solid weapon on her or anything that could possibly be used as a distraction.

Pretty much giving up on the entire endeavor and sending up a prayer for Dorin's soul, she chucked the stone and the so-tiny-it-was-worthless knife into the trees as far as she could.

"What was that?" George stopped on his way into the cabin and looked in the direction she'd thrown the contents of her pockets.

"Deer, I'm sure," D'Aboville said. "Now, search."

Gritting her teeth, Brielle tried to think of something else to do.

But it turned out she didn't have to.

Shouts erupted from the cabin, and a flurry of movement passed the cabin windows, and then Dorin was fighting off Javier and another two guards with what appeared to be Brielle's best shovel. The guards' short swords clanged against the shovel.

"I will see your blood on my blade, Soul Crushers!" Dorin shouted in elven. Soul Crushers was what the rest of the world called the Broyeurs.

Dorin had shed the cloak and—wait, what was on his back? Dark emerald dragon wings protruded from his elven back. She gasped, the shock of seeing his bare, elven flesh against the beastly joints of those massive wings almost difficult to look at. So strange. Swallowing, she held herself tightly. Was he truly the only one like this? Why was he currently half elf and half dragon? Is that how it had been in the time of the dragon goddess Nix?

Though a shovel was obviously not ideal, his expert fighting skills managed to drive back George as well. D'Aboville snarled a curse and launched himself at Dorin, but then the heir to the elven throne was in the air, flying into the foggy peaks.

Brielle ignored the shouts, questions, and arguing of the guards and D'Aboville. She kept her eyes trained on Dorin until he flew out of sight, his fantastical silhouette disappearing into the morning's purple sky. A long sigh left her lips, and she wanted more than anything to follow him.

CHAPTER 4
DORIN

Dorin sped over the green and gray foothills and into the last of the night's shadows, dark places the rocky cliffs of the mountains hid from the morning light. He was flying. Flying. How? His wings felt natural to him, moving in tune with the rest of him without much thought.

He shivered, horrified. What had he become? A monster. Brielle had been kind and seen the blood on his hands, but she didn't know how he was covered in it, morning after morning. Now he knew why. He was a killer. What had he done as this monster? Killed innocents? It was surely possible. He had no memory of being a full dragon, but if Brielle was telling the truth about seeing him in her courtyard, he had times when he was completely changed over into such a creature. Was this why he'd always been drawn to dragons?

His mind hit him with another confusing thought. Brielle was Wylfen.

How could he think of her as a kind person if she was one of them? Of course she wasn't kind. With their trained scar wolves, her people were responsible for slaying countless innocent elves. If it hadn't been for Princess Aurora, his brother's wife, the Wylfen would have destroyed all of Dorin's kingdom, ripping and tearing their way across Balaur. No, Brielle might have saved him, but she could not be trusted any more than he or his bloody hands could.

His eyes burned in the cold wind as he landed on an outcropping far from any village or goat farmer's stead. Though he was an elf and the cold didn't usually bother him, he shivered. Shirtless in the mountains wasn't his idea of a wise health choice. He needed to get supplies to remain at this altitude. At least he was safely in Balaur now.

A break in the rocks proved to hide a slender passage that opened into a cave. Beams of daylight shot through cracks in the rock above, and he paced the floor, trying to figure out what to do. Part of him longed to find Filip and get help. But what if he changed into the beast when he was at home or in Lore? He might kill the very people he loved the most. No, he had to stay away from everyone. That was certain. But he would need supplies. Already his stomach growled with hunger, and he couldn't stop shaking from the cold—or from distress; he wasn't exactly sure.

A shudder rocked him suddenly, and he fell to his knees.

The flavor of what had to be dragonfire touched his tongue, and heat lashed across his back as sparks of magic spun around him in a dizzying circle. He reached over his shoulder. His wings were gone. The magic's light died away, and he was left himself once more, fully elven. He touched his face, the memory of Brielle's fingers there tingling and warm. Smooth scales, hard and real, ran like armor along his cheekbone on one side and over part of his temple and forehead. Oh. So he wasn't fully elven. Not anymore. He shuddered. What curse had been set on him? How had this happened?

He had to travel to a village for food and clothing. Perhaps the scales wouldn't be noticed if he wore a cloak with the hood pulled up, but he had no cloak. He'd pulled the borrowed one off when his wings had reappeared in Brielle's cabin closet. He'd have to visit the nearest village at dusk, then. It would be an incredible risk to the people there, but he had to get provisions.

And no one could find out who and what he was.

What would happen to Balaur if the truth of its heir were discovered? At some point, he'd have to think of a long-term plan, but for now, he'd find what he needed to live here in the remote regions of the mountains and learn what he could of his condition. He would seek out dragons again and study how they reacted to him and his magic. Maybe they'd find him abhorrent and kill him. That would be one way to take care of the problem that was his life now. But maybe there would be an answer there that he hadn't thought of yet.

Two small questions nagged him.

What had drawn him to Wylfen Castle and Brielle, and would it happen again? If it did, there was good chance the soldiers of Wylfen would be the end of him.

CHAPTER 5
BRIELLE

With the men busy pointing and arguing about Dorin's escape, Brielle slipped out of her hiding place and hurried back into the tunnel. At the tunnel's end, Celeste and Father waited.

"Daughter, I hear you have been doing your own hunting." The tone of his voice was a dare. But what did he want? For her to admit she'd been helping someone with magic or to claim it was all a plan to capture the elf, a scheme that went awry?

"You know my curiosity, Father," she said, giving him a shallow curtsey and not for a moment missing the disdain in his gaze, the look that traveled over her trousers, shirt, and muddied boots. "I simply wanted to study him for a day before giving him to the Broyeurs. I thought perhaps there might be more like him."

The pleased gleam in his eyes turned her stomach. "Of course." He crossed his arms and rubbed his mustache and the small beard that covered just his chin. "And what did you find out?"

There was little use holding back. A witness had observed magic, and the men at the cabin had seen Dorin's wings. They didn't know he was the crown prince of Balaur though. She'd keep that bit to herself. "Not much of anything. D'Aboville ruined my chance and the elf flew away."

Celeste dropped the stack of clean clothes she'd been holding.

"Flew? And he was an elf? I heard about the magic, but not this," Father said.

"I'm sure you'll have a fine report from D'Aboville," she said, her words exactly as sharp as she wanted them.

Father's mouth twitched in irritation, a mannerism she knew as well as the back of her hand. "Shed your hatred of the man," he said. "He works for me, Brielle, and that should be enough for you."

Her teeth were going to crack if she gritted them any harder. "The person in question was an elf, and he transformed into a dragon."

Celeste crumbled, and Brielle caught her. "Never in my life..." the maid mumbled, her face pale.

"Never in anyone's life." Father snapped his fingers, ordering two servants waiting in the shadows to help Celeste.

Brielle followed Father up the stairs and into the castle. The bump and bang of servants finishing up the last of the morning work carried down the corridor, the pungent scent of the lemons and oils they used for cleaning cutting the air.

"Tell me exactly what you witnessed." He led her away from her chambers.

"I thought I'd be locked in my room for my behavior."

He waved a dismissive hand. "You are no child. I know you leave the castle when it suits you. Let's pretend no longer."

She stopped, shocked. Was he actually saying he allowed her to do as she wished?

"If you're doing the work of a Broyeur," he said, "even if incompetent, you should be permitted to train in the position and should report to me or to D'Aboville."

Ah. Of course. There was the truth of it. Hunting and killing for him would earn her the privilege of freedom. She couldn't repress a foul shudder.

Father whirled and pointed a finger. "Enough of that, Princess. You are to become a Broyeur today, a crusher of all that is unclean. You cannot shy from the violence of the job."

"I don't want to be a Broyeur, and you know it."

His pointed finger curled into his fist and his mustache bristled. "I..." A vein in his forehead throbbed.

"What about marriage?" Of course, she would never marry anyone he chose. She'd run away to Khem forever before that happened.

His face smoothed, and he straightened, walking again like he hadn't almost lost his temper and throttled his own daughter in the window's lovely morning light. "I haven't yet secured a husband for you. Until I do, you will work for D'Aboville and me. If you are determined to get your hands dirty, you might as well help your kingdom while you're at it."

Brielle always raged at everyone who crossed her, everyone except for Father, because he didn't bluster and fuss or back down when faced directly with opposition. He would have her punished, whipped, maybe even killed. She'd had a cousin once, brother to her dear traveling companion and fellow rule-breaker, Gabe, who was currently sneaking about the northern regions. This cousin had been caught in the forest on the border with his elven lover, not far from her cabin. The young man had been run through the next day, a supposed hunting accident. Brielle knew the truth. Father had arranged his murder. If she raged at him, he would do the same to her without batting an eye.

"Why are we going to Apothecary's chamber?" Brielle secretly called the underground room full of bottles and bubbling cauldrons the potions chamber. After all, the blends of herbs and substances performed their own kind of magic, didn't they? Putting people to sleep, helping those with bad vision see more, calming anxious folk, easing muscles, catching fire, causing explosions. Seemed like magic to her, but she knew enough never to verbalize that thought.

Father swung the black door open, and the scent of anise, sage, and charcoal made Brielle cough. "Apothecary!" He smiled at the wizened old man standing over a smoking black pot. The man was only ever called Apothecary. Brielle had been told that when a person accepted this position, they shed their former life entirely. With their new life almost completely spent in this one chamber, they kept the castle's secrets safe from spies.

Apothecary turned and bowed. "Your Majesty. Princess."

The man moved like a skink, quick then frozen. It was especially unsettling considering how old he was. How did he move like that? And why? Probably the result of being around powerful concoctions all day.

"I assume you're here to see the new blend." Apothecary skittered over to a row of pale blue-green bottles set into a wooden frame. He lifted one, uncorked and sniffed it, then handed it to Father.

He replaced the cork, then raised the bottle to the hanging oil lamps, using the light to examine the bits floating in the substance. "This, fair daughter, is Magebane."

"Of course," she said wryly. He'd tried countless times to create a concoction that would incapacitate those with magic. None of them had worked.

"No, this blend has been tested and proved. Let's have a demonstration, yes?" The smile on Father's face was death.

Dragging her feet, Brielle followed him and Apothecary to the dungeons.

She hadn't realized the Broyeurs had caught another witch or water mage. She always attempted to help them escape. Never once had she been successful. Father seemed to know every time she was about to attempt it, and he'd cut her off by calling her to the throne room or to a meeting, sending his closest men to escort her so she couldn't make excuses. Once she'd managed to pay off a new dungeon guard to leave a water mage's door unlocked, but D'Aboville had discovered the error before the beaten woman could make her way out of the cell.

A foul stench loomed in the dungeons, telling her as much as the moaning. This was a place of suffering. Some of the folk here might have deserved imprisonment. Murderers. Those who hurt their children. But those with magic certainly didn't. When Father died, perhaps Etienne would follow through with the ideas they'd discussed over wine late at night three years ago. Maybe Etienne really would stop the hunting of those with magic and end the atrocities their father so enjoyed.

Led by the dungeon guard of the day—a man built like a deerhound—Father and Apothecary approached the last cell down the long, dank row. The basket of bread and apples Brielle had had Celeste bring down sat untouched just outside the reach of any prisoners. Brielle's jaw clenched. She would have to make sure the dungeon guards were ordered to give the food to the prisoners next time.

Kicking the basket aside without so much as a flicker of emotion, Father took the keys from the guard and unlocked the cell. Inside, a young woman about Brielle's age shivered in the corner, oily, dark blonde hair hiding most of her face. She wore what had once been an apron and a dress of homespun wool but was now a torn and stained rag of filth.

"She's too young to be here," Brielle said.

Her father's gaze whipped through the dimness. "She is a witch."

Like that was reason enough to destroy a person. He only hated magic because he didn't have it and he couldn't control it. Well, he could control it if he killed everyone who wielded it.

As she rubbed a finger over the runes carved into the

stone in her pocket, half of Brielle's mind drifted toward thoughts of the dragon elf. Where had he flown to? Had the Broyeurs' sword cut him? Was he flying away with blood seeping from half a dozen wounds? Elves were difficult to kill, so maybe he'd be all right, but he might be dying at this very moment.

Hate for D'Aboville pulsed in her heart, joining the terrible, constant drum of anger for Father and Apothecary. What wonders would this world have if those three didn't exist? This witch would be practicing her power, and an elf-dragon would be learning how to deal with his magic, possibly with her help. She gripped the rune stone hard, fingers trembling.

Apothecary removed one of the tiny, pale blue-green bottles from his royal blue robes, uncorked it, and drank a measure while Father produced an oaken wand from the folds of his cloak. He gave it to the witch, who snatched it from his hand and immediately spoke a spell, her words too quick to be deciphered.

But the spell did nothing. No plume of smoky power spread from the end of the wand. The witch gripped at her throat like she was choking, then she dropped her magical weapon and crumbled to the floor, weeping. Brielle knelt beside her and set the young woman's head on her leg. The witch wrapped her skinny arms around Brielle like a child, the small fingers of one hand hooking desperately onto Brielle's pocket.

"You see?" Father's teeth were bright in the dark. "Magebane suppresses magic. We finally have a weapon against the filth of this world."

His gaze flickered over Brielle, and she knew he was

disgusted by her kind treatment of the prisoner, but she didn't give a rat's tail. He could lose both eyeballs staring as hard as he liked. She wouldn't leave this poor woman until bodily forced to do so.

Brielle suddenly hated herself for not doing enough for these magic-wielding prisoners. She should have tried harder to help them escape. She should have railed. Would it have worked or would she be as dead as her cousin by her father's own hand?

The witch's fingers brushed the rune stone. The young woman sat up. Her dirty hair shielded her eyes as she jerked the stone from Brielle's pocket, lunged for her wand, and spat a spell that had Father and Apothecary frozen, only their chests moving with their breaths. The witch stood up, gasping in shock. She stepped back, slipped on a puddle created by the leaking ceiling, and dropped the rune stone.

Father and Apothecary were instantly freed. Father reached for the witch, snatching her arm. Brielle took advantage of their distraction to nick the rune stone and slip it into her pocket again, her mind clicking through the events and what they might mean.

"How did you do that?" Father shouted in the witch's face.

She only wept and shook, keeping the truth of what the stone had done to herself. Smart woman. Father and Apothecary must not have noticed the stone in her hand. It was dark, with only a single small oil lamp that barely fought off the shadows, so it stood to reason they had missed that part entirely.

When the witch refused to answer, Father threw her to

the floor. He whirled to face Apothecary, who was sniffing the bottle, white eyebrows bunched in thought.

"Increase the blend's potency," Father snarled, "then send word when you believe it is finished. We will try this again when you do. Do not fail me in this, Apothecary."

The old man nodded and started out of the cell as Brielle's mind worked over what she could possibly do to help the witch. If she suggested the witch go with Apothecary, he might perform terrible experiments on her. A shudder shook Brielle as she left the cell and the deerhound-looking guard locked the door. Father gripped her wrist as she tried to meet the witch's eyes, but the woman turned away from the door. As Father pulled Brielle down the corridor, she silently berated herself. Once again, she had failed to help the innocent.

At least she still had the rune stone. How had the stone negated the effect of the Magebane?

"Once Apothecary tweaks the blend," Father said, "Magebane will inhibit magic approximately a mile around the Broyeur who drinks it."

"A mile?"

"That is what our former experiment proved," Apothecary answered as they made their way up the stone steps into the castle proper. "We tried it on a water mage near the river. She could do nothing."

A dimple appeared beside the small beard on Father's chin. A man like him shouldn't possess a sweet dimple. It somehow made him even more frightening. "She only wept," he said proudly. "Couldn't even stand when Apothecary came close."

"I guess that witch was made of tougher stuff?" Brielle never could resist poking the bear.

His mouth twitched. "I suppose. But Apothecary will see the blend made stronger. We won't have any more mistakes like that, will we?"

"No, Your Highness," Apothecary said.

Morning light streamed through the windows on the middle floor of the castle, brightening the red rugs to match the color of freshly spilled blood.

"How did it feel to be frozen by a spell, Father?" She used the sweet, dulcet tones of a doting daughter just to make sure the question hurt his pride further. "I can't imagine how such a tiny woman could so completely incapacitate a king."

His lips curled, and Brielle took a sliver of delight from his irritation.

"It was nothing. But I do feel dirtied from the experience." At the branching of the corridor that led up to Father's royal apartments, he dismissed Apothecary. "I'm off to wash this filth away. I suggest you do the same, Daughter. And if I catch you in those dungeons without orders to be there, Celeste will be relieved of her duties."

Cold speared her chest. He meant to have her maid killed if she disobeyed. Loathing this entire moment, Brielle curtseyed, then left Father's presence as fast as her feet could carry her.

She had to get Celeste out of the castle tonight.

CHAPTER 6
DORIN

When the waning sun painted the sky the color of sapphires and rose quartz, Dorin— barefoot and fatigued for a thousand reasons —arrived at the nearest farm. As the couple who ran it locked up their red-brown chickens, he kicked in the side door to their small cottage. He'd watched them for hours, making certain they had no children or workers. It was such a small place, which made it easier to keep this morally bereft quest simple with as little extraneous damage done to the victims as possible.

"I don't even know who I am."

He hated himself more than he had when he'd woken each morning with blood on his hands because now he was fully conscious. The High Prince of Balaur was a common thief. Shaking his head and trembling with frustration, he dug through the farm couple's chest near the kitchen window, their shelves near the bed. Then, in a dark corner where none of the window's last light could reach, he saw a winter cloak. It was too heavy for anything but the worst of the mountain's weather. He took it and tied it at his neck, the fur already warming him.

"Who's there?" A man's voice, touched with the rural mountain drawl, came from the broken side door. "We want no trouble. Take what you need and be gone or taste the end of my shovel."

Dorin pulled the hood over his head and emerged from the shadows, feeling exactly like the low thief he was. "I must take this. I apologize. I will see you paid somehow. I swear it." The cloak had probably cost the couple a half year's wages. If they even made money here. They most likely bartered with their nearest neighbors and only visited Low Spike for the market once a season.

The woman peered at Dorin over her husband's shoulder, her kerchief tied tightly around her graying hair. "We'll need a replacement by winter if you don't mean to starve us, rich one."

"Ana-Maria!" The man scowled at his wife, and she elbowed him hard, her eyes gone steely. They moved aside so he could leave the way he'd come in.

Dorin gave them a nod and strode out of the tidy cottage and into the spring evening. The dusk sky had gone a midnight blue, and soon he would transform, if Brielle had been speaking truth. What she had said was madness, but it also made sense. How else had he ended up in a cave at Spike Peak completely devoid of clothing and bloodied? Did that mean he had to disrobe before the magic stole his body away?

Swallowing his rage and frustration, he ran into the higher elevations, heading for the second cave. It wasn't on

Spike Peak but was still very remote, and he could only make it there if he utilized his full elven strength and speed. Perhaps if he exhausted himself enough, the dragon inside him wouldn't rise. The thought gave him a feather's weight of hope, and he ran faster.

At the cave, he realized he'd completely forgotten to find anything to eat. He'd had nothing all day. The stars blinked in the young night, and a shudder shook him. The magic was coming. He shucked his newly stolen cloak and borrowed trousers, then folded them and set them on a flat boulder inside the cave.

Thus disrobed, he faced the mountains and waited, shivering and afraid. Filip's man Drago would have had a festival of a time seeing the proud Dorin like this. Dorin wished he could laugh, but his stomach growled, and he had no idea what—or whom—he would hunt tonight. Maybe if he repeated his own desires, the dragon in him would listen.

"I don't kill elves or humans or fae. I am not a murderer. I respect the animal life I take, dispatching it quickly and with mercy. I will only kill what I can consume."

Like the phrases could save him from the darkness beginning to cloud his mind, he repeated the words over and over and over again, his jaw set and his gaze straight ahead.

A heat only a lightning strike could replicate struck him down, and he knew no more.

THE DRAGON SOARED OVER THE STARLIT FORESTS AND

farms as hunger overwhelmed the desire for sleep or finding a mate. He longed for the taste of warm blood in his mouth and a full belly. Movement caught his eye, and he hovered, wings tipping vertically and beating the wind at a sharp angle to keep him aloft and steady. A small, pale shape moved in the silvery light, and the soft bleat of a sheep rose to the dragon's ears. Stomach rumbling, mouth watering, the dragon dove. Almost as silent as an owl, the dragon swooped low, his muscles bunching as he readied to change angles and snatch the animal in his talons.

Another creature appeared walking on two legs. Human. The figure walked quickly but calmly toward the sheep. The human didn't even see the dragon. Perhaps it was time to taste human and see how they served as dinner.

The human screamed shrilly as the dragon extended his talons and grabbed sheep in one set and the human in the other. The weight made rising into the air difficult, and the dragon worked hard to fly back to its new cave. He deposited the human and the sheep at the mouth of the cave, their small bodies rolling and both of them calling out in their own way. The human hit his head on a stone and went quiet. All the better. The screaming and shouting turned the dragon's stomach and put strange images in his mind of a redheaded woman and a male elf's hands that felt familiar somehow. The dragon shook his head and set to eating the sheep. He would taste the human later, maybe roasted by dragonfire. Such treatment had made the mountain goat he'd feasted on last night very delicious indeed.

With the sheep gone, the dragon licked his lips and

searched for a place to lie down. Fatigue tugged at his eyes and wings like he hadn't slept in days. But surely he had. Blinking, he realized there were gaps in his memory of yesterday. And the day before that. He must be fighting off an illness of sorts. All the more reason to get some sleep.

The scent of elf was in the air nearby. On a rock, a pile of human clothing sat folded. He sniffed it and recoiled, mind whirling. How did these clothes smell like humans and elves, but also like himself? Scenting the clothing again and again, he couldn't make sense of it. That strange image of familiar, male, elven hands flashed behind his eyes. He truly was coming down with a sickness. Sleep would fix him. His instincts told him rest was imperative.

Ignoring the clothing for now, he curled into the back of the cave. Spiked tail wrapped around his body and wings stretched over him, he cracked one eye open to check that the human remained quiet. The man had stirred at some point during the dragon's meal and was now huddled against the cave wall, knees pulled up to his chest.

An ache spread slowly across the dragon's chest, and he lifted his head to study the human further. The human glanced over, then quickly away, a shudder rocking the small thing's form. The ache grew sharper and turned into a strange pain. He didn't like seeing the human afraid. Why? In the gray shards of his inherited memories, he saw moments when humans butchered fallen dragons for teeth and spikes. But this one wasn't dishonoring dead dragons. He had only been tending sheep. This man most likely consumed sheep like the dragon. They had that in common. The urge to communicate with this human bloomed inside the dragon's chest, a fluttering excitement that soothed the pain of seeing the human's suffering.

The dragon let out an inquisitive growl, just something to denote a willingness to communicate.

"Please!" the human squawked. Tears ran down the man's face now. He no longer seemed capable of being calm.

How did the dragon understand the man's words? They were clear as the dawn to his mind. Maybe the dragon could speak? No. Of course not.

So the dragon tried to speak with his mind. *Do you understand me?*

The words seemed to fall into an imaginary crevasse, useless, unheard. The human stared, standing now with his arms out as if to fend off the dragon. Ridiculous human. Enough of that. It was time to sleep.

CHAPTER 7
BRIELLE

A memory of Mother's face—soft cheeks, sad smile—drifted across Brielle's mind. She pressed a hand to her heart, the ache of missing her taking her breath.

"Why did you have to leave me, Mother?" she whispered, unshed tears burning her eyes.

If Mother hadn't died, maybe they could have changed things here. Etienne might have stood up to Father. Mother and Etienne together might have made Wylfenden less of a terrible nightmare.

Brielle still wasn't sure if Father had killed Mother. She'd been attempting to train the scar wolves in a more humane way when one had snapped—its vicious treatment at the hands of Father's trainers overcoming its senses—and gone for her throat. Brielle hadn't witnessed the event, so there was no way to know if the tale was true or not. For a time, neither she nor Etienne had spoken to Father, both of them silently wondering about his role. She had been ten and her brother thirteen, old enough to think for themselves.

Father wasn't going to have that witch as his next victim. Brielle would gather her things and find a way to get the woman out today. Together, they would flee to the mountains, away from Father, and hopefully, they'd find Dorin. The memory of the hooked barbs on the tips of his dragon wings blinked through her mind, the jade green of his massive wings. That click of a talon on her window. The pained look in his golden, elven eyes. He'd looked like a cursed man, a man who hated himself. But he was a wonder, and she would help him see that.

At her chambers, she hugged Celeste so hard she probably cracked something.

"My lady!" Celeste choked out.

"Thank you for being you. Now, we must say goodbye. You have to leave the castle now and forever. I am once again up to some very dangerous mischief, and I can't handle anyone dying on my behalf."

Celeste sighed heavily. "Why is everything you find entertaining deadly?"

Brielle patted Celeste's arm. "I'm sorry my penchant for adventure destroys your peace."

"It truly does." Celeste picked up the crumpled blanket Brielle had accidentally cast to the floor when the dragon —Dorin—had tapped the window.

"Maybe someday I'll take up embroidery." Brielle shrugged, then grinned thinking of what Zahra—her friend from Khem—would say to that. It would definitely involve eye rolling and requests for wine.

"If you do," Celeste said, "please send for me. That sounds divine."

"No goddess I've heard of enjoys stitchery."

Celeste sniffed as she folded the blanket. "Perhaps those are the goddesses that don't make it into the history scrolls. They're just minding their business, doing their goddess work, and settling into bed at a reasonable hour." She seemed reluctant to leave the room.

"Perhaps you're right, dear friend." Brielle enveloped the woman in a hug. "I'll miss you, but I'll find you again when it's safe. All right?" Celeste smelled of baked bread and clean linens.

"You can't be serious. I'm not leaving you. I haven't worked outside this castle in a decade!"

"Please. Just leave for now. I'll send word of where to meet once it's safe." Brielle opened her armoire and pulled out a bag of coins. She set it in Celeste's hand. "Take this."

"No. I can't." Celeste tried to push it away, but Brielle was stronger.

"Yes, you can, and you will. That's an order."

Frowning, Celeste took the bag and studied it. "Can't you tell me what is happening? Why are you so set on going against your father? Can't you simply hang on until..."

Brielle knew what she meant to say. Until Father was dead and Etienne was on the throne. "The whole situation is in play now, I'm afraid. Your leaving can't be put on hold. We must go. Now. Tonight."

The old woman's head drooped, and Brielle rubbed her back. "I know where to send the message."

"Oh, yes, at my—"

Putting a hand over Celeste's mouth, Brielle shook her head, then jerked her chin toward the door where George and Javier might be listening. "I know," she whispered. "Now, go. Please."

After tucking the bag of coins into the bag on her belt, Celeste placed a prim kiss on Brielle's forehead. She trudged to the door, her eyes watery. "Until then, my lady. Please don't die."

"That's at the top of my list of actions."

Celeste laughed sadly. "Do you know why your father hates magic?"

"I suppose there are countless reasons. The reason passed down to us all is that Wylfenden can't abide that which is not easy to control."

"True, but there is a reason specific to your father."

Brielle had heard whispers of a run-in with a witch when he was younger, but never any details. "Tell me."

Celeste took a breath and glanced at the door. "When King Raoul was still Prince Raoul, newly married to your mother, father to tiny Etienne, he fought in the wars in Lore. Somewhere, deep in the forest of the fae, a witch ensorcelled him, or so the story goes."

"What did she do?"

"She drew him away from the fighting and took him to bed. At dawn the next day, she revealed herself to be an old witch. She laughed at his ignorance, shamed him for loving the very magic his kingdom fought against."

Her father had lain with a witch? "Did mother find out?"

"Many in the castle know the tale, so I assume she knew. But shortly after he returned, if my tallying is correct, and it always is, your mother grew pregnant with you. They must have been happy at least for a time. But it is said that his hatred for magic sprang from that spell set on him in Lore."

"I wish you had been with me from the start. Mother would have loved you as I do."

"Oh, your dear mother wanted nothing to do with nurses. It was well known that she bit the very heads off those who dared claim that noblewomen shouldn't be nursing their children. She wouldn't let anyone lay a hand on you or Etienne, so they say."

A laugh bubbled from Brielle. "I can imagine that."

Celeste gave her one more hug. "Be well, child. I'll see you someday."

"I'm sure you will."

Once Celeste left, Brielle began to plot in earnest.

ONLY A FEW MOMENTS INTO HER PLOTTING, HER DOORS sprang open, and D'Aboville appeared with two other Broyeurs.

Anger cracked across Brielle's chest, and she saw red. "I'm dressing. Please leave at once." He had no right to burst in here like this.

D'Aboville grinned. "No need for a change of dress, Princess." He snapped his fingers, and the men grabbed her and began dragging her from her room. "Your father has ordered your official ceremony to become one of us, and it's time for your Marking."

Bile rose into the back of her throat as they pulled her down the corridor in the direction of D'Aboville's office.

"No!" If only she'd had time to ready herself. She'd only meant to wash before dressing and donning her throwing knives. "I won't go through with it."

"You speak as if you have a choice, Princess. You do not."

D'Aboville shut his office door with a slam and gestured to the hearth. The Broyeurs didn't meet her gaze as they forced her to her knees beside the crackling fire.

"You can't let him do this," she hissed at D'Aboville's minions. "My father will see you punished and Etienne will as well."

"Don't threaten my Broyeurs, if you please, Princess." D'Aboville turned away and rummaged about in a chest behind his oaken desk. Then he began to whistle.

A deep shiver ran through Brielle. The first time she'd heard him whistle was the day he'd been set as personal guard to her, just after one of the many wars with Lore. D'Aboville had been a basic palace guard at the time, not yet the head or even a member of the Broyeur force. Father had given him the duty as extra protection for Etienne and Brielle, just in case of an assassin. She'd only been a small child, eight or nine maybe, and while D'Aboville's back had been turned to talk with Mother about Etienne, Brielle had fallen into the river. D'Aboville had been there in a heartbeat, snatching her by the hair and keeping the current from taking her. But when he could have pulled her to safety, instead he had whistled and ducked her head below the water. The water had burned her throat and nose, and he had yanked her out, the pain of his grip like fire on her scalp. She had lain panting on the banks as Mother and Etienne ran to check on her,

D'Aboville still whistling ever so quietly. "She's a naughty one, that princess is. We'll have to keep her close, won't we?" he had said to Mother.

Eyes shut, Brielle shuddered at the memory as the whistling came closer. She opened her eyes, and D'Aboville stood above her, his wolfish features sharp in the uneven light of the hearth. He held a long, metal pole that ended in a two-inch version of the Broyeur symbol—a black, fisted hand backed by flames.

"Your father's only requirement was that we brand you in a place unseen so that it won't affect any possible marriage proposals in the future."

Brielle spat into his tunic. "You're a worm, D'Aboville, and you'll never have the power you pretend to hold."

His face reddened, and he drew the pole back as if to strike. The man on his left made a noise, and D'Aboville pressed his eyes shut, lowering the pole.

"Expose her back," he said quietly.

To the underworld with this. Brielle stood, surprising the guards and loosening their grip. She slammed a shoulder into D'Aboville's gut, then launched herself toward the door. Hands sweating, she gripped the doorknob, but it wouldn't turn. It must have a mechanism that locked on closing. Whirling, she looked for a weapon, but the Broyeurs were too fast and the room too small.

"Stop fighting it. It is your fate that I become your overlord in this one duty."

She pulled at their hold on her arms and wrists, but there was no breaking free. "I won't hunt people for you or for my father."

"You will. In time, you will learn the horrors of magic

and how it must be crushed in order to retain the proper order of the world." He set the brand into the fire, his eyes dancing. "We can't allow just anyone to rule simply because they are born with magic. It's madness."

"You are the mad one." The stone of the floor chilled her cheek as they pressed her flat on her stomach.

D'Aboville made a small tear in the upper back of her day gown, and three round, silver buttons clicked to the floor and rolled into the dark corner. He pressed the brand into her skin, at the base of the back of her neck, and the piercing, blinding pain pulled every name she'd ever wished to call D'Aboville or Father from her mouth. As soon as they released her, she scrambled to her feet and lunged away from them. The searing agony of the Broyeur symbol forever etched into her skin nearly brought her to her knees, but she fought the black spots dancing in front of her eyes with the fierce determination to get back to her chambers to prepare to leave this place once and for all.

"Help her to her rooms," D'Aboville said as he returned to his desk, eyeing the brand like it was a favored pet.

"I don't need any help. It's a burn the size of my thumb, not a broken leg."

Though her dress wouldn't appear torn to anyone not eyeing her back, servants in the corridor stared as she walked. She must have been pale and sickly-looking. Pain throbbed in time with her heart as she went around the corner and up the short set of stairs leading to her floor. George and Javier both held out a hand. She waved them off.

"It's fine." Then a thought occurred to her. "Did you know he was going to do this?"

"Do what, Princess?" Javier asked, and George's features echoed the same innocence.

"Never mind. See that no one disturbs me."

After pouring cool water over the burn as she stood in the bath basin, then drying the burn as carefully as possible, Brielle went to her bed in a low-backed shift and leaned on a stack of pillows. Her temples pounded from both the pain and the fury lashing through her blood.

They would pay. Someday, they would suffer for this.

A knock sounded. "Apothecary is here to apply healing ointment, Princess," George said.

"Send him away."

But the doors opened, and the old man walked in anyway.

Brielle gripped the bedsheets. "I don't want your concoctions. Shove off!"

He tilted his head like he didn't understand and held up a pale white bottle. "The king ordered me to apply this rare and expensive healing ointment to your Marking."

Snarling, Brielle shot out of bed, the burn tugging and making her hiss through her teeth as she stood. She turned her back to Apothecary, and he applied the foul-scented stuff.

The pain kept her from striking the man, held her frozen in place.

Soon, the scent faded, and the sound of Apothecary's boots tapped across the room. The door opened and closed. Brielle stared out the window that Dorin had cracked with his talon. She would never admit it to anyone, but that ointment was definitely doing its job. The pain was already easing away, and she could move without wincing.

"Princess," a voice whispered from the dark corner of the room.

Brielle's heart seized, and she spun.

CHAPTER 8
BRIELLE

"Celeste is on the road, Princess." Soot marked the little brunette's cheeks and hands. Lisette was Brielle's best spy here in Wylfen Castle. "Saw her from the top floor myself."

Brielle hugged the steward's chambermaid. "You just saved a life, Lisette."

When she pulled away, the spy grinned. "And ma mère always thought I was worthless."

Heart stinging for the girl, Brielle gave Lisette one more hug. "You're worth more than gold, little one. If you can manage to love yourself, that's all you'll ever need."

The spy slipped from the room, the surprised questions from George and Javier making Brielle chuckle. Lisette would be just fine.

Now, it was time to find the dragon lord.

Brielle dressed in a thin robe that would keep George and Javier from wanting to question her. They always grew incredibly skittish when she showed any skin at neckline or ankle. Like cats in a room of rocking chairs.

Under the dress, she slid on her two knife holsters, one for each thigh. All ten of the small knives were sharpened to a deadly point. Mother's voice echoed in her memories as she smoothed the dress over the weapons and checked to be sure the holsters weren't visible. *You have to feel the target. Know that you will hit it. No doubts. The eye. The throat. And right here...* Mother had shown her where exactly to strike to incapacitate and kill. "I will never leave without them again, Mother," she quietly promised. Mother's old lullaby fluttered through her mind.

"No matter the blood that runs through your heart, / You are my daughter, and we'll never part..."

Brielle supposed the blood line referred to Father's blood. Her parents hadn't had a happy marriage. Who could be happily wed to a man like him? Not her sweet, fierce mother, that was certain.

As prepared as she could be, Brielle swung open one of the double doors. "Guards, I'm dying for a snack and want to select it myself from the kitchens so—"

But neither George nor Javier was there.

In their place, a man as big as a trebuchet stood to one side of the doors. He faced her, and she looked up—and up some more—past wide shoulders, a square jaw, to a set of dead eyes. Absolutely no emotion leaked from their placid depths. Of course, Father had placed this new man here. This guard had no nerves about what she was wearing. Sadly, it seemed walking corpses didn't care about scantily clad women.

"I'm here to escort you should you need to do any Broyeur business, Princess." The man bowed neatly.

Whirling, she went back inside and slammed the door.

Flaming stones of the underworld. What now?

Father would have told this new guard what she could and could not do. The king of Wylfen was no fool.

She poured a glass of water from her rock crystal ewer, then set it down hard, the silver gilt base chipping the edge of the polished wood table.

A wicked smile pulled at her lips.

Shucking off the dress, she found her adventure clothing and patted the rune stone in her right pocket. A strange, feathery feeling skirted up her fingers, and a memory surfaced. One night in the library, she had stumbled on an illuminated page folded and hidden inside a history of Wylfen's apothecaries. The illustration had shown a gryphon and the creature's golden tail had sent that same sort of feeling through her hand. Could that have been magic too? Why would she react to magic? She was a basic human with zero fabulous powers if one didn't count temper and knife skills.

Shrugging off the time-wasting trip down memory lane, she finished dressing. With the long shirt on and her knives now in place over trousers, she tied on a proper cloak.

Then she kicked her armoire and howled like a broken wolf.

Knocking sounded at her door. "My lady, are you hurt?" the corpse said, voice muffled through the wood.

She yowled with more fervor, and her door burst open, the latch's frame breaking into two under the big man's force. Brielle was waiting, ewer in hand. She didn't want to leave any knives here. She bashed the corpse guard's nose, wincing at the sound as he reeled back. After she struck him again on the back of his head, the man collapsed onto her floor.

Wasting no time, she hurried out of her chambers, doing her best to shut the partially splintered door before setting out for the dungeon.

A different guard stood watch at the dungeon, his yellow beard oiled and styled for a great hall instead of a grimy place of misery. "May I help you, my lady?"

"I must see the witch." She schooled her features to show distaste.

"My orders are to keep everyone out until morning."

"Father says I must...I must take her finger to him to prove my dedication to the cleansing of magic in our kingdom. Today, I became a Broyeur." She forced her eyes to tear up, keeping her chin defiant so as to be more believable. Any tales this guard had heard of her would have made it clear she was not in the habit of obeying or hurting prisoners.

His gaze flicked to her hand to check for the brand.

"They branded me on my back because of my ranking."

"Ah. Yes, Princess." The guard turned to lift the keys from the hook over his desk.

Brielle took his moment of distraction to snatch the wand sitting beside his cloak and hat. Heart pounding, she tucked the wand into her cloak's inner pocket beside the rune stone and followed the guard to the cell.

The witch shivered in the corner, but her gaze lit up at

their arrival, eyes focusing on Brielle. Could the witch sense the wand in her pocket?

The guard opened the cell, then handed Brielle a knife. What a nice happenstance. She wouldn't have to dirty her own blades.

Recalling the times she'd spent training with blade and bow alongside Mother and then later with Zahra in Khem, Brielle spun and lodged the knife between the guard's ribs, a wound that would hurt and bleed but not kill the idiot so he still had years to live to grow some brains. If Father let him live.

"You shouldn't hand weapons out so freely."

"But you're the princess," he croaked out.

She raised one eyebrow. "And you know my reputation."

He fell against the wall. Brielle threw the wand to the witch. The witch stood and hissed a spell spoken too quickly for Brielle to pick up. The guard's mouth froze in a call for aid, and then the women were running.

"This way." Brielle led the witch out of the dungeon's staircase and into the corridor the servants used for the carts of fouled laundry.

When the corridor opened into the laundry lit by smoking tallow candles, a dozen red-cheeked faces looked up at them. The witch was wise enough to hold her wand against her side, but she couldn't hide the stench and filth of the dungeons. Brielle held one finger to her lips.

They walked through quickly but calmly, not a word spoken in the entire chamber. Only the sound of bubbling pots and the labored breathing of hard work told Brielle the witch hadn't frozen the room.

And then they were out the side door and into the cool, bloom-scented spring air.

Behind them, voices rose in the laundry, gasps and questions to the head laundress, no doubt. But Brielle couldn't worry about that. There were bigger giants to topple.

The southeast courtyard held the stables and an eon's worth of mud. Brielle picked her way across the boards set in the muck like poor bridges.

"My palfrey, please," she said, using her most imperious voice on the middle-aged stable hand. "And a pony for my friend."

The man glanced at the witch, then at the other two hands who were mucking stalls, neither of whom had even bothered to look up. Brielle rolled her eyes. If it had been Etienne here, they'd have been scrambling over one another to have a bowing contest.

At a snail's pace—no, at the pace of a snail wrapped in cold molasses—the hand finally saddled the mounts.

"Don't gallop," Brielle whispered to the witch as she nudged Juliette's spotted sides and started for the castle's back gate. "Keep your head high and act like you are royal too." If the word hadn't spread about the breakout yet, they might just escape. She longed for the day when escape wasn't the main activity of each and every day.

The guards let them pass, but it was too easy. Glancing over her shoulder as Juliette picked up speed, Brielle had to wonder if Father had something up his sleeve. Surely, she hadn't killed the corpse guard. He'd most likely already told his tale and raised the alarm. So why was all quiet in the castle?

"How long will your spell on the dungeon guard last?" she asked as the witch caught up. Stones, the woman rode like she had been born on a horse. Just lovely.

"I can only hold it when I can feel the heart of him," the witch said.

"That makes no sense to this non-magical person."

A grin tugged the woman's small mouth up at one side. "The spell faded in the courtyard."

Brielle groaned. "Time to get a move on, then!" She urged Juliette into a full gallop.

The witch, not missing a beat, rode right alongside her down the rock-lined road into the mountains.

The fact that they weren't yet being followed didn't mean they'd escaped cleanly. It only meant Father was devising a plan that wouldn't allow for her to slip away unscathed. At this point, Brielle was sure of it. This time when Father sent D'Aboville, she would either kill or be killed. Fear was a rusty, vicious blade scratching across her nerves. She shoved the feeling down deep and rode on.

They were at the river crossing by the time the moon was high.

"What is your name?" Brielle asked as they removed the horses' saddles and rubbed them down as best they could with dry grasses near the riverside.

"Maren."

A name that referenced the sea. "Do you sail? Did you grow up by the sea?"

"Yes. My family..." She coughed, and her hair fell over her face, shielding her expression.

"Did D'Aboville hurt them?"

"They died defending me."

Brielle shut her eyes and said a silent prayer. "I'm so sorry for your loss. They died heroes."

Maren nodded quickly, finished rubbing her black gelding down, then began to pick berries, her movements quick and practiced. "The Broyeurs tried to get me to hurt my mother." She shook her head and wiped her eyes with the back of her hand. "They hunt us witches for a living, but they don't even know we can't injure close relatives with magic."

"I didn't know that either."

"The magic rebounds on itself." She cleared her throat and held out a full hand of the berries, obviously ready to change the subject. "These are edible, Princess."

Brielle knew that but didn't want to be an arrogant arse —especially considering how open Maren had been in sharing her terrible experience—so she simply said, "Good that you know that. I'm starving." She let Juliette's reins drag the ground, the horse munching the fresh spring greenery that grew in clumps near the muddy banks. While they ate the berries, Brielle tried to decide what to tell Maren. "Do you want to keep going on your own or stick with me? You choose. I do have a ship I sometimes take to Khem, so if you want a job that uses your sailing skills, I can send you that way with my ring and a note. If we can find some writing material, that is."

Maren shoved her hair away from her face. "Truly?"

"Yes. I myself have a plan that involves a dragon, so I'm not sure you want to continue on with me."

"A dragon?"

And so Brielle told Maren everything.

"Suffering gods," Maren murmured as she cupped a

handful of river water and drank. "How do you plan to find him, and why in the name of the goddess Nix would you want to?"

"He needs help."

"You like saving people, don't you?"

Brielle had to snort at herself. "I suppose I do. There are worse habits." She took the rune stone from her pocket. "Like being obsessed with digging up ancient magical artifacts when your father is a renowned killer of anyone with magic." She handed the stone over.

Maren touched the runes. "This stone helped me work magic in spite of the Magebane."

"I saw that. I wish we knew more about how exactly that worked."

The witch nodded like she was thinking. "These are powerful. Someone with amazingly strong magic carved them. I hear—"

"A hum?"

The witch grinned. "Yes. You hear it too? Do you have witch blood?"

"No. Definitely not. I wish. Father would perish where he stood if he knew I could hear magic."

They laughed though the subject was dark, two women whose lives had been twisted by evil.

"Can I smell your hand?" Maren asked.

"Umm." Had her time in the dungeon stolen her mind?

Maren gestured impatiently, so Brielle lifted her palm toward the witch. Inhaling and touching each digit, Maren frowned. Then she dropped Brielle's hand and shrugged.

"You don't smell like a witch."

"I'm just your typical human over here."

"Sure you are, Princess."

"What do you mean?" Brielle asked.

"You're something magical." Maren sniffed the air again, then studied the rune stone. "I just don't know what."

"You've met enough witches to know the scent of your kind?"

Nodding, Maren ran a finger over the stone's last rune. "It's pretty distinctive."

That was an evasive answer. Brielle didn't blame Maren for protecting other magic workers and any information about them. After all, Brielle was King Raoul's daughter.

Holding the stone to the sky, Maren asked, "This is solid jade, isn't it?" She returned the artifact to Brielle, eyebrows lifted and mostly hidden beneath her thick, tangled hair.

"I think so. It most likely belonged to the Jade dragon clan during the time when the gods and goddesses lived here in physical form." Brielle had studied the Jade dragons aplenty.

"Did the stone lead you to Dorin? Oh, no, you said he flew into your courtyard. That must have been incredible to see."

Brielle turned the rune stone over in her hand. "I handled the artifact earlier in the evening. Perhaps..."

"Did you say anything over the runes? While you touched them?"

Brielle had to think. She couldn't remember. "Maybe? I puzzled over the meaning of the runes. I asked them to help me." The memory of Dorin's scowling face, his powerful arms roped in muscle, and his emerald-colored wings spread across her mind like a wildfire.

Maren clicked her tongue and held up a finger. "You called the dragon." She leaned over and pointed to the first rune. "That is a rune of calling. This," she set her pinkie finger on the third rune, "is for aid. I think this stone called your dragon elf. I've used the ancients' writing in plenty of magic. I've no doubt that if you want him to show up, all you need to do is whisper your call for help over those runes. So you're certain he won't decide we're for feasting? What if he still doesn't know himself in dragon form?"

"If you want to leave for safety's sake, I don't blame you." She removed the sigil ring that showed her house's wolf and gave it to Maren. "My crew is docked at Genette in a ship called the Oiseau Noir or perhaps with no name. It depends on what they're up to while I'm away. We make use of a lot of paint."

"I'd rather stick around and see the dragon," the witch said. "But if it comes after us, I'm on this horse and gone."

Brielle stood and cupped the stone in both hands. "I wouldn't blame you."

Maren slipped the ring onto her first finger and nodded.

The wind whistled in the trees, and the rune stone's hum rang quietly as Brielle called the dragon.

CHAPTER 9
DORIN

That strange pull hooked the dragon's heart, the same feeling he'd had the night he'd traveled to the human's castle. As he flew the direction the sensation demanded, he blinked, confused. He couldn't remember the rest of that adventure into the humans' territory. He was assuredly still ill with a sickness that didn't want to leave his body. The wind buffeted the back edges of his wings as he soared lower and lower, heading for a spot near the river. He smelled fish, spring onions, tart berries, and humans.

A pair of horses startled and dashed away at his approach. Two female humans stood on the bank, and something pulled him toward the one with fiery hair. His emotions twisted and fought one another. Anger at being summoned cut him, fear of doing something wrong—though he didn't know what action could be wrong—whirled, and an overwhelming desire to protect this woman who called to him with what had to be magic grasped his heart and shook it hard.

Fine. He'd protect them, but he would do it from his cave. Enough of this flying near human territory. Those creatures made him nervous, and he didn't care for the way they covered their bodies with the same kind of garments he'd found in his cave, the ones that smelled like himself and confused him further.

Dragonfire kindled in his belly as his frustration mounted, the heat of it glowing in his chest and shining a dull light on the females as he grabbed them up with his talons. The light-haired one had powerful magic. She drew a wand, and magic struck his talon with the heat of a thousand suns, pain licking up his leg. He dropped her, and she scrambled into the woods, fleeing even as he flew away with the fire-haired human in his grasp.

At his cave, he gently released the human whom he strangely longed to protect. She landed on her feet. Impressive balance, he thought begrudgingly. Where was the male human he'd captured earlier? Had he eaten him during one of his memory lapses? Doubtful. He never ate humans. Or at least, he didn't think so.

"Dorin!" the female reached out a small hand, fingers like flower petals. "It's me, Brielle. I know what you are. You told me yourself when you were in your elven form. I'm here to help you."

Help? What nonsense was she spouting? A pounding started in his head. He snorted and lunged, and she backed up as he'd wanted her to do. He needed no human's assistance. Besides, the magic she'd worked to call him indicated she was the one who required aid, not him.

Sniffing, he searched for the magic. The sound and smell of it was dwindling quickly. She produced a stone and showed its gleaming, green, dark surface etched with runes.

This was the magical object causing all of his problems.

He snatched it up with his mouth, his teeth grazing her hand, and tossed the foul rock off the cliffside outside the cave.

"No! We might need that!" The redhead threw up her hands and growled like a bear.

No. That wasn't her growling.

A bear came barreling through the back of the cave, snarling and foaming at the mouth. The creature was sick, its eyes rolling as it completely passed the dragon without notice and lunged for the human female.

Three thoughts shot through the dragon's mind.

She is my captured prey.

I must protect her.

Let the bear have the loud woman.

He acted on the first thought, shooting forward and clasping the bear by its haunches, his dragon teeth digging through the tough hide. As he threw the bear against the side of the cave, the screaming human wielded small knives, throwing them and narrowly missing the bear's eyes but hitting the throat. The bear wasn't going to die that easily though. They were a tough kind—and this one smelled like sickness. He prepared to slice the bear open with a talon, but the human threw another volley of knives, and the bear jerked backward to avoid a hit and slammed its head into the cave wall. A knife struck its throat, finishing what the wall had started, and the creature dropped, dead before it hit the ground.

Whirling, the dragon eyed the back of the cave. An opening farther inside must have been wide enough for this crazed animal to pass through. He would have to fix that.

The redhead panted as she retrieved her blades with her trembling, flower petal fingers. Once she'd finished, he used one set of talons to drag the bear to the cliff's edge and toss the animal as he'd done to the rune stone. Branches cracked as the bear fell, and the dragon let out a breath. He was thirsty now and desperate to wash the stink of sickness from his mouth.

"Thank you," the redhead said, "for helping me." She looked over the cliff's edge, not appearing to care that she had a dragon at her back. "That poor creature must have had the foaming rage."

Why was she speaking to him like she knew him? As if he really had wanted to protect her? It was only the leftover magic of that rune stone that had had him thinking that earlier. It was quite worn off now. He contented himself in believing he'd killed the bear to protect his prey—the woman. Not out of some bond between them.

He snorted smoke out his nose, which made her freeze in fear, then he stalked into the back of the cave hoping to find dripping water and to close up the opening the bear had nosed out. He didn't want anyone surprising him while he slept. And he was so very tired. Maybe he had the beginnings of the foaming rage too.

"Dorin, do you understand me?"

Swiveling, he let out a puff of smoke as a warning. She needed to stay away from him. He didn't think he would eat her, but she confused him. That nagging magic still bothered him. Yes, that was it. He couldn't have some strange bond with a human. Shaking his head and growling loud enough to draw dust from the cave's cracks, he continued into the cave. Thankfully, the woman didn't follow.

After three tight turns, wings tucked for passage, he located a nice, steady stream of mountain water coming from a spot where two large rock formations met in the darkest region of the cave. Working only on scent, he set his muzzle beneath the flow and drank his fill of the near-freezing water. He was too tired then to find the opening the bear had used, so he curled up and fell asleep near the streaming water, content to spend a while in the dark, away from a certain annoying human.

DORIN WOKE WITH A START, HIS HEART BEATING WILDLY and his hair in his eyes. His face, neck, and chest were wet, and falling water splashed nearby. Where was he? How long had he been sleeping? He stood and began searching for clues, vaguely remembering the night sky and...

Oh, Rigel and Ursae save him. Had he captured two women?

His head spun, and he spread his hands to steady himself before walking onward. The scant light of the cave led him to an alcove. Ah. His clothing. He remembered folding them and placing them here. Squinting, stomach twisting, he tried to see if he had blood on his hands. There didn't seem to be any, so he dressed as quickly as his chilled body allowed. He hoped to all the gods that he hadn't hurt anyone last night.

The cave opened into a larger room, one he remembered.

"Dorin!" Brielle, the Wylfen princess, ran toward him, and his heart leapt at seeing her, though whether that was due to frustration, anger, or desire, he wasn't sure. "Do you remember finding me?" she asked.

"What are you doing here?"

"It's the rune stone." Her eyes were emeralds. He shook his head, still spinning with confusion. "The stone I unearthed at the foothills, it's what called you to my courtyard the first time, then again last night by the river's edge."

Anger boiled in his chest. "Why did you call me? I am not yours to beckon as you wish. It's a fool thing to do anyway. I could have killed you. You should have escaped me while you were able." A plan grew roots in his mind, and he took her arm, ignoring the spark of pleasure touching her gave him. "You are now my prisoner, Princess Brielle. If I must be cursed, I can at least do something for my kingdom while I work out a solution."

She jerked away from him. "Ha. As if you could keep me here. You're half out of your mind, and you sleep more than anyone I've met. But if you're hiding proper chains or cages in your back pocket there, perhaps you'll prove me wrong."

The woman was laughing at him, her pink lips drawn into a cocky grin.

He backed her up against the rock wall. Staring up at him, she glared as he pressed closer, torn between wanting to toss her off the cliff and hoping he could stay and breathe her honey and blossom scent in for eternity.

"You were right," he growled out, forcing himself not to look down at her chest as it brushed his. "I am a dragon, and so I will use the cursed skills set on me." During his research into dragons, he'd discovered their tremendous tracking ability. It made sense he had that skill set now as well. "I have scented you, Princess Brielle, and there is nowhere in the world where you can hide from me now," he said, bluffing. "Stay, and I will see you returned to your father with a peace treaty in place. Leave, and I can't promise you the beast in me will treat you as anything other than prey."

"Dragons don't prey on humans." Her jaw worked as she gritted her teeth. Stars, she was brave. The steel in her look was directly in contrast to the soft curves of her cheeks and the gentle slope of her chin and throat.

He swallowed. "They also don't shift into elven princes."

Pain burst across his groin, and Brielle twisted away. She'd kneed him between the legs. As he coughed and set a hand on the wall, she snickered.

"Give up this game, Dorin. I've seen evil. I know it well. The night you woke in my courtyard, naked and shivering, your true self showed in the kindness of your stupidly gorgeous, golden, elven eyes. You don't scare me."

He had to bring his plan to fruition, and to do that, he needed several items. Rope to tie the foul Wylfen princess and keep her here. Parchment, ink, and quill to write his letter to her evil father. And food for them both. Despite her confidence, he truly feared the beast in him might devour her if she angered him while in dragon form. He was more than willing to ransom her for peace for his people, but the thought of hurting her made him sick. The sooner this nightmare came to an end, the better.

He turned, thinking to tell her to remain here, but her jutting chin and angry, emerald eyes said she wouldn't listen and he'd be wasting his breath.

With one last glance, he leapt from the cliff's edge and landed on an outcropping, heading for the farmer's croft he'd visited. If he couldn't manage that, he'd find another farm or trader's post.

"Where are you going?" she called out.

Ignoring her, he eyed the distance between the horizon and the sun. He had plenty of time to seek supplies, well, if everything went according to plan. Of course, he'd sprouted wings from his elven form so nothing about his life now was predictable. He just hoped he wouldn't unleash dragonfire onto any innocents.

"Answer me!" A knife stuck in a sapling beside him. He spun to see Brielle standing with her hands on her hips.

He only growled and walked faster.

CHAPTER 10
BRIELLE

Brielle started to follow him, but the dark stains on the cave floor pricked her thoughts. She bent, and with her cloak pooling at her boots, she touched the dried puddle. It was blood.

"Is it animal or human?" a voice said, making Brielle jump.

Maren climbed into the cave, face washed clean and dark gold hair pulled into a tight braid.

"I thought you were gone for good. How did you find us up here?"

With a wink, Maren approached the blood and extended her wand. "A witch has her ways." She set the end of the wand in the center of the stain. "Common animal or human, you will reveal. Upon this stain, I lay my seal." A flash of gold and black magic shot across the cave floor, and a gray cloud formed the shape of a sheep and a man.

Brielle's stomach turned, and she looked to Maren. "He killed a man."

"He ate one, most likely." Maren sheathed her wand in the vines she wore as a belt at the waist of a homespun dress.

Perhaps she had magicked the dress into being? It was certainly an improvement from the rags she'd been in. Magic was so handy, Brielle thought idly. "Dragons don't eat humans."

"If you say it enough, it might become true."

"No, really. They don't. I've studied them. All the records show that dragons don't enjoy the taste. They only bite when threatened, and even then, they release the victim or kill them outright. They don't consume them."

"That's three times toward making it true. Keep on giving that a go. I think it'd be wiser for you to come with me and escape this awful cave, but it's your life." Maren looked Brielle up and down. "You've lost the rune stone. I can't hear its magic anymore."

"He threw it off the cliff."

"Too bad. It was a powerful artifact."

The loss pressed on Brielle's history-loving heart. "I know," she said miserably.

"So you're staying here? With the dragon elf? Last chance. I'm going to take you up on the sailing offer."

"He says he'll hunt me down by scent if I leave. I'd only be placing you in danger. I'll get through to him."

"Even if he weren't a shapeshifting dragon, he's still the heir of Balaur, your greatest enemy."

How could she explain? The golden scales on his strong-boned face brought to mind the dragon-shifter goddess Nix and the time of the great elven god Arcturus.

Dorin could take to the skies, rule his realm with fire. He had the blood of powerful ancients, blood that held a magic thought to be lost forever. He was the most exciting, fascinating, beautiful creature in the world, and there wasn't a chance she'd leave here for such a piddling thing as her safety.

"Maren, what do you live for?"

"Well, I just now had my life returned to me. Thank you for that. I might have to think a bit on the topic."

"Understandable. I live for adventure and for exploring the secrets of the ancient world. I love the power and mystery of it. Many times, I've risked my life to sneak away to my ship and sail to Khem. I dare to walk the streets of that island to visit Zahra, a member of the first family of Khem, a woman who could order my head lopped off on a whim. I do it simply so I can seek the treasures of the past. Every moment, my heart beats for history and for the thrill of discovery. Dorin is the past come roaring back to life."

Maren's eyes had gone wide. "So you're staying."

Brielle grinned, shaking her head. "Yes."

"Even if the handsome dragon elf with ancient power decides you'd be delicious."

"Even if. What a way to die!"

Clapping Brielle on the shoulder, Maren nodded. "Thanks again for the rescue and the position on your ship. I hope you don't get to die in your chosen manner and that we meet again on the sea."

Brielle had to laugh at that. "Will you just stay for a day?"

"And risk my neck for history?"

"He won't hurt you."

"Says the girl standing in blood."

"It's not a lot of blood," Brielle said. "It could mostly be from the sheep and the man had a wound."

"A wound made by dragon teeth."

"Or farm tools."

Maren nodded. "Know a lot about farm tools, do you?"

Glaring, Brielle tried to decide whether she liked Maren or wanted to kick her off the cliff. "Just stay until nightfall. Then you can slip away while I distract him."

"Why do you want me here?" Maren asked.

Brielle considered that carefully. "Well, if things don't go the way I want, you could defend us with your magic. And honestly, I think having the two of us here might help Dorin feel more at ease."

Maren wiggled her black eyebrows. "Is it a little tense between you and your vicious enemy? I know what resolves such tension."

Warmth coiled in Brielle's belly as she recalled the feeling of Dorin pressed against her, his gold eyes flashing and his broad shoulders blocking the light. "No. It's not like that."

"Right." Maren dropped onto a boulder near the entrance and crossed her legs. "Fine, I'll stay. I don't know why, really."

Brielle crossed her arms. "Because you owe me your life, perhaps?"

Tilting her head, Maren tapped her finger on her pointy chin. "I think it's a sick curiosity, really. I want to see how in the names of all the goddesses you plan to get through to this cursed elven prince."

"He's not cursed," Brielle said. "He's blessed."

Maren's eyes narrowed. "With the ability to gobble us both down in a blink."

"Please stop."

"Aye, aye, Captain."

Brielle pointed at her. The witch had to keep that to herself. "That's a secret."

"So don't mention your ship and Khem and this royal Zahra lady in front of the scary dragon elf?" Maren asked, fluttering her eyelashes.

"No, please refrain."

"As you say, my lady."

Cocking an eyebrow, Brielle eyed this woman who'd slid into her life so easily. "I might talk him into eating you first if your tongue proves to be a continuing challenge."

"Oh, my tongue has nothing on yours, Fire of Wylfenden."

Teeth grinding together, Brielle tried to remember folk didn't know how much she hated that nickname. "You'll fit in just fine with my crew, witch."

Maren had brought a small pouch filled with unopened flowers, faeberries, and a cold, cooked rabbit leg.

"You've been busy."

She handed Brielle some flowers. "This is plantain lancéolé. A little bitter, but good."

They ate in companionable silence, the spring breeze teasing their hair and bringing the scent of the pines and the smell of the snow that never quite melted on the highest peaks.

For a moment, she pretended that she wasn't the daughter of an evil king. She was just Brielle, the one who sailed to Khem to see Zahra and spent her days digging in the dirt for long-forgotten secrets, a woman who was lucky enough to see the first dragon shifter in one thousand years.

CHAPTER 11
DORIN

Dorin left the shelter of a large pine and hurried toward a different farm three hours' walk from the cave. The farmer and his three nearly grown boys were tilling the strips of terraced land and were far too busy to notice an intruder. Their dog, however, was having none of Dorin's thievery.

A growl emanated from the brindled pup, a cur who didn't seem to know how small he still was. The farmer had tied the young dog to a post in front of the house.

"Easy, fellow. That growl is impressive. And that's coming from someone who spends time as a dragon." Dorin held out a hand to let the dog sniff, hoping the animal might sense the lack of aggression in Dorin.

The pup came forward, reached out its nose, then snapped at Dorin's fingers.

"Ah. Careful now." He stood and set a hand on the house's door, but the dog erupted into mad barking.

"Curses." Dorin gave up stealth and rushed inside. "Bow. Arrows. Where do they keep you?"

He took up a shirt hanging near the hearth that had apparently just been mended and tied the sleeves and hem so it created a sack of sorts. Snagging a pile of berries from a basket near the window, he began to fill his bag. A round of cheese. Day old bread. A crock of something unlabeled. His prisoner would have to eat. He couldn't have her dying before her father had the chance to promise peace with Balaur. There was no parchment to be had in the house, so instead, Dorin tore the bottom from the one scroll they possessed—a list of seeds, looked like—and nabbed the bit of charcoal they'd been using to scribe. It was rough, but it would do.

The pup was still destroying the day with its racket. He had to hurry.

Finally, he spotted a bow and a quiver against the far wall near a straw mattress. Feeling miserable and sick for the toll he was taking on this family, he grabbed the weaponry as well as a length of rope and a small bag with a flint and striker, then fled out the door past the barking dog.

"Prince Dorin?"

Dorin skidded to a halt.

A lad around fifteen or so eyed him. He didn't look familiar, just an average elven farm boy. "Your Majesty." He dropped to one knee in the style of royal messengers. "I ran missives from Balaur Castle to your exploratory group during your first summer with the dragons. That was before my father inherited this farm from my uncle."

Clearing his throat, Dorin tried to appear less thief and

more prince. A hundred places he'd rather be at this moment flashed through his mind. Having his arm burned off by angry dragon younglings. Experiencing frostbite in every single one of his toes. Dancing with Costel's sister. How did one attempt to look regal and deserving of a crown when one held stolen items? It was impossible.

"I'm sure you notice," Dorin said, "I'm holding items from your home, and for that, I sincerely apologize. All I can say at this moment is that I'm in a situation that cannot be understood by myself or anyone else. I will endeavor to rectify the loss to your family as quickly as is elvenly possible. On my honor." Dorin touched his heart and dipped his head.

The lad stared. "Whatever we have is yours, Your Majesty."

With one more nod of apology and a chest full to bursting with self-loathing, Dorin hurried into the forest.

THE CAVE WAS EMPTY. ANGER ROSE INSIDE HIM, HOT AND wild. Perhaps it was more like panic. Brielle was gone, and so was his one solid chance at finding peace for his country. Why did he make a mess of everything in his life?

CHAPTER 12
BRIELLE

Brielle and Maren searched the forest floor for the rune stone, Brielle shifting through pine needles among the gnarled, raised roots while the witch checked a cluster of glossy-leaved bushes that didn't grow in Wylfenden.

It was odd to be in Balaur, in the enemy's kingdom without any guard. Her people called all of these mountains the Ecailles, but this stretch and beyond belonged to the elves, and she knew it well. She'd never been to war, but images brought on by what others had told her filled her head. Warriors like Dorin with swords that moved as fast as the wind. Their kind could leap impossibly high and were immune to most strikes, their flesh far stronger than a human's. And sometimes they had fae at their sides, ready to use healing magic. She couldn't hate the elves. Her kingdom had always been the aggressors, not the elven armies. Here she was, in their land with their heir, sharing a secret that would change

Balaur forever. A thrill made of fear and freedom zipped through her. She had the power to help Dorin and his people deal with this development of his. Whatever occurred later, she had to make certain Father never caught him.

Was Father looking for her now, or had he sent D'Aboville and the Broyeurs? Most likely the latter. Father didn't tend to do his own hunting. He only enjoyed the kill.

"How long before the Broyeurs track us down?" Maren's mind must have been following a similar path to Brielle's.

"Depends on how messy you were on your way up to the cave."

"Oh, that's nice talk considering I'm here out of the pure kindness of my heart."

"Sorry. But that's the truth of it. If you broke branches on your climb, if you scratched a hand on a rock... The Broyeurs' hunting dogs can locate their quarry on a surprisingly limited supply of clues."

Maren wiped her hands on her dress. "That explains a lot."

Brielle's heart ached at the tension in her new friend. The woman had been through so much. Brielle wouldn't press for more of the tale. If Maren wanted to tell it, Brielle would listen. If not, so be it.

The sun drifted through the forest canopy, and the dappled light hit a shining object.

"There!" Brielle darted toward the base of an ancient willow. The rune stone was warm to the touch, another sign of magic.

"Found it, did you?" Maren grinned in that funny way

she had, with just one side of her mouth. "You may not be a witch, but you definitely have witch blood somewhere in that princess heart of yours."

Brielle stood and pocketed the stone.

Maren was touching the willow's pale green leaves and frowning. "Surprising how leafy this tree is."

"Why?" Brielle started back the way they'd come, up a narrow animal path lined in yellow grasses that hadn't yet grown green with spring's warmth.

"It's early. Willows don't usually leaf out before the weather's been warmer for longer. And I don't like the ivy twisting around its trunk."

"Ivy kills trees, doesn't it?" The tree seemed incredibly healthy despite the parasitic growth.

"It does. I truly don't like this tree."

"Well, come on, then, and let's leave the unnatural thing to its evil business."

"You jest, but your words might be closer to the truth than you think."

A chill as cold as the dungeon's walls crept up Brielle's spine. "What do you believe is causing the early growth and the ability to withstand the ivy?"

"Magic, of course. And it feels off."

"Off how?" Brielle grabbed a small ledge on the steep rock slope leading up to the cave.

"Foul. Wrong. Dark."

"Good thing we have a dragon at our beck and call."

Dorin crashed through the trees, his elven hands bending branches out of the way and his hood shadowing most of his face. Goddess above, but he was glorious in his rage, all graceful speed and undeniable power. The light caught the scales on his cheek, and for a moment he was a history scroll come to life.

Warmth curled in Brielle's stomach and moved lower. If he would just listen to her, they could have so much fun together learning about his magic and this new ability he'd developed. She could just imagine him grasping her in those muscled arms and flying her into the heavens, his dragon wings wide behind them, their green color as dark and lovely as it had been the day he'd slipped D'Aboville's clutches. She was so glad he'd escaped. To see him on a pyre would be horrifying. Of course, could one burn a dragon? Maybe not.

"You're positively thunderous," she said, giving him a sly smile. "What has you all worked up? Ransom not working out the way you'd hoped?" She pushed past him.

"You could've been taken by wolves," he said, his voice a snarl.

"During the day? Doubtful."

"You saw that bear," he said. "The foaming sickness could have spread."

"I'm touched at your concern, but we're fine here. And we located the incredibly powerful rune stone you so foolishly tossed from the cliff."

"Who are you?" he demanded of Maren.

"This is Maren," Brielle said. "She is a witch who escaped my father's dungeon."

"With the Princess's help." Maren grinned and waved her wand.

He looked at each of them, lips tight. "How did you get down here anyway?" His gaze flitted up to the cave's entrance, then he glared at Brielle.

She snorted. He thought them weaklings. "Humans aren't elves—"

"Or dragons!" Maren piped up from the back, one finger lifted as if to make a point.

"As I was saying," Brielle murmured, glancing sideways at Maren, "we aren't elves, but we can still climb. Especially those of us who have spent our lives sneaking out of castles."

Unable to fight the part of herself that loved showing off, she hurried toward the cave, childishly hoping Dorin was watching her climb so expertly, but when she turned to check on him, he was staring at the sky. What was going on in his head?

Maren had her wand out and was gripping the roots of a cliff-side tree, her feet scrambling for purchase on the animal path. "Only with magic am I able to do this. I don't understand how you're managing."

"My mother used to call me her kitten because I would climb the trees in the castle courtyard, then cry for someone to fetch me down."

Dorin grabbed a handhold in the rock face beside the path and outpaced Brielle easily. He didn't glance her way even once.

She hated how much that bothered her. Curse him for being so interesting. She didn't want to care about his fascinating scales, the fact that he sprouted wings, and how he could morph into the most dangerous creature in existence, but she most certainly did. What would it be like to kiss a legend come to life?

CHAPTER 13

DORIN

Back in the cave, Dorin scowled as Brielle finished the climb, removed the rune stone from her pocket, and proceeded to ogle the old—and most likely evil—rock like it was the finest gold. He snatched the stone and shoved it into his cloak's interior pocket, ignoring her indignant gasp.

"You had better not toss that thing away again!" she snapped.

Using every bit of elven speed he had, he ripped the knife holster from her right leg. She shouted in his ear and slammed a knee into his ribs as he moved to tear the other holster free. Another knee, this time to his solar plexus, pushed all the air from his lungs. He stood and threw the holsters and knives out of the cave's entrance, off the cliffside.

Her lips drew back, and her glare burned. "Those were from my mother."

"And you can have them back after the peace treaty is signed and you are returned to your father."

With the farmer's flint and striker, he lit a torch he'd made from the shirt and a smear of flame leaves he'd obtained near a spring below the cave. Torch in hand, he grabbed Brielle's arm and started dragging her toward the back of the cave.

"Witch Maren," he said over his shoulder. "I suggest you leave while I allow it."

"Don't have to tell me twice."

He didn't miss the witch's wink to Brielle. He'd have to make sure she didn't return to rescue Brielle.

"What are you doing?" Brielle kicked the back of his knee, and he almost stumbled, his elven agility keeping him from falling.

"I'm going to tie you up back here, out of sight, so if I shift into a dragon again, I won't hurt you."

"You're hurting me right now."

Feeling ill, he loosened his grip on her arm. But she was Wylfen. Why did he care? Her people had killed so many of his fellow warriors and innocents too, camp followers who had been in the wrong place at the wrong time. A nagging voice inside his head reminded him that she had saved him, but he silenced the voice. So she'd acted kindly and bravely once—that didn't mean she was good. Her Wylfen blood would rise at some point and she would surely stab him in the back.

"You are my enemy and the key to peace for my people. Nothing else matters."

"Then why care if the dragon in you gives me trouble?"

"Because he might do more than cause trouble," Dorin said. "He might take your head."

"I don't think he will."

"I didn't ask what you thought."

She snorted. "I don't wait to be asked for my opinions, Prince Dorin."

The cave path led to a three-pronged passage. Dorin noted the two massive stalactites to remember the way, then took the first opening since that passageway would be too tight for his dragon form and thus would keep her safe from him. The walls pressed close, and Brielle's body pushed against his, her hair tickling his cheek and her hip brushing his. His blood rose to the feel of her, his stomach tightening and his breath quickening.

"Dorin. Please. I can take care of myself. You don't have to do this. I want peace too."

"Wylfen lie."

She exhaled, shaking her head. "How many Wylfen do you know who save witches from the king's dungeon? Hmm?"

He doubted that was all there was to that story. Brielle had been offered something valuable in return. It hadn't been kindness. Wylfen hated magic. Thought it to be blasphemy against the natural earth, the fools. She'd only saved him to keep herself out of trouble. Now, well perhaps she was following him, hoping to help her father's men find him.

"You had no idea Maren was a witch until you saw her on the climb with her wand out," he said.

"Fine. Believe what you want. I'm not the begging type.

I'll get out of here though, and you'll regret treating me like this."

"I will feed you, and I'm only putting you back here to protect you from my curse. I'm treating you far better than any Wylfen deserve."

"You don't have a curse."

"We've been through this."

He tossed her to the ground, set a foot on her thigh firmly but without the pressure to injure, then went to work lashing her to a stalactite. His fingers grazed the rib beneath her chest, and he heard her gasp. "Is that too tight?"

"It's fine, you idiot. I could be your ally, and here you are mistreating me. I might be the only one willing to help you in the entire world, clod head."

Ignoring the heat of her skin through her clothing and the delicate lines of her neck and shoulder where her dress had fallen a bit, he tied a proper knot, then turned to leave. A twinge of guilt hit him, right in the heart.

"If you need aid," he said, "shout my name. I'll ensure the cave is secure from other predators before I return to the entrance. I'll bring you some food shortly."

She glared, the torch's fire reflected in her green eyes. He could almost feel her anger like a spear headed for his chest. He'd have liked it better if she'd railed more or hurled curses at him.

Forcing himself to leave her, he went to the back of the cave. Taking up small rocks, he secured the crevices and spaces that could allow a predator entry. He maneuvered the maze of passageways and left to hunt with a bow and arrows.

The scent of the witch was almost nonexistent, so she must have truly left the area unless she had magic and will to cover her presence. Did this Maren actually have a bond of sorts with Brielle? She still might return to attempt a rescue—especially if what Maren had said was true, that Brielle had helped her escape the dungeons. No. It just couldn't be that simple, that pure. Surely, Maren had offered something to Brielle for help. It had been an exchange and that was over now.

Dousing the burning unease flickering around his heart, he set to finding a deer path and locating his quarry.

The sun lowered and bled color across the sky through the pines and budding maples, beeches, and oaks. A large stag nibbled the new growth on the ground, his ears twitching. He'd heard Dorin, it seemed, but only for a moment and hadn't scented him or he'd have been off and running minutes ago. Dorin nocked an arrow, focused on the stag, and let fly.

The wind rose as the arrow shot through the air, and the arrow hit the stag at a bad angle. The animal shrieked and dashed into the darkening forest. The scent of blood caught Dorin's nose as the sun disappeared.

He shook violently. Heat flamed across his chest and down his back.

"No. No, no, no."

Why couldn't he control his own body?

"Stay alert. Remain yourself," he said to himself. He repeated the phrase three times before sparks encircled his arms and legs. The black took him.

. . .

WHEN HE OPENED HIS EYES, HE SAW COLORS HE'D NEVER known existed. A shade somewhere between emerald and ruby, but bright as day... Another hue like the sun on the river in Dragon Wing Pass but with hints of yellow. He shook his head as a strength rose in him. He gasped, rocking backward. A tail whipped out behind him, and he shouted. He was still Dorin, and he was a dragon.

The scent of blood called to him like a song, and he forgot everything else, rushing after the wounded stag. The musk of the prey made his stomach growl, and the spark of dragonfire warmed his chest and brought a taste similar to southern citrus fruits and wood fire to his tongue. He was on the stag in a heartbeat, and he neatly bit the throat, killing it quickly. Stepping back from the deer, he let out a crackling burst of flame, torching the prey and filling the air with the glorious smell of cooked meat. After devouring his meal, he looked up. Stars danced above the trees. For a time, his thoughts flitted away...

And then he came back to himself and looked down at the dark blood on the forest floor. There was no going back to the cave now. He could lose himself, hurt Brielle, and ruin everything. Tucking his wings, he searched out an open spot, somewhere to lift off. He couldn't believe this was happening. He was a dragon that could summon dragonfire from his belly and fly into the night sky, traveling farther in one night than he previously could in three. At least. He could easily make it to Balaur Castle and his family.

An ache spread in his chest, and he had to catch his breath.

If only he could go to them and ask them what to do.

They had to be worried about him. He'd been gone for far too long with no word sent by any messengers. They'd have sent out search parties.

This was a nightmare.

If it led to peace between Balaur and Wylfen, then it would be a useful nightmare. Yes, he had to refrain from visiting Balaur. He couldn't risk hurting his family. And he had work yet to do. He'd fly all night and approach the cave near dawn when hopefully he would transform back into his elven form. Then he would write the message, return to the messenger lad he'd found at the farm, and move forward with negotiations with the King of Wylfenden. It would work. It had to. If not, this entire horror of an existence would be nothing more than grief and more grief.

He stretched his wings and flew toward the stars.

Flying was as natural as walking in this form, but it did nothing to calm his fears. The night air whipped past his face, the chill not at all bothering his scaled hide though he did have a strange longing for fire, for intense heat. Following that desire, he let his intuition guide him. The dip between two peaks led to a plateau hidden by the way the mountains came together. But it wasn't actually a plateau; it was a caldera. His dragon instincts drew him toward the center of a former volcano. The scent of sulfur rose into the wind, and a curling tail of steam undulated from a crack in the ground. He tore at the crack with a front talon. Hot steam blew into his face. The elf in him drew back, but the dragon urged him closer. The heat tingled across his scales and helped relax the muscles he'd used to fly.

A pop sounded, and earthblood—golden and bright in the darkness—gurgled from the opening. He settled down beside the incredible heat, feeling better than he had in ages. Hopefully, the monster that reigned over him would be gone by sunrise.

CHAPTER 14
BRIELLE

The moment Dorin was gone, Brielle exhaled, and the rope tied around her loosened. Having traveled and lived through some wild times with Zahra in Khem, she knew the tricks. She worked one arm out by lifting a shoulder and wiggling.

Had Maren left? She certainly wouldn't have blamed her. Freed, Brielle touched the inner pocket of her cloak and cocked her head to listen for the hum of the runestone. Yes, its magic was there, almost impossible to perceive.

She'd enjoyed picking the pocket of a dragon elf.

Setting her hand against the wall, she began to search her way out of this small section of the cave. No slouch with direction, she soon walked into the dim light of the main, wider passageway.

The sun set as she made it to the entrance, the sky going purple over the snow-capped peaks. A shiver shook her, and she pulled her cloak closed.

Voices carried from the forest below the rock face. Hunters? Dorin? Who was out here at night?

Going to her belly, she scooted toward the edge of the cliff. Torches bobbed in a line not far from the animal path that led to the cave. She focused on the voices, the sounds disjointed with the echo and the distance.

Finally, she heard one word.

"Princess?"

Her heart jumped. She rolled over, hiding completely. It was D'Aboville.

What now? Aside from cursing everything and raging out of here to get one kick between the captain's legs before she was taken and forever trapped in a life of misery, into being a Broyeur and hurting those with magic... No, she wouldn't do it. She'd die first. No way she could live as one of them. She'd strike out against Father, and to the underworld with the consequences.

Time for her one good kick.

Wincing, she remembered Dorin chucking her throwing knives off the cliffside.

"Flaming stones. Stupid, miraculous dragon elf."

Instead of amazing knives that were honed to perfect, she grabbed a rock and began slipping as quietly as possible down the rock face toward the Broyeurs. At the base of the rise, the line of Broyeurs ended with D'Aboville. She threw the rock into the forest beyond them, and they all turned toward the noise. Rushing D'Aboville, she leaped onto his back and wrapped an arm around his neck, choking him as Zahra had taught her two seasons ago.

Forget kicks. Throttling was far more effective.

D'Aboville dropped his torch, grunted, then shifted his

weight. He dropped a shoulder and slung Brielle over and cast her to the ground. The earth hit her back and expelled all the air from her lungs in a painful blast. Stunned, she watched as he grinned, teeth white in the near dark.

He put a boot on her throat and held up his hands to stop the other Broyeurs' questions and shouts. "Unless it's a dragon you spotted up there, hold your tongues. I have our true quarry here. For it's one of our own, our newest Broyeur."

Sputtering and wishing to every god and goddess that she had the power of dragonfire, Brielle tried desperately to shove his boot from her throat. No air would pass, and spots danced in front of her eyes. The hum she had felt when she'd whispered over the rune stone echoed in her ears and vibrated her chest. So strange... Just when she thought she was going to faint, he released her and yanked her to standing with a rough hold on her hair.

"I'm sure you didn't intend to attack your captain, Princess." He released her but stayed close.

"I'm sure I did. If you're going to take me back, then you'll have to do it with force. Just remember how mercurial Father can be when it comes to his offspring. He might just forgive you for hurting me. Or he might decide your limbs would look fantastic arranged just so above his hearth."

The Broyeurs didn't flinch at her statement, but they weren't attempting to restrain her either.

She faced D'Aboville. He had drawn his sword with his branded hand—the Broyeur dark fist in flame spread over his knuckles, a match to the one on her upper back, at the base of her neck.

D'Aboville flipped the weapon. He was going to hit her.

Body buzzing like a swarm of bees, she slammed a palm into his nose. He fell back a step, then, quick as a snake, struck her across the face with the flat of his blade. Heat preceded an agonizingly powerful throb of pain as she tumbled to the ground.

A roar sounded from the trees.

She lifted herself on her elbows to see Dorin as a Jade dragon, furious and hovering, his belly flickering with the light of dragonfire. D'Aboville yanked her to standing, then threw her between him and the dragon prince.

A blaze of blinding light seared her flesh like the sun itself had fallen from the sky, then darkness stole her mind.

CHAPTER 15

DORIN

ine! he shouted in his head. *This place is mine!*
The humans shrieked and ran before his
dragonfire could do more than set their
clothes to smoking, and he began to fly after them, but a
sight stopped him.

A woman with fire-red hair lay still, one side of her
blistering from burns.

Recognition hit him like a strong wind, blowing his
wings back and felling him like a tree. He pitched
downward and smacked the ground. Sparks cracked and
snapped around him, magic coursing through his blood and
bones.

Shaking himself, he found his feet, once again an elven
prince, no longer a dragon. How he had managed to shift
now was a puzzle he had no heart to solve at the moment.

As he ran to her and knelt, she flickered out of sight,
then back again. He gasped. What was this magic?

"Please." His voice trembled. In the name of the god

Arcturus... He'd never injured someone so directly in a time outside of war. His stomach rolled. Even though she was a Wylfen, this was too much. Too harsh. "I didn't intend to hurt you. I wasn't myself. I told you I was cursed. You should have left when you had the chance, you stubborn thing!" With no thought left for how he had not a stitch of clothing, he lifted her inert form. She was an enemy, but he couldn't allow her to die like this. This felt too much like cold-blooded murder.

Her head fell back, showing her pale neck and the edge of the burn that ran down her side. "We'll go to Balaur Castle. I'll bring you there during the day. We'll have Princess Aurora's fae ladies come. They can heal you. Filip can bring them quickly on his dragon, Jewel."

An itching feeling joined the sweat of panic that ran over him like a fever. He'd seen dragonfire burns during his time studying the creatures in the remote regions of these mountains. He'd seen men die from infection, from shock too. And he was so far from the castle and even farther from any fae that could heal. There wasn't enough time.

If only he could force his wings to expand from his back but keep this elven form as he had during his escape at the cabin, then he could carry her safely and quickly.

He shouted, furious, then a twig snapped, and he fell silent, studying the darkness, using his elven vision to see in the night.

The witch, Maren, walked out of the woods. "Need a hand? Or should I say, a wand? I can't heal. That gift isn't in my blood as it is in some rare witches. But I can do some good here, I think."

She whispered something and pointed her wand. Magic

blinked gold and smelled of sage as it wavered through the air, then his dragon wings burst from his body in a feeling much like stretching after a long trek. The soft wool of trousers brushed his skin from waist to ankle, then something tickled his neck—the ties of a thick winter cloak the stark gray hue of the cliffs.

"Showing up naked would be delightfully interesting, but I think you'll have enough to explain without that bit. Or should I say, bits?" She grinned wickedly.

Brielle was limp, and fear shook him. He ran five steps, then stretched his wings and caught the spring breeze, taking off into the sky.

"My thanks to you," he called out. "Flee as quickly as you can. The hunters are nearby. Or do you need me to come back for you once I find help for her?" He didn't want her to suffer at the hands of the Wylfen.

"I'll find my own way. Don't worry about me." She saluted him like a warrior as he took off, then the night swallowed the sight of her far below.

Dorin drove hard toward the stars, holding Brielle against his chest and desperately trying to hear her breathing between beats of his wings.

Over snowy mountaintops and beyond great canyons where spring wildflowers swayed in the starlight, Dorin flew, the dragon in him just barely restrained and fury boiling his blood. The beast in him hated the fact that those Wylfen men had crossed the border into Balaur to hunt him and possibly Brielle too since she had helped him escape. His elven self was not as territorial, but even that side of him understood the implication of their actions.

They felt free to cross into his family's kingdom and do as they saw fit. He would have revenge.

The purple of a bruise stretched from her jaw to her ear where one of the heartless fools had struck her. Not that he was any better. As a full dragon, he'd nearly burned her to death. She could very well still die, and it would be his fault entirely. She had saved him, and all he'd done was tie her up to use her as a ransom and then unleash dragonfire on her.

He was a demon from the underworld. Worse, because he knew how to behave in a civilized and honorable way. But he needed to use her to gain some sort of agreement with Wylfen. And despite the fact that she'd rescued him, she was the Princess of Wylfenden. She was an enemy.

But would the Wylfen think Brielle was dead?

If so, they'd only strive to find the beast that Dorin was so they could kill it, the murderer of their princess. If those magic hunters reported Brielle dead to their king, the man would never believe she'd lived and that Dorin was the prince and that he held her, alive. Dorin wouldn't believe it himself if he wasn't living through the truth of the story. He'd made such a mess of the entire situation.

Muscles quaking with fatigue and throat parched, he spread his wings and held them tilted to catch the wind as he landed in a rocky clearing. He set Brielle gently on the ground, easing her head down.

Her eyelids fluttered open, and she groaned in pain, her hand going to the worst of her burns, above her elbow.

Stopping her hand so she wouldn't make the injury worse, he whispered, "I am so sorry." She was an enemy—he wouldn't forget that or the fact that he was a monster—

but she had been innocent in this one situation, and he'd done a great injury to her. He would do what he could to heal her in gratitude for his rescue, in apology for the injury, and to protect her as his prisoner. It was the honorable choice.

Breathing unevenly, she let her eyes close again and went limp.

He had to find something to ease the pain. Recalling everything his mother, Queen Sorina, had taught him of herbs and healing, he searched the perimeter for springleaf and mariblush. He rooted out some popweed. Its seeds could be ground and boiled in water to create a pain reliever. Under a stand of wild ivy, he came across springleaf's fat blades. Second only to magic, the viscous fluid in the large leaves was the best treatment for burns. No rose-gold mariblush plants grew in the area, unfortunately. They would have been good to combine with the springleaf. He'd have to make do. He didn't want to leave her by herself with the possibility of predators hunting nearby.

After gathering kindling and dry branches, he stared at the would-be fire. He had no flint. Brielle shivered beside him, her skin pale as moonstone. She needed warmth.

Swallowing, he closed his eyes and focused on the spark of dragonfire in his belly and throat. The taste of citrus and smoke touched the back of his tongue. Could he bring it forward in this mostly elven form he now held? His wings remained, but the rest of him was just Dorin, elven prince. Could his elven skin handle the dragonfire, or would he bring it from his chest only to do such damage to himself that he couldn't help Brielle?

"Dorin..." Brielle's voice was almost too quiet to hear, the sound of his name cracked like ice on a spring pond.

"Bless me, Rigel and Ursae. Bless me, Nix." He focused on the spark of heat inside him and imagined it rising, growing, flickering. His throat grew hot, but the feeling wasn't painful. Was that a good sign?

The dragonfire licked its way up his throat, dragged itself into his mouth and over his lips. He exhaled, and fire rippled from him like a river of light. The kindling and branches exploded into flame, and Brielle jerked, eyes going wide.

He started to touch her good arm but pulled away. "It's...all right..." He tried to give her more assurances, but they wouldn't spill out because they were lies, and he knew it. He might hurt her again. If the dragon took full hold of him tonight again, he could very well end her life in this clearing.

Gods and goddesses, it was unbelievable. He'd summoned dragonfire.

His stomach turned, and he pressed his hands against his temples, his head pounding. The first time he'd witnessed a dragon using fire had been his second trip to study the creatures in the far north, on the very edge of Balaur. There had been a mottled, female dragon—blue and green and white—with an egg she guarded day and night, seemingly with no sleep because the mated male was dead. Dorin and his team had located the male not far from the dragon's cave, his body unnaturally wasted in the same way as two other dragons he'd found the year before. When they'd approached the female, unaware of the egg, she had blown fire across their vantage point and set one warrior's pack ablaze and severely burned a second elf's torso and face. The burns hadn't wanted to heal either. It had taken work from five fae to restore the second elf's flesh, and even then, the fellow had scars. Brielle would have scars if she were lucky enough to survive. Well, scars weren't bad. They were a visual reminder of the person's fortitude.

Dorin set the popweed seeds on a stone and began grinding them into a paste. With the water from the bubbling spring beyond where he'd obtained the springleaf, he created a drink for her cupped in a boar's ear leaf. The low bush had soft, large leaves that he and Filip used to pretend were drinking horns when they were little, longing to be adults enjoying the mysteries of fruit brandy and wine. He had no way to boil the seeds for Brielle, but hopefully, the popweed drink would still beat back a measure of her agony.

When he faced her, he realized she was humming faintly. The tune seemed familiar, but he couldn't place it. Supporting her head, he helped her sip. She coughed and spat most of it out, but it was the best he could do for now. She slumped back into a tortured sleep by the crackling fire. After tucking her cloak snugly around her, he also covered her with the magicked cloak Maren had spelled into being for him. He made sure to keep Brielle's injury open to the air.

Removing the burned cloth from her injury with careful movements, he prepared to apply the springleaf's juices. He broke open three leaves and squeezed them over the wound. Opaque drops fell onto her burns. She shivered with every dose. He then flattened the springleaf and set the insides against her wounds like a wrapping, tucking his cloak over the area. With a drop of springleaf on his thumb, he gently dabbed her split lip.

Anger coiled in his chest, the dragon stirring the desire to find and promptly destroy the ones who had done this to her. That rune stone magic still held him, that odd feeling of the need to protect her. It was as if she'd created a bond between them by using the runes. There was powerful magic in the artifact, and he was glad he'd most likely dropped it somewhere near the caldera.

He propped himself against an ancient willow—an odd tree to grow up this high and so far from a river's edge— and kept watch as long as his body allowed it. He could do nothing to ensure the dragon wouldn't rise to do evil, but he couldn't leave Brielle exposed either, so he stayed, and eventually sleep dragged him under.

CHAPTER 16
BRIELLE

Brielle existed in flames. Pain was her king now, her ruler, her torturer. Her wounds throbbed, and she dove into the darkness to escape.

The dark spit her out, and she opened her eyes to see fire flickering right in front of her. She scrambled backward, pain gripping her arm and shoulder like hands of flame. Her stomach rebelled at the overwhelming torment, and she was sick. Just bending over was another unbearable action. She fell back, and her gaze landed on the person beside her.

Dorin. Asleep. Winged. Bare chested. Eyebrows drawn together as if he dreamed of her suffering. He was terrifying. And incredibly beautiful.

She hadn't forgotten—the dragon in him had burned her. In her memory, he hovered above her and the Broyeurs, his deep green wings fluttering and his eyes bright. But he hadn't intended to hurt her. Anguish blurred her mind... Had she been dreaming of flying? She shook her head, desperate to keep her thoughts straight.

D'Aboville had found the cave, and Dorin had been defending his hideout, and D'Aboville had thrown her into the path of Dorin's flames. He hadn't had time to react, or most likely, hadn't realized she was there. He wasn't at fault; she knew that fact like she knew her own heart. Yes, he was deadly, but Dorin was a good soul. After all, here he was sitting beside her without his cloak. His garment now lay half on, half off her wounded body. He must have put it there to help her stay warm in the cold spring night. Her mind fogged thickly again, and her injured arm trembled. The stars blurred as her burns screamed in pain. She dropped back into the darkness, grateful for the relief.

When she woke, the sun had risen, and Dorin was covering the campfire with dirt, scraping the earth over the flames with his bare foot. Her mind turned slowly as she sat up. She couldn't think past what was happening right that moment. The wind on her injury. The ever-present pain. She shifted with every beat of her heart. Was that her heart beating or was it the pain throbbing? Was there a difference?

Dorin said something to her, but the sounds garbled and twisted, sliding off her ears and onto the ground as the drier bits of scattered dirt flew away from the smothered fire and into the wind.

He crouched in front of her, eyes like gold coins, his full lips moving in a question, based on the lift at the end of the phrase of twining sounds that didn't make words... Wincing against the pain, she tried to understand. Shaking his head and murmuring, Dorin lifted a leaf to her lips and helped her drink a cold, sweet liquid. She drank it down and shut her eyes, allowing her head to fall onto his solid, warm chest.

"Not a curse. Blessed," she murmured. "You smell like Khem oranges and wood smoke."

Strong arms lifted her, cradled her, hands and fingers gentle against her thighs and upper back as they lurched forward as one. Opening her eyes just a bit, she watched the wisps of clouds grow larger. They were flying again. Dorin's arms were warm and secure, and whatever he was giving her to drink was dulling her pain. She couldn't think straight, but she didn't wish for death anymore at least. She tried to thank him, but her mouth was filled with clouds...

WHEN SHE OPENED HER EYES AFTER WHO KNEW HOW long, she lay on a bed of long grasses. Dorin stood in front of her, his wings stretched wide as if he were protecting her from something in the line of towering pines beyond a meadow dotted with bright pink wildflowers. The wind stirred his golden hair and shook the thin membrane between the bones of his wings. The muscles in his calves strained against his trousers. With his broad shoulders, long arms—and of course the dragon element—he was an elven prince built for war. And though she was his enemy, here he was taking care of her.

No, her mind corrected. He was only protecting her so he could ransom her for peace with her father's kingdom.

She shuddered.

If the need to destroy her arose, he would do what he

had to for Balaur, for his people. She couldn't decide if that infuriated her or if she understood.

"What is it?" she croaked out, gaze on the pines.

"A mountain lion."

"Lion versus dragon elf. Sounds like an entertaining final show for this princess. I'll take it. May goddess Nix be with you."

Dorin looked at her over one clawed wingtip and raised a thick, blond eyebrow. "You're not dying."

She shut her eyes as she trembled viciously once more. "Stop bossing me about. I've had quite enough of men bossing me in this life. Perhaps my existence in the afterlife will see me free of bullying fools."

"I doubt that. Haven't you read the tales of the Shadow King?"

A frown tugged at her dry lips. Dorin was sharing folktales now? The lion must truly be readying for attack if the elven prince was trying to distract her with stories.

"My father didn't permit underworld scrolls to be housed in the Wylfen Castle library," she said. "I know nothing about the dark lord of the afterlife."

"Everything I've read leads me to believe he is rather domineering."

"Takes one to know one?"

Dorin sniffed, a sound that was almost a laugh. "I'm going to take this animal down now. Stay here and stay quiet."

"At least you're consistent." She was surely sick considering she was teasing him while a deadly beast hunted them. Taking a deep breath and keeping an eye on Dorin, she tried to relax and remain still.

A pale shadow emerged from the forest, one large paw lifted and body coiled to attack. Dorin's wings shot out, and he careened into the air, breathing dragonfire. Brielle bit down a shriek. How was he breathing fire in his partial elven form? His flesh wasn't melting from the bone, but how?

The lion launched at Dorin and swiped a claw at his leg, the animal leaping several feet from the ground after his winged opponent. Dorin wasn't breathing fire anymore. Why not? He flew over the lion's head, and the creature rotated, tail lashing out like a whip with the quick movement. One paw caught Dorin's leg, and blood gushed from three jagged rips in his trousers as the dragon elf lifted higher into the air to escape. The lion roared, and the fine hairs on Brielle's arms stood on end, a primal fear chilling her heart and begging her to run.

Before she realized what she was doing, she was crouched and preparing to do just that. The lion's glare locked onto her.

Dorin shouted, but with the wind and the painfully loud beat of her heart, she couldn't decipher the words' meaning. He flew between her and the lion and struck at the tawny beast with the tip of one wing. The claw tore across the animal's back as it lunged for Brielle, then the lion moaned a guttural growl and turned to face Dorin. Blood dripped from the animal's wound as well as from Dorin's leg.

Why wasn't he using fire? From the fear and frustration on his face, she guessed it was because he couldn't manage to summon the dragonfire again for some reason.

In a burst of speed, Dorin flew at the lion and snatched

its tail. He tugged the end and the lion curled in on itself, then twisted to lash out at the dragon elf with both front paws. Dorin shouted as the lion pounced and hit the prince in the chest, bringing both of them down in a tangling, snarling mess.

Fear pounded through Brielle like a war drum. She couldn't hear. Couldn't see clearly. Hot and cold flared through her blood, and she collapsed to her knees, gasping.

The lion had Dorin pinned to the earth, the dragon elf's arms stretched out to hold the lion back. Only Dorin's magical dragon strength must have been keeping the beast from ripping his throat out. A spark of that magic flashed around Dorin's throat and hands, and suddenly he had talons on the ends of his large fingers that pierced the lion's chest, and fire rippled from his mouth as the scales on his cheek shimmered.

The lion screamed and rolled off Dorin, dead before it fell to the muddy ground.

Dorin slowly got to his feet, his wings drooping and mud cloaking his side and bleeding leg. The cuts must have been very deep considering the toughness of elven flesh. He limped toward Brielle, his eyes looking more dragon than elf.

"I would say thank you for all of that, but—"

"But I'm only protecting you to ransom you. Yes. You're right."

She forced herself not to flinch at his suddenly cold demeanor. Was it a dragon thing? Or was it just as he said? He lifted her into his arms and readied to take off into the sky.

"You're feverish." His eyes pinched together, and his

pupils went from slitted to round, the dragon fading with what she guessed was worry for his ransom prize.

"Told you I'm dying."

His jaw muscles worked along the sharp lines of his handsome face, and he grunted with effort as he spread his wings to fly.

If he couldn't see a way to peace beyond giving her up to a man who would at best keep her forever imprisoned in the royal dungeons, then he was an obstacle. She would have to work around him to find a permanent escape from Wylfen. Perhaps she could find an ally at Balaur Castle? More likely, someone there would murder her in the night while she was sleeping. How could she convince those in charge that she wasn't like Father or D'Aboville and that she absolutely could not return to Wylfen? That there had to be another way to keep the peace or use her knowledge to forge a treaty? One thing she knew. If they saw the Broyeur brand on the back of her neck, they'd kill her immediately. The Broyeur reputation extended across the world. Even the people of Khem knew of them and feared them.

Her heartbeat pounded in her ears, and she leaned into Dorin's chest even though he was an arse of a dragon elf. She just felt so awful. Dying was really not a fun adventure.

CHAPTER 17
DORIN

Dorin's mind latched onto one truth and refused all else. He was a monster. He had done this to Brielle, and she couldn't argue the act was nothing so terrible and begin to trust him. There were so many reasons—their kingdoms being at war, the fact that they didn't know one another at all—but the most important reason she couldn't be allowed to trust him was that he was a monster and could just as easily kill her as save her life.

Wait. Why did he care if she trusted him? He shook his head and squeezed his eyes shut. He was losing his mind over this woman!

Like slamming a door, he closed off his emotions and let the cold air inspire his actions. He would be practical, stoic, and he would get this job done. The fae called to Balaur Castle would heal her. If she lived, he would ransom her to the Wylfen king for peace, then Dorin would disappear into the highest peaks and never bother anyone ever again with his twisted magic.

The world whirred by as he flew past the familiar trails and villages near the castle. He soared high enough that few would notice him in the night sky. He didn't want his kingdom knowing the heir to the throne was a wild monster. It would throw them into chaos, and Filip would have a terrible burden to bear seeing as Dorin's father, Mihai, was too sickly at this point to do much more than continue as king in name only.

Fingers tightening on Brielle's soft form, he gritted his teeth. He should have been back at the castle, working for the kingdom and taking responsibilities. It was his fate to rule Balaur, his burden to bear. Filip and their mother had to be mad with worry at his absence.

Brielle's rosebud lips parted in a moan of pain, and Dorin swallowed against a lump in his throat. Her proud cheekbones shimmered like moonlight, and her thick eyelashes fluttered in her fevered sleep. A feeling pounded on the mental door he'd slammed shut—longing. She smelled like the forest and some fine perfume, made from lavender perhaps, but it wasn't her scent or her looks that tugged at his soul. It was the way she'd so bravely confronted him even after seeing him as a dragon. Or maybe it wasn't bravery but foolishness. The wild redhead had no thought for consequences to her actions. It was as if she didn't care what happened to her. But she did care for others. She had helped that witch escape, that much was certain. So maybe it was her kind heart that appealed to him—that and the fire in her eyes that blazed with the desire to be heard and to act. She'd never be happy caged in a castle like the princess she was.

He shook his head to clear it and imagined blasting that door shut again. She was his ransom prize. That was it. The end.

He took in a shaky breath, and she shifted in his arms, her warm body pressing into his. Her slim, delicate fingers curled on his chest, and he wondered what those fingers would feel like at the back of his neck or sliding down his torso.

Rigel, god of elves, and Nix, goddess of fire, save him. He was the worst sort of elven prince. He couldn't stay focused for even one single minute.

As Brielle's breathing grew more labored, Dorin at last landed on the roof of the west wing at Balaur Castle—the stronghold that was home to his family as well as the heart of the mountain elf kingdom.

Holding Brielle securely, he closed his eyes and tried to will his wings to shift away. Recalling the feel of the sparks of magic, he visualized them disappearing into his back, but they didn't budge. He couldn't enter the castle like this. He had to keep his condition a secret. It was the only way to secure the kingdom. Filip could take Dorin's place once the treaty with Wylfen was signed. Again and again, Dorin mentally pushed the wings inside himself, willed them into invisibility, prayed to any god that would listen that they would just be gone. But it was no use. The wings were staying.

With a growl of frustration, he used one foot to lift the rope handle of a wooden square set into the roof's floor.

Underneath, a passage led him down worn stone steps. Brielle's skin blazed under her clothing, her flesh sticky where it met his. She gasped, then thrashed, and he had to hold firmly to keep from dropping her down the stairs.

The scant moonlight from the opening above his head reflected off an unknown object, then the prick of a blade touched the base of his throat. His heart stuttered, and even Brielle stilled in his arms as if she somehow knew there was danger.

"Who goes there?" a guard said.

Dorin pushed past the man, too tired to fret about being slit from ear to ear. "Your prince has returned, and I suggest you find my brother before I arrive at my rooms, or you'll be on chamber pot duty at the armory tomorrow."

The man stammered. So finally he'd noticed the wings.

"Go on," Dorin barked. "And keep my...appearance to yourself. That's an order."

After a hasty bow, the guard ran down the right-branching corridor.

This wing was mostly deserted, with cobwebs glistening at the corners of the arrow slits in the walls and rusty hinges on the doors leading into the living areas. A spiral staircase brought him to a seldom-used corridor that branched off toward the kitchen and the main passageway.

Two guards froze at the door to his chambers, their eyes matched in shock. "My lord prince," one managed to whisper. "You should know the king has been asking for you."

No doubt, and sending parties to search for him as well. "Let the king and queen know I am here and in one piece.

Then arrange for the castle maids to tend to this lady. She will sleep in my bed. I will retire to the green guest rooms below once she is settled. And men..."

"Yes, Your Highness?"

"Keep my appearance a secret from all. Even from my king and queen."

"As you say, my prince," they replied.

The secret wouldn't remain so for very long. Not after the maids saw his wings.

A voice in Dorin's head asked why he wanted Brielle to sleep in his bed, but he treated that question like he did his emotions and locked it away to deal with at another time.

Her head lolled as he lay her carefully onto the damask coverlet. He drew a fur-lined blanket across her, and goosebumps rose over her forearms. Cheeks bright red, she murmured something in Wylfen. He leaned close to her lips to try to understand.

"Ce n'est pas ta faute," she rasped in her people's tongue. *It's not your fault.*

His chest tightened, and he straightened, taking a breath. It most certainly was. But he wouldn't burn anyone again. He would do his duty, then live far, far from anyone. She knew it was his fault too; she was simply too fevered to think clearly. After removing her muddied boots and tucking her chilled feet back under the covers, he turned to see a veritable army of maids behind him. They curtseyed in unison, most looking horrified at his appearance, faces drawn tight with fear.

"Your Majesty," one maid squeaked.

Filip walked into the room and rubbed his eyes. "I suppose we have a few things to discuss." His gaze traveled from the tips of Dorin's wings to his hand—thankfully, no longer showing talons—still perched on the bed post near Brielle's neatly covered feet.

"Indeed," Dorin said grimly, his stomach twisting. What a disaster.

CHAPTER 18
DORIN

Dorin followed Filip through the crowd of maids and servants and into the corridor.

"You've always been the prince in black leathers. I never guessed your style would move toward flamboyant." Filip's tone was light, but his eyes burned with curiosity and were pinched at the edges with concern.

Running his hands through his tangled hair, Dorin paced the rectangle of moonlight shimmering on the stone floor. "I've been unwell for a while now. I had hoped to keep this from you and from our people, but..."

How could he explain this?

He faced his younger brother, a memory from their shared childhood surfacing. During Frostlight when Filip had been no more than five years of age and Dorin just seven, Filip had wandered into the raucous crowd of nobles gathered to watch the sword fight competition in the castle's inner bailey. Their nurse had started shrieking in panic, and Dorin had waded into the mass of adults, sweating and sick with worry. Even though the nurse believed Filip to be her charge, Dorin had always kept Filip safe. The wee thing had a bad habit of climbing walls and getting himself stuck in frighteningly high places. Dorin had shoved past two laughing guards, their noses red from the cold and their eyes puffed from too much fruit brandy, but he still hadn't been able to find Filip. He'd ignored the nurse's shouts and threaded through the nobles, dodging the inevitable pats on the head until he'd found Filip hanging upside down from a roof beam in the public stables. Filip had slipped just as Dorin had walked in, and he'd raced to try to catch his little brother, his heart in his mouth. Filip had landed atop Dorin, and even though the piles of straw had cushioned the blow, Dorin had broken an arm. Filip had been fine though, giggling and hugging Dorin's neck like everything in life was a grand adventure.

Now Dorin was the danger. Instead of being the protector, he was now the problem. A hollowness echoed in the depths of his heart. Was this truly the end of his life with his dear family?

"I am cursed," he said, emotion choking him. "For the past moon or so, I've opened my eyes each morning with the blood of what I hope were sheep on my hands. I don't know how this happened and what foul magic touched me or if it's something I did to deserve this, but I can't control it."

Filip touched the scales on Dorin's cheek. "It's fascinating." He stepped back, that familiar light of jesting in his gray eyes. "You spent too much time chasing dragons. They decided to make you one of their own." With a sudden movement, he pulled Dorin into a hug, his hand snagging the edge of a wing. "We will figure this out together, Brother."

Love swelled in Dorin's chest, and he hated the monster in him even more than he thought possible. Unshed tears seared the corners of his eyes. "Thank you, Filip."

But Dorin would leave at the first moment it made sense to do so. He couldn't drag his family or their kingdom into his curse.

Dorin broke from the hug. "I will sleep chained in the west wing tower. It won't protect everyone from me completely, but it's the best we can do for now because there's no time. Night is when the curse tends to take my senses and I shift completely. But nothing about this curse is predictable. Sometimes, I'm aware. Oftentimes, not. I don't know what to expect as the magic settles into me. It seems to be changing." Chills raked his arms and back, and he swallowed a bitter taste at the back of his tongue.

"Then quickly tell me about the woman before we tuck you into your cozy prison."

Dorin huffed a laugh that had little humor in it, then told Filip all about Brielle rescuing him, about D'Aboville, and about his plan to secure a peace treaty that would forever protect Balaur from Wylfen violence.

Filip rubbed his chin as he listened, nodding as Dorin detailed the message he'd meant to send via the farm boy in the rural passes. "This will work. Even the worst of men, and I have to believe the King of Wylfen is just that, won't permit an enemy to hold one of their children. Perhaps only because of pride, but..."

"Yes, I doubt the Wylfen king is a kind father, but he

has certainly shown pride, and I do believe he will bend if he finds out we have his only daughter. How much? Well, time will tell. We can at the very least trade for a peacetime that will last long enough for our people to harvest again from the new farmlands your marriage brought Balaur."

"Just two years would fill our barns and bellies, then we can be ready to fight them and their trained wolves again."

The Wylfen army's scar wolves were a horror and incredibly difficult to defeat. Filip's wife, Magelord Aurora, had helped the Balaur and Lore armies beat them back for the time being, but the enemy never stayed gone for long.

"How do you see this playing out?" Filip asked.

"We show proof of Princess Brielle's presence here and the fact that she lives. We hold her for the length of the peace and keep her healthy and well-tended."

"Well-tended," a new voice said from the shadows. Fae Prince Werian approached, his ram horns reflecting the moon's silver luminescence. "That could mean so many things." The fae winked. He was incorrigible.

"I didn't realize you were here. Can you attempt to heal Princess Brielle? I'm sure you've already heard the gossip and whom I've brought home."

"I do have my spies as well."

Dorin felt his lip curl. "One day you may go too far with your glibness, Prince Werian."

Werian waved him off. "Calm yourself, dark and stormy, I mean no harm. We are friends here. All friends. For your information, I healed Brielle a fraction just now. She'll need further attention throughout the night, but Princess Aurora's fae ladies arrived yesterday in preparation for her stay here with Filip, and they are with her now until morning." The fae picked at one of Dorin's wings. "And what magic, pray tell, did you get into while skulking about the mountaintops? Looks serious."

Dorin turned away from Werian and faced Filip, relief that Brielle was being tended cooling his blood. "I am off to take care of my lodgings for the night. I'll write the missive for the Wylfen king tomorrow at dawn. Will you meet me in the throne room then?"

"I will. Mother will be angry you didn't stop by her chambers to say hello, but I'll cover for you until you're ready to explain."

He grasped Filip's shoulder. "Thank you." With a quick nod to the fae prince, Dorin left to find chains that might prove strong enough to hold the dragon hiding in his skin.

"He likes that Wylfen ginger," Werian whispered not so quietly to Filip as Dorin stalked away.

Dorin fisted his hands and refused to rise to the fae's bait. He was a good person, Werian was, but he was far too casual considering his rank and role here in Balaur, and someday when less pressing issues were at hand, Dorin would make that very clear.

DORIN SAT ALONG THE EMPTY WALL OF THE DIM chamber in the west wing, waiting to be fully chained up. He couldn't manage the final lock on his own. "Drago! Hurry up!"

He was grateful to Drago for agreeing to aid him, seeing as Dorin trusted Filip's band of knights more than the newer recruits assigned to him during his absence.

Dorin was keenly aware of the fact that he was distant and closed-off, unable to form a bond with his men. Filip did it so easily, and Dorin had no idea how to go about it. When he tried, it felt false and silly. He'd stopped trying years ago.

The door squeaked open, and instead of Drago, his mother, the queen, walked in. His stomach knotted.

"I didn't want you to see me like this. Who told you? I'll have their head. You have to leave. Now. It's not safe." Images of Brielle's burns flickered in his mind.

Mother touched the chains that looped through the cuffs on his wrists, cuffs that would likely not fit when he transformed. But he didn't care. If it hurt him, so be it. At least there would be a measure of protection against him crashing through the castle setting everyone on fire.

"You don't have to do this," Mother said, her voice thick with emotion as she clicked the final lock shut.

"I do. I can't bear the thought of hurting anyone." A flash of magic burned down his arms and fingertips, turning his nails into talons.

Mother leapt back, her hand going to her chest. She met his eyes, and he turned away. He didn't want to see what she thought of him now. Her fingers found his chin, and she turned his head to face her.

"No. You are still my Dorin, my boy."

"I'm not though." His throat constricted. He sucked a trembling breath as more magic surged in his blood and he tasted dragonfire in the back of his mouth.

Mother pressed a kiss to his scaled cheek. "You are. And I will check on you at dawn. Porridge with paprika and a soft-boiled egg?"

Chest aching with worry for her, he tried not to shout, to demand that she leave before he lost his senses. "That will be perfect. Thank you."

She gave him a sad smile that he absolutely hated—he wanted a smile of pride not pity—then she left the chamber, locking the heavy oaken door behind her.

Then his mind went hazy. Last time he transformed, he'd been able to retain his elven wits, but now, everything was fading. Dragon magic was horribly unpredictable.

CHAPTER 19
BRIELLE

D reams of Dorin's strong arms and the imagined scent of oranges and smoke dissipated as Brielle woke in a soft bed with three people staring down at her. The warmth that coiled in her belly at the thought of Dorin's touch, his gentleness, the way he'd fought off that lion—it faded fast and left her in a panic.

Mind clearing and pulse ratcheting up, she scooted back against the headboard and raised her fists. "Where am I?"

One woman moved closer, and the twinkle of an earring flashed at the tip of a pointed ear. Horns arched above the woman's head. The window's dawn light illuminated the ethereal beauty of three horned women currently laying hands on Brielle's arms and legs.

Fae. She'd met one fae in her life. Prince Werian. He'd been wonderful, but who knew if these would be as ready to accept her as Werian had? He'd had reason to ignore the fact that she'd come from the kingdom that had killed so many fae. He'd been up to no good, and she'd been his rescue to a point.

Tightening her fists, she readied to strike out. "Who are you?"

"She certainly lives up to her nickname," one of the fae said. "Fire of Wylfenden."

Brielle ignored the reference to her hated title and instead studied the leafy inkings covering the closest fae's forearms. The muscles under her sleeves showed she hadn't simply been doing embroidery at the fae court her whole life.

"I'm Gytha," the tattooed fae said, "a former member of the Fae Court and one of Princess Aurora's ladies."

The oldest-looking of the three fae ladies grabbed for Brielle's hand. "And if you'd sit still, we'd be finished cleaning the ill humors from your blood already. Did you tell Prince Dorin you have witch blood?"

"I don't." Yes, Maren had guessed Brielle had some sort of magic hiding inside her veins, but Brielle had yet to decide if she believed that.

"You do," the older-looking fae said. "Your magic sleeps, but it lives in you. And here you are a Wylfen, completely against all magic." She snorted.

Well, if she did have some slight magic that was apparently dormant, what did it matter? The mystery of some weak ability was the least of her problems here.

"Sit still, please," the fae woman snapped.

Gytha pointed a thumb at the older fae. "That's Hilda. You'll get used to her sour nature and short temper."

Hilda glared, and her lip curled, silver hair falling away

from the knot on top of her head. Two small horns curved backward behind her pointed ears.

A round-cheeked fae peered between Hilda and Gytha, her head not quite to their shoulders. "I'm Eawynn. I'm so excited to meet a Wylfen princess!"

But they had to hate her after the war. Brielle knew exactly how many fae Father, D'Aboville, and the rest of the Wylfen army had slain. Father bragged about it regularly. She put a hand on her stomach, realizing they were speaking her language. "You speak Wylfen."

"Of course we do," Hilda snapped, closing her eyes and pressing the heat of healing magic into Brielle.

Brielle gasped. More magic. Did they grow used to their powers and being around such amazing miracles every day? She never would even if she did manage to permanently escape D'Aboville and Father.

"We are taught all the world's languages at the fae court." Eawynn grinned proudly. She smoothed a scarred hand down Brielle's ankle, and magic bloomed beneath the fae's touch.

That scar across her knuckles... Brielle's kingdom had done that to her. But the fae had killed many Wylfen too, men forced into the fighting for Father, who threatened to burn their farms and their families if they didn't comply. The urge to explain that pushed against her lips, but she held back on saying too much too soon. Life had taught her to keep her cards close to her chest.

A feeling of wellbeing rushed through Brielle like a cool wave, and she was reminded of the coast in Khem. They had indeed healed her. She owed them gratitude at the very least. "Thank you."

They stepped back, giving her room to swing her legs around and sit up properly. "Of course," Hilda said. "And you should know it was done by the order of Prince Dorin."

"With our lady's Prince Filip's blessing too." Eawynn took a scone from the folds of her simple gown and handed it to Brielle.

Stomach growling, she took it with a smile. The scone was flavored with rosemary and was still warm. She moaned with pleasure. "This is amazing."

Gytha pointed to a tray by the roaring fire across the room. "There are plenty for you and a pitcher of watered wine as well, my lady. You should eat up, too, because King Mihai and Queen Sorina have some questions."

The scone soured in her mouth. "When am I to meet with them?"

Stars above, what was she going to tell them? The wrong word and they might decide Dorin's ransom idea was rubbish and they'd rather see her run through right in the middle of the throne room. Honestly, she wasn't sure which fate she'd choose. Going back to Wylfen now was a death sentence as well. Father would never allow someone who embarrassed him as much as she had to live a long life. That was if she managed to survive D'Aboville and the Broyeurs who were surely tracking her as best they could. She choked on the scone, and Eawynn hurriedly fetched a horn cup of the watered wine for her. The liquid cooled her throat, and a powerful thirst overcame every other thought.

"Not too much." Hilda took the cup and refilled it.

"Just one more, or you'll be sick at the king's and queen's feet."

Brielle squeezed her eyes shut, willing the whole morning away.

The door burst open, and there was the man from her dreams, chest heaving and eyes narrowed. "Is she alive?" His claw-tipped, emerald-green wings twitched, possibly showing annoyance. "Move," he ordered the attendants in a booming voice, tucking his wings in tightly. With dark talons where his fingernails had once been, he ran a hand through his sleep-mussed hair. "I must see her."

The fae ladies scurried out of his way as he pressed forward and dragged his gaze across her body and face. The light from the arched window touched the gold scales on his cheek and the back of his right hand. Those were new.

He studied her, asking the fae questions in quick elven tongue, which, even with her education, she couldn't decipher. His gaze fell on her bared shoulder, still pink from the healed burn, then he glanced at her leg. His look was a rough hand, and she clearly recalled the feel of his fingers on her thighs and side as he'd flown her here to Balaur Castle. It was all coming back, and though it was a fine mess with D'Aboville and being here in enemy territory, she couldn't help the curl of excitement unfurling in her heart. Perhaps his obvious concern meant he had come around to the idea of them working together for their kingdoms.

She braided her hair over one shoulder, ideas about how to deal with the Broyeurs already springing to life in her head. "I'm doing quite well, thank you. The fae here—"

"As long as you're alive to serve your purpose for the treaty." Dorin's golden hair fell over one slightly slitted eye, then he turned on his heel to leave. He slammed the door shut, and the chamber fell into a tense silence.

Hauling herself out of bed, she shouted at the closed door, her anger hot and her fists clenched, "It won't work! You're a fool if you think it will!"

Gasping with rage, she spun to see the fae gaping. Well, she had just shouted at the heir to the Balaur throne. And she had to meet with his royal parents soon. Fabulous. Should she play along with the peace treaty idea? Father wouldn't cave for her. He might pretend for a while though, and that could be to some advantage to Balaur. But could she truly betray her kingdom? Not everyone in Wylfen was horrible. Just those in charge of the military.

Exhaling, she tried to calm down.

"He doesn't really feel that way," Gytha said quietly, gaze on the door.

"Gytha, hush," Hilda scolded.

"Please," Gytha said. "The Prince never acts like that, and did you see—"

Hilda gripped Gytha's arm. "I said *hush*."

Practically snarling, Gytha bobbed a shallow curtsey. Hilda must have outranked her in some fae manner of things.

Eawynn put a gentle arm around Brielle. She smelled like chocolate. "Let's get you into the bath and ready to see the king and queen, aye?"

They couldn't bathe her. They'd see the Broyeur brand. "I'd rather do that myself, please."

"But—" Eawynn looked from her to Hilda.

Hilda smiled primly. "That's just fine. Eawynn, get the water."

Eawynn took a bucket from a maid who'd popped in and set it next to a large tub in the adjoining room. Brielle followed the fae through the open doorway. The scent of lavender filled the air.

"Prince Werian himself completed your first round of healing. Did you know?" Eawynn asked.

That was kind of him. He obviously hadn't told anyone he knew her. Perhaps he had a good reason for that. She'd play ignorant. "I'm sorry. Who?"

Gytha grinned. "He is a rogue, fae prince and the heir to the Illumahrah throne."

"I take it you like Prince Werian."

"I do. He sees rules as I do," Gytha said. "Bendable, negotiable, and incredibly fun to shatter into pieces."

Hilda rolled her eyes and set a folded bath sheet on a stool. "Once you finish, come into the bedroom again, and we'll ready you for the king and queen. Would you like to slip your shift on yourself as well?"

They were so kind not to question her habits. "Yes. Thank you so much."

Gytha fetched a clean shift and tucked it under the bath sheet.

The bath was warm and wonderful, but Brielle wasted no time soaking. She washed in a hurry, then dried and pulled on the shift.

In the bedroom, the fae ladies elaborately braided her hair in two ridiculous piles on either side of her head, then dressed her in a plain, vanilla-hued gown edged in red symbols. She grabbed the hem of her skirts to examine it closer. It was a set of stars—the sigil of the mountain elf kingdom. Maybe she'd been wrong to tell Dorin the ransom wouldn't work. Father might agree to anything to get that symbol off his property. She knew well that was what she was to him—yet another of his possessions. It was an old lesson, but the hurt from that truth never seemed to leave her heart.

A knock sounded at the door. "Our guest must meet King Mihai immediately!" a deep voice said from outside.

Eawynn fussed with Brielle's hem while Gytha swung the door wide to show another elven lord, this one with an eye patch and the grin of a man who likes trouble.

He bowed. "I'm Drago, Princess Brielle, and I'm to escort you to the throne room," he said in elvish. His expression said he'd enjoy taking her behind the nearest tavern for a hug and a little more.

"As long as you keep your hands where they belong, I will follow you willingly."

Drago's lips parted, then he recovered from his shock and eyed her seriously. "I don't force myself on women. I understand the power of courting."

Gytha crossed her arms and smirked. "By courting, you mean the finest pint at your favorite pub."

He spread his hands wide. "What's wrong with that?"

Brielle traded a look with Gytha, then headed off on her own.

"You don't even know where you're going!" Drago caught up, eye wide. "Stay by my side, Princess," he whispered. "I'm not flirting now. I'm giving you a tip. There are those who would love to see your blood all over this floor."

A chill swept across Brielle's back. She'd thought about that herself earlier but had been caught up in Dorin and the fae and everything else since. "Of course. I'd go down fighting though, I can tell you that."

Drago chuckled. "Ah, the Fire of—"

"Don't ruin our budding friendship, elf."

"Not keen on your nickname, eh?"

"No, no, I am most assuredly not keen."

"Why? I think Fire is a rather powerful title."

Brielle stepped to the side, and he nearly tripped over her silken slipper, only catching himself because of his goddess-blessed elven agility. "Don't, Drago. Just...don't."

They walked down a wide set of stone stairs, and Brielle did her best to ignore the glares coming from several servants as well as two well-dressed nobles. A corridor decorated with bright banners and wreaths of vines and wildflowers brought them to an impossibly tall set of doors.

Drago nodded and opened what she assumed was the door to the throne room.

"Your Majesties," he said to the dim room, extending a leg in the Balaur-style bow. "I present Princess Brielle of Wylfenden."

A knife flew through the air.

CHAPTER 20
DORIN

After checking on his prisoner, Dorin had Filip's man Costel lock him up again. The dragon wanted to unleash its frustrated fury on everything, and it was just too dangerous to roam the castle today. He rubbed at the red skin where the chains had been. Perhaps he hadn't shifted fully during the black nothingness of last night. It was so incredibly frustrating that he didn't know.

"Thank you, Sir Costel," Dorin said as clearly as he could.

"It's nothing, Prince." The man's frizzy hair caught the daylight from the window. "And if you don't mind me saying so, the Jade dragons were always known as the best warriors in the time of the gods and goddesses. Makes sense that you would have their magic, Your Majesty."

It was kind of the man to say as much, but Dorin didn't have the focus to answer. As Costel carefully shut and locked the door, Dorin fought the dragon inside, mentally pushing the feral thoughts to the back of his mind and imagining snuffing out the magic with his icy will. A shiver shook him, making the chains rattle as his talons retreated and his fingers became his own once more. Then a roar sounded in his ears, his heart...

For while, he knew nothing. Just the swirling confusion of his two minds.

Blinking awake, he realized he was lying on the floor. He must have fallen at some point during his fight to remain himself. He stood, nausea threatening to return him promptly to the flagstones. His chains scraped the ground as he paced, an animal caged in mind and body. His fingers throbbed as if the talons might thrust through the skin, and spines of crystal were just moments from bursting from his back.

"No," he said to himself through gritted teeth, the sound more growl than word. "Don't give in. You can't give in."

Magic crackled along his arms and down his spine between the wings he wished would disappear. It seemed the horrible additions to his body were now permanent. Sweat trickled down his forehead and nose, and he bit his lip, his sharp elven incisors drawing warm blood. Trembling, he prayed to every god and goddess he'd ever heard of and made up a few for good measure, then he switched to focusing on those he loved. This struggle was for Mother and Father. For Filip. He would beat this cursed side of him for them. For all of them.

Brielle's voice echoed in his memory. *Not a curse. Blessed,* she'd said.

He barked a laugh that had teeth. "Blessed indeed."

The beast refused to submit. He was out of control and had proven as much when he'd burned Brielle. And he'd been so sloppy as they'd traveled here, not hiding evidence of the campfires or brushing their footprints away. The Broyeurs would follow; they would cause trouble soon, no doubt about it. The dragon poacher he'd caught had been a Broyeur. He remembered the brand on the back of the man's hand—a dark fist surrounded by flame. They were expert trackers and could travel the mountains faster than one would guess a human could travel. If their entire purpose hadn't been to crush everyone who had magic in their blood, he'd have guessed they had a power of their own.

His dragon magic surged again, and he pressed his forehead into the cold wall, his fists aching from clenching them so tightly. Chills ripped through his muscles, his body longing to shift, begging to shift. His head pounded, and his eyes felt like they were bleeding.

"I can do this. I can."

But the memory of Brielle's awed voice distracted him. *Fascinating*, she had said of the small scales on his face. She was likely no better than any other Wylfen and longed to burn the dragon out of him, to crush his power and watch his destruction gleefully.

But could he be wrong? At the Wylfen castle, she'd saved him from her father and the Broyeurs. She didn't want to crush him. Her fascination was innocent, genuine.

What drove her enthusiasm for this magic his blood had somehow dragged out of the tombs of old? The magic twisted his elven form into an entirely different species. It was horrible, and yet she thought him fantastic, alluring. The woman had problems.

Where was she now? Was she in his chambers still? Going through his scrolls, his books, his chest of keepsakes? Gods knew she was a curious sort. She had probably unearthed everything there was to know about him already. When he thought of her soft skin, the fire in her eyes, her courage and kindness, heat spun down his chest to his stomach, then lower. What was it about her that possessed him? She was an enemy with an absurd way of thinking. He refused to care about her. It was foolish. Abhorrent. He would not.

Magic swamped his thoughts, and he battled to keep the bread he'd eaten in his stomach.

His skin rippled with power, light dancing across his flesh. It wasn't painful until he tried to will it away again. Overwhelmed, he fell against the wall, crushing his wings. Pain burst across his back, and darkness swallowed him.

CHAPTER 21
BRIELLE

The knife peeled back the tension in the throne room as it flew toward Brielle. With a movement faster than she could see clearly, Drago lunged and blocked the knife's path. The weapon hit his leather gauntlet and clattered to the floor. Across the room, there was a shout, then two other elves had a knight pinned to the floor.

Brielle bent to retrieve the knife, but a frizzy-haired, male elf plucked it from her hand with a shaky, shallow bow and a polite smile. "I'm Costel. G-Glad you didn't die."

Touching his eye patch as if he wished he had two eyes to see, Drago stared at the captured elf on the ground near the dais, the one who had presumably thrown the knife. Then he looked at Costel, and they traded a heavy look that told Brielle they knew the one who had attempted to murder her. Brielle's heart was beating too quickly to think straight.

"She is Wylfen!" The captured elven knight thrashed under the hold of two of his fellows, his long, dark hair falling over his proud nose. "She killed my brother!" He went limp, giving up the fight. "I'm sorry, King Mihai and Queen Sorina." The other knights stood him up, a man on each side. He was a lean elf and taller than everyone in the room.

The king, gray-haired and too thin, remained on his throne while his bright-eyed queen walked with a quick stride toward the captured knight. She placed a hand on his shoulder. Not a good sign for Brielle.

"Sir Stephan," the queen said, "We don't allow such violence in this room, and well you know it." She murmured something, then Stephan was escorted out of a side door decorated in metallic runes. "Tell us, Princess Brielle of Wylfen," the queen continued, "why we should allow your presence here in Balaur Castle."

Brielle's stomach twisted as she faced the queen. Queen Sorina stood now at the base of the dais steps, her dark crown sparkling in the light of the oil lamps. Wind whispered through the wooden ceiling beams and drew up the scent of honeyed fruit and damp stone.

"Firstly, Your Majesty," Brielle said, "I had no choice in coming here."

"That was my son's doing."

Brielle inclined her head. "He was kind enough to allow me the opportunity to heal under the expert hands of the fae, and I will forever be grateful."

The queen waved a hand impatiently. "But what is your goal now that you are here? Do you know what Prince Dorin had in mind? It is established he has claimed you as his captive. But do you know the purpose?"

What could Brielle say? If she revealed the truth—that Father most likely wouldn't agree to peace for her, that he nearly hated her—her life was worthless to them. How would these elves handle her own personal truth? Despite the fact that they were incredible warriors and frighteningly dangerous, she'd always had a bizarre fascination with Father's greatest enemy. Now that she'd met Dorin, though, she realized they were just like humans in that some seemed capable of good and others of evil and most existed between those extremes.

"I hate the way my father treats those with magic. I am not loyal to him." At the base of the back of her neck, the brand tingled like it could understand her words. If they saw it, they'd never believe her.

Eyes narrowing, the queen crossed her arms over her waist-length, fur cape. This woman could finish what Stephan had started at any moment.

Brielle swallowed and forced herself to hold eye contact. Elves were known for their courage. Surely, their culture valued bravery over all else. "I don't believe the king will agree to a peace to save my life. But I believe, because of his pride, he will care if you threaten to mistreat me."

The queen's arms fell to her sides. Her fingers moved as if she wished for a sword. "He views you as property."

"Exactly."

A spark flared between them, the warmth of understanding and the rage of being underestimated as a woman. It wasn't friendship. Certainly not. But it was an agreement of sorts, or at least, that was how it felt.

The queen swept forward, her dress dragging along the stones with a rushing sound, then she clasped Brielle's hand. "I welcome you to Balaur Castle. You are our guest as long as you aid us in establishing the best bargain we can manage with your father's kingdom."

So the moment Brielle was seen as going against Balaur, she would be killed or imprisoned. Or worse.

"Understood. Thank you very much." Brielle gently squeezed Queen Sorina's cool fingers and bobbed a curtsey.

The queen looked to Drago and the frizzy-haired elf. "Please tell Prince Filip I must speak with him."

The two bowed low, then left with quick steps out the double doors, their striped fur and woolen cloaks rippling behind them.

"Come," the queen ordered, leading Brielle toward the dais where the king looked on, austere and pale as milk.

Claiming her throne beside her sickly husband, the queen settled herself. "Now, Princess, please tell us first, what your kingdom has planned for their next attack and second, what type of message might prove best for our communication to your father."

The faces of Etienne, Celeste, George, and so many more flashed through her mind. Could she betray them? There was no way to ensure the good people of Wylfen wouldn't suffer because of Brielle's actions here in Balaur. Such a dream was something she would've thought possible as a child, but she'd seen enough of wars and politics to know that dream was completely impossible.

"We need a way to shut down my father's military

advances before he can arrive here. We need a new ruler for Wylfen."

"Will your brother make for a more peaceful ruler?"

Sighing, Brielle searched for the right way to explain Etienne. "Yes."

King Mihai coughed. "You don't sound like you believe that."

"It's not that I don't believe it, Your Majesty. Etienne is young and hedonistic. He isn't necessarily a good or bad man. He is, however, far too fond of fine things to long for war as my father does."

"That I do believe." Salt and pepper hair tangling in the peaks of his thick crown, Mihai glanced at his wife, and they exchanged a quick whisper.

"Hmm." The queen tapped a finger on her lip.

Her cool gaze reminded Brielle of Dorin's features when he refused to believe he wasn't a monster. What did his parents think of his dragon magic? Did they see him as she did—fascinating and wondrous? Or did they believe he was cursed? Had they visited him? That look in Dorin's eyes when he shut down his emotions... She shuddered. He was good inside. She knew that. But when he took on that coldness, fear gripped her heart and she remembered well the horrors his magic could inflict.

"And what of the message to your father, the king?" the queen asked.

"Dorin may have already sent one."

"I am fully aware of what my son has and has not accomplished. That's not what I asked."

Brielle rubbed her hands on her gown. "Tell him you will put me on my knees to scrub the chamber pots of the lowest-ranking elven knights. Inform my father that you will also force me to shout accusations about the Wylfen throne every day at noon in the outer bailey while tied to a post just like the ones he uses to burn witches, fae, and elves."

The queen and king shifted in their thrones. "Should we follow through with such a threat?"

Trick question. If Brielle said yes, then she would be suggesting the royal pair treat their guest like the worst prisoner, a terrible act in the Balaur culture if Brielle's research was accurate. But if she said no, then she would be asking the queen and king to betray their honor by lying.

"Give King Raoul one moon to send a peace treaty signed in blood before you take action against me."

"That's only asking them to attack." Prince Filip walked out of the shadows and approached his parents with a bow. He nodded toward Brielle, his gray eyes bright with what she presumed was interest in the developments of this situation.

Leaning against the tall back of her seat, the queen tilted her head. "We could then intercept them as they approach."

Filip shrugged and ran a hand over his black braids. "Possibly. I think we should discuss this with my brother and without our guest."

"Agreed. You've been honest with us, Princess Brielle," the queen said, the king nodding in agreement. "You will continue to be our guest, and we will have a feast tomorrow evening to welcome you. It will fit in nicely with the first of our seven days of Primāvara Noroc Festivities."

Brielle sighed. At least they weren't stringing her up by her neck today. She'd enjoy any wins she could find.

"Maybe a feast will tug Dorin out of his darkness," Filip said quietly, his eyes downcast.

"Oh, I will be doing that whether he likes it or not." The queen studied Brielle like one would a faded scroll, then she looked to a servant waiting in bright blue and black livery marked with the stars of the Balaur court. "Take the princess to the guest wing. I assume they've been prepared as I ordered?"

The servant bowed. "Of course, Your Highness."

"Rest a bit more. I'm sure you need it. I will send for you soon," the queen said to Brielle.

Brielle let them lead her from the room and into the chilly corridor. Birds sang outside the long windows set high in the stone walls.

"Where is Prince Dorin now?"

"Apologies, Princess, but we've been ordered to keep that information to ourselves."

"By Prince Dorin?" But she received no answer. These servants were loyal and wise enough to hold their tongues, much to her frustration. She wasn't about to remain stuck in some guest chamber all day when this was her first real foray into the elven kingdom and a dragon prince was out there somewhere with all the wrong ideas about his magic. She was finally inside a fascinating moment in history instead of simply reading about it. No way she was being a good girl and waiting in her gown to be fetched for a feast.

They led her across the main stretch of the castle, through an open foyer complete with suits of metal-studded leather armor—from the fourth century, if she guessed right—and dark banners showing the house sigil. Tapestries of onyx-eyed ravens and starlit pines cloaked the hallways and winding stairwells.

"Are we going the long way to confuse me? Don't answer that. I know the answer already."

One of the servants cleared his throat as if he might be covering a chuckle. They were definitely trying to get her lost. Good luck, she thought with a perfectly mischievous grin. She had the best sense of direction of anyone she had ever met. It was the one thing her friend Zahra envied, and now she would use that inborn skill to sniff out a handsome dragon.

As the servants left her, setting what sounded like just one guard at her door, she plotted how exactly to distract the unfortunate elf.

CHAPTER 22
DORIN

Aknock sounded on the chamber door where Dorin lay exhausted from fighting down the dragon inside him.

"Go away."

"Not a chance."

Oh, gods, it was her. "Be gone."

"If you don't tell me where the key to this door is hidden out here, then I'll show Filip the parchment hidden in your chest."

He lifted his pounding head. Which parchment? Wait. He didn't care. He turned away from the door, rolling to his side and wincing at the pain in his right wing. He'd hit the wall too hard on that side earlier.

"The parchment that shows all the lovely elven ladies."

His drawings. "I was a child!"

"Right. Anyway, as I said, if you don't tell me where the key hides..."

He ignored her musical voice. If her voice had been

more nasal or grating, it would have been an easier job blocking her out.

"Fine. I'll find it myself. It can't be that difficult a task. Down here..." Her words grew quiet as sounds of her moving about outside the thick door shuffled through the air. "Ah, maybe this loose stone? Hmm. No. If I were a far-too-serious elven prince, where would I hide a key? Or did your jovial brother hide it? Or maybe the fae prince even, the one they say can charm the trousers off anyone in ten seconds flat?"

Dorin pressed his forehead against the cold floor and begged Goddess Nix to take this human away along with his curse. At the moment, he couldn't decide which was worse.

A wicked laugh crawled under the door, and he jerked. Who was that?

"I found it!" she crowed before laughing that horrible laugh again.

"What is that sound? Gods, woman. You are murdering me."

The key clicked in the lock, and the door swung wide to show Brielle, her red hair loose around her shoulders and going all the way to her calves. Her delicate lips curled into a smirk. Longing coiled in his belly, and a flush crawled up his chest. What would that swan neck feel like beneath his mouth? Would she smirk if she knew how he responded to her presence? He snorted, knowing the answer. Yes, yes, she would.

She raised an eyebrow and crossed her arms. "Don't like my victory laugh? Come now, it's endearing." The question sounded more like a royal command. Her quick temper flared in her eyes.

He stood quickly, head spinning. "Be gone, pest."

She bared her teeth, and he was reminded of scar wolves. "Watch it, elf. I'm not known for my patience. You're lucky you're interesting."

Turning away, he looked out the window at the last of the morning's glow peeking through the scraps of woolen clouds. Why was she here? How could he get her to leave?

"I thought burning you would be enough to persuade you to keep your distance."

"Psssh. You didn't intend to burn me, and you never would."

"You do not know that. I don't even know that." He glanced over a shoulder. She stalked the chamber like a lioness, watching him like prey. Straightening to his full height and expanding his wings, he strode toward her and showed the edge of one sharp tooth. "Don't forget who is predator and who is prey here, Princess."

Her lips curved, eyes glittering like she wanted to fight and in fact loved such sport, and he forced himself not to gasp at her fierce beauty. "I'd like to think we can both have a turn playing said roles."

"I don't have any idea what you mean." Irritated, he shuffled his wings and sucked a breath at the pain in the right one.

"You're injured. I'll go get the fae ladies or Prince Werian."

"No. Just go. I'm not a project for you to pore over. Be. Gone."

"So you don't want to know what I learned about

dragon shifters? Fine. I'll go, you pompous, elven arse-face."

Whirling around, he focused on her glimmering eyes. "What are you talking about?"

"I assume you met with not one but two powerful princes, not to mention your own parents, and not a one of you thought to do some research into history about your magic. Elves and fae really are the most arrogant species in the world."

Dorin rolled his eyes. "Enough with the dramatics. Did you find anything of use?"

"How about an *I appreciate your efforts* first? I'm sure your mother taught you manners."

"I appreciate your efforts," he said through gritted teeth.

She flew at him, red hair billowing around as she stopped. "Just because I'm your prisoner doesn't mean you get to treat me like your lesser. I want to help you, but I will do absolutely nothing if you don't mind that tongue, Dorin."

The way her mouth formed his name tugged at his middle, and he wanted to hear her say it again. And the wildness, the challenge in her voice...

The dragon in him longed to see if he could tame her. He reached up to touch her chin, her fair skin looking like the softest thing he'd ever seen, but his chain stopped him short. She glanced at his outstretched fingers, and her lips parted in a silent inhalation. Heat built between them, a sparkling sensation that reminded him of being in a field just before a lightning strike. His entire body was on alert, eager, anticipating the step that would close the sliver of distance between them and start down a path he had never imagined. A journey traveled alongside a Wylfen princess.

He recoiled from the near kiss, then turned away, shutting his feelings away. "I don't care about what you think you discovered."

Footsteps sounded outside the half-closed door.

"Your escort arrives," he said. "Please see to it that you don't leave your room in the future without permission."

"Your Majesty!" a guard said. "Apologies for allowing your guest to walk without an escort."

"She is not my guest but my prisoner. Ensure it does not happen again."

"My lord."

Brielle let out a string of Wylfen curses as the guards forcibly removed her from his chamber.

When Brielle and the guards' steps faded, the room was too quiet. Dorin wished they had locked the door behind them. He'd been too distracted to order it before they'd left. At least he hadn't shifted in front of anyone. Perhaps because he was so exhausted from fighting the magic all night and this morning.

"Have you slept at all?" Werian's voice surprised Dorin.

"What do you want?"

"My lord." Werian bowed gracefully, then straightened and held out a scroll that was crumbling along its edges. "I secured some information about the tales of old. About the dragons who had an elven form. This is supposedly a rewrite of the god Arcturus's research with the goddess Nix."

Dorin looked at the scroll but didn't accept it. What was the point? He was cursed. He was a danger to all he loved. Once this deal was made with the Wylfen king, he would leave. No research necessary.

"You've given up before we've started, have you?" Werian hitched himself to the doorframe and crossed his arms. The window's light couldn't quite reach the shadows his ram horns casted.

"What do you care?" Dorin eyed the keys that Brielle had set on the window ledge.

"My dearest cousin is married to your brother. We are family."

"We are not." The fae were crafty and certainly not of the fine elven blood that Dorin and his family had flowing through their veins. Fae were solid warriors, but unlike his brother, Filip, Dorin did not trust the fae.

Werian picked up the keys and proceeded to unlock Dorin's shackles. Dorin allowed it because the day was full now, and, hopefully, the dragon would remain quiet for the time being. There was work to be done.

"I beg to differ, Your Majesty. Perhaps not by blood, but you are part of my chosen family. That's more important to me. Perhaps not to you, but I don't follow your orders."

Werian winked, and Dorin's blood boiled.

"This is the elven kingdom, fae prince. Watch yourself."

Werian held up his hands. "I know, my lord. I apologize for my bluntness. But at least you know I speak only the truth to you."

Dorin walked out of the door, his legs like Frostlight pudding due to fatigue. "Am I to receive an endless string of folk who believe they know the answer to my curse?"

"Oh, who else kindly offered to help you?"

Glaring, Dorin muttered, "The prisoner."

"You mean your mother's guest? The one we are feasting soon?"

Dorin stopped, and Werian bumped into him, most likely on purpose. "What nonsense are you babbling?" Dorin asked.

"I think I've had enough of your disrespect, Your Highness. If you want answers, you can find them yourself." Something snagged Dorin's wrist, and warmth rolled across his skin, soaking into his bones. He forgot everything else Werian had said.

Werian was healing him.

"You don't deserve this, you tumult of determined agony," the fae muttered, "but at least you might be able to function as an actual prince."

Dorin started to pull away, but the magic hummed pleasurably along his tired limbs and relaxed the knotted muscles in his shoulders and back. Sparks burst along his wings, and they disappeared. His body had returned to that of a normal elf! Thank the gods. At least he could be seen now without frightening everyone. It still wasn't safe. He could shift at any moment, but he looked himself.

"Thank you, Prince Werian."

Werian was good enough not to grin too proudly. "You're welcome, Prince Dorin." Then the fae walked away into the shadows.

Taking a breath and enjoying his lack of wings, Dorin walked slowly to the doors of his personal chambers, where two guards stood. "What is this about a feast?" he asked them.

The guards glanced at one another, the slimmer one stammering.

Heat built behind Dorin's eyes, and the taste of dragonfire touched his tongue. "Answer me!" He took a breath again, trying to calm himself. This curse stoked his already quick-to-blaze temper.

"Your...the queen... She called a feast in honor of Princess Brielle."

Dorin threw the man against the wall, then released him, barging into his chambers. "What insanity has captured this castle? They aren't afraid of what they should be, and they invite murderers to their hearthside!"

Filip appeared, greeting him with a nod and a goblet. "You stowed your wings away. Wise move. That way we can walk among the people without too much gawking."

Dorin took the goblet with a quiet thanks and downed the watered wine, the feel of the vintage smooth against his irritated throat. "Stop changing the subject."

"Mother wants to hear more about what the princess has to say of her court and father. It's wise," Filip said.

"Brielle is no fool," Dorin replied. "She won't fall for any simplistic tricks like pretending to befriend her."

"Did you just call our mother's plan foolish? I'm telling."

Using half his strength, Dorin punched Filip in the gut. Filip doubled over, laughing.

"Unwise or no, we have both been commanded to attend pre-feasting activities starting at noon, so take a rest as you need to now, Brother. We will be wrestling in the great hall after luncheon."

Dorin waved in two new manservants. They stripped off his fouled clothing and filled a tub. Filip detailed what they'd discussed of the message they'd send to the Wylfen king and what Brielle's suggestions had been last night.

The scalding hot bathwater felt like a blessed afterlife, like some unknown paradise of the underworld. "I like the plan."

"Well, once you're finished in here, we need to talk, Brother."

Shutting his eyes, Dorin ground his teeth. "What's the point?"

"You were missing for a long time," Filip said. "We thought you were dead."

"I'm sorry you worried for me."

"You should have come to us right away."

As Dorin opened his mouth to argue, Filip left the bathing chamber. Dorin exhaled and slipped beneath the surface of the hot water. He didn't want Filip wasting time trying to solve this. There was no solution. Was there? His chest tightened, and he winced like an arrow had pierced him through. If he allowed himself to hope he might have his life back and it didn't work out, the pain would certainly kill him. Maybe someday he'd be strong enough to search for answers, but he didn't have it in him yet. Everything was pain. The concern in Mother's eyes. The way he'd had to avoid Father for fear of upsetting him in his ill health. Filip's pitying gaze. Brielle's fascination. It hurt. All of it. And though he'd never thought of himself as a coward, he supposed he was now because all he longed to do was run away, to run and run and run until he couldn't think anymore, until exhaustion overcame the hurt.

His men dressed him in black as was his custom, and he met Filip beside his hearth where a tray of food had been set for them. Dorin's elven half wasn't hungry. He was too frustrated to want to eat. But the dragon in him...

"Whoa, beastly brother," Filip said with a laugh. "That is the loudest stomach growl I've heard in all my life." He tossed Dorin a hunk of black bread.

Dorin sat and bit into the warm, thick-crusted bread but didn't lean back and relax. "I will answer any questions you have of me."

"Good." Filip ate a piece of bacon and propped his boots on the stone edge of the hearth. The coals glowed bright orange, and small flames licked at the pale wooden log. "When did you first notice this happening? The memory loss you spoke of?"

Dorin went over the details he remembered, but they were foggy and vague.

"What purpose might this curse hold for you?"

"What kind of question is that? I'm ruined. I'm a mad beast. Not a true dragon. Not an elf. I'll never be who I was again."

Filip shrugged. "You can't possibly know that for sure. Even if you do stay this way, it might be an advantage."

Throwing the remainder of his bread on the tray, Dorin stood.

Heat prickled his back and throat, and he stared Filip down. "How in the name of the gods Rigel and Arcturus could accidentally burning my entire family to the ground be an advantage?"

Filip rose slowly, eyebrows lifted and hands spread like Dorin was a spooked horse. Dorin's jaw ached from clenching his teeth. "Because perhaps you could instead burn our enemies to the ground."

"I have no control over it! You don't understand!" The bright heat of magic unfurled across his chest, and he spun, gripping the chair and trying to breathe.

"Eh, Brother. It's all right. I don't understand, but I'm here, and I'm not leaving you alone with this challenge the gods and goddesses have set on your shoulders."

"You're being ridiculous." Dorin was practically growling now, but he did nothing to change his tone because Filip needed to recognize the danger here. "I wish you would leave me alone in this."

"No, you don't," Filip said. "Not really."

"I do! Did you not see what I did to the Wylfen woman?"

"She is our enemy. Who cares?" His words said one thing, but the spark in Filip's eye said another. He was trying to ferret out information from Dorin. That look on his face was the same one he'd had as a young lad when he'd tried to find Dorin's secret path out of the inner bailey and into the forest beyond the castle grounds.

Dorin shoved the chair, flipping it over easily, then he stormed out of his chambers, scattering the guards as he went. They tried to keep up, bowing and asking him what he needed and informing him of messages left for him. He walked faster, ignoring them and Filip's call of his name too.

He headed for the castle library, eager for information now that Brielle and Werian had set the idea in his head—though he would never admit that fact to either of them.

Hope was permitted to last just this one hour. If he found no information about another elf suffering from such a curse and a way to cure it, then he would crush any further thought or outside mention of hope.

"It's pointless, I'm sure anyway," he muttered as he kicked the library doors open, making a scribe yelp in surprise. "Apologies, Master Hemm."

"What can I find for you, Your Majesty?" Hemm scurried over, squinting and bowing as he went.

"I'll be fine on my own. Thank you. Just see that I'm not disturbed for the next few hours."

"Exactly as you say, my lord."

Dorin was fairly certain Hemm was immortal. The man had been old for as long as Dorin could remember. He was the head scribe at the library and kept immaculate records of the Balaur history, folktales, military achievements, language, and on and on. Not a hair left on his wrinkled scalp, he shuffled back behind his desk and picked up a quill, murmuring as he did so. Dorin's shoulders relaxed at the familiar sound, reminding him of the days when he and Filip had spent hours here with their tutors. Filip had constantly been in trouble for fidgeting, but Dorin had never had difficulty sitting for lessons.

The first section of the towering wooden shelves held recent histories and documents, copies of the treaty with Lore—secured by Filip's marriage to Princess Aurora—as well as lists of studs in the royal stables and the lands gifted to varied noble families after the last war.

Dorin strode past that section and a half dozen more, searching the painted tablets hanging from hooks on the end of each set of shelves. The final section, more sparsely lit than the rest of the chamber, was labeled *Gods, Goddesses, and the Magic of Lore.*

Running a finger along the scroll cases on the first shelf, then the next five or so, he found writings on goddess Vahly and the god Arcturus aplenty, but nothing on the dragon goddess, Nix.

Itching with frustration and with last night's fatigue pulling at him, he fell into a green velvet chair at the end of the section. The towering collection of scrolls sheltered this resting spot, and just one high slit of a window lit the space, albeit weakly.

A table stood beside the chair, and on it, an odd piece of wood with a metal placard. Fighting a jaw-cracking yawn, he lifted it. The faint remains of claw gouges marred the edge. Someone had spilled liquid on the piece, and the wood had gone darker here and there because of it. His finger brushed the placard. It said:

"Artifact from the Dragon's Back Tavern. First taken from the Silver River."

Dragon's Back Tavern? What was that? He'd never heard of such a place.

The yawn finally won as he stretched, glad to have his elven form back if only for a moment.

He wasn't sure when he fell asleep, but at some point, he realized he was dreaming.

Greetings, elven prince, a lapis-lazuli-hued dragon with eyes the color of the setting sun whispered into his mind.

CHAPTER 23
BRIELLE

Shaking with frustration, Brielle longed to lash out at these elves and rail against how they were treating her considering Queen Sorina had deemed her a guest. It'd be pointless. She was a guest in name only. But, oh, how she relished the thought of kicking this goddess-cursed door down, grabbing Dorin by his delicious shoulders, and dragging him into her life.

Sinking onto the bed, she shook her head. Doomed, that's what she was. Doomed to argue and pine over this dragon elf creature until his people had her strung up as the enemy they knew she was.

"Don't look so glum!" Eawynn, the curviest of the fae ladies who'd healed her, bustled into the room. "Princess Rhianne of the Fae Court is here to keep you good company and help you prepare for today's Primāvarā Noroc festivities."

Rhianne! Of course, she was here with Werian. Brielle had met them together during their adventure to Khem.

Granted, Rhianne had most likely been sent here, just like these fae, to keep Brielle close and watch her every move, but still, it was lovely to see a familiar, friendly face.

Dressed in green velvet with a wand tucked into her belt, Rhianne entered the chamber and smiled widely. She went to Brielle and embraced her.

"You know one another?" Eawynn asked.

"We met a long time ago," Rhianne said quickly, giving Brielle a look that said *play along.* "Human business, you know. Such are our strange ways, to meet with enemies in lands far away."

"Yes, yes. Good to see you again," Brielle said.

Rhianne pulled her dark brown hair over one shoulder.

"How did you and Prince Werian end up together? If you told me, I forgot."

Rhianne clasped her hands in front of her and smiled prettily. "Well, Prince Werian captured my heart."

Eawynn directed a young maid to set out a midnight blue gown on the bed beside Brielle. "It is one of the greatest fated loves in the history of the Matchweaver," the fae said, fluttering her eyelashes.

The Matchweaver... Brielle had heard of this woman, but she'd thought the witch who matched fated loves together was an old hag who had caused a multitude of problems for Lore.

"Our Princess Rhianne is the new Matchweaver."

"Everyone makes their own match now if they choose it, Lady Eawynn," Rhianne corrected, a soft smile gracing her lips.

"That was clever magic," Eawynn said.

"Thank you."

With no clue as to what these two were going on about, Brielle removed her sleeping gown and shift. The cool air touched her skin, and she was glad to slip on a clean shift, careful not to let anyone see her brand. She truly needed to tell them and at least attempt an explanation, but fear held her tongue. "What is involved in these festivities everyone keeps crowing about?"

Rhianne chuckled. "With the mountain elves, it always starts with fighting."

Eawynn laughed and took the job of lacing Brielle's gown. "The princes will begin the holiday with a wrestling match at noon in the great hall."

Whipping around, Brielle looked from Rhianne to Eawynn. "Dorin agreed to that?" He was so worried about losing control of the dragon in him... How could he now think wrestling was a good choice?

"His mother the queen decreed it as the first event." Rhianne's tilted head and the spark in her eye said that Queen Sorina's word was law.

"Ah. I see." Brielle fluffed her skirts, enjoying the lack of weight to the gown. "Is this the Balaur style?" It was different from Rhianne's elaborate velvet situation over there.

"It is," Rhianne said. "They like their females to move more easily even at court."

"I like it."

"I do too," Rhianne said, eyeing the gown wistfully. "But Werian loves to show off, so I'm humoring him during the spring holiday." She ran a hand down the embroidered front of her dress, then lifted the hem to show—

"You're wearing boots!" Brielle had expected court slippers.

"I have to draw the line somewhere. This isn't the Forest of Illumahrah with its leafy paths. Balaur is still spring mud, and Werian will want me at his side to watch the outdoor events later. I'm not freezing my toes off and sticking to wooden planks all day."

Brielle grinned. "Does that mean I get boots too?"

Eawynn groaned. "You two sound like Gytha. She hates court shoes."

"You rang?" Gytha, the lean and mean-looking horned fae with the vine tattoos popped her head into the room. Then she held up a pair of slim, black boots topped in fur. She tossed them at Brielle.

"How did you know?"

Gytha jabbed a thumb backward and yet another woman walked in. "Princess Aurora saw you in boots climbing a mountain trail. She made a guess you'd need some footwear attention in this place where males forget we need to get around comfortably."

Aurora of the Court of Lore. Brielle had heard so many stories of this Magelord Princess. Of her water power, her ability to see things in water, her brash ways, her so-called evil magic. The woman's silver-white hair had been pulled into three knots that sat high on her head. Her eyes were as blue as the Wylfen Castle lake, which was fed by snowmelt from the mountains.

"And I saw you throwing knives, Princess Brielle." Aurora didn't nod or bow her head in greeting. Instead, she glared at Brielle, rage shooting from those eyes like bolts from a crossbow. "I do hope you aren't armed at present. Surely Queen Sorina saw to that."

"She did." Brielle wasn't about to be cowed even if this lady was a living legend. She lifted her skirts to show a bare thigh. "No knives hidden here, Princess," she said tartly.

The corner of Aurora's mouth twitched like she was fighting a smile. "Good. Rhianne and I will be at your side at all times today. Don't get any cute ideas about strategy, Wylfen."

"Aury..." Rhianne started, her face imploring.

Aurora held up a hand. "None of your kindness needed here, Princess Rhianne."

Gytha whistled low, and Aurora threw a warning look at her. "This is our enemy's daughter," Aurora said, "and the moment we forget that is the moment we become fools. I've been on the battlefield with her kinsmen. Watched them run swords and arrows through my friends from Darkfleot. They nearly killed the heir to the throne of Lore and Filip too. Filip was thrown from Jewel's back and..." She closed her eyes, and when she opened them again, tears glittered in her lashes. "It's disgusting what you do to the scar wolves, how you train them. I hope you at least treat your children better than you do your animals."

Anger sparked inside Brielle, but guilt kept the fire from growing out of control. "I hate what my father does with the wolves. I have no part in that."

Aurora snorted as if she didn't believe Brielle.

"Why do you think I learned to throw knives? I could have taken a trained wolf to my side at any moment I chose, but I denied my father's offer every time he brought it up. It's my father you hate, Princess Aurora. Not me.

Not my brother, Etienne, either. He isn't like Father in that way."

"In that way. Then in what way *is* he like your father?"

She was a quick one, this Aurora. "Etienne enjoys attention, a crowd that showers him with praise."

"Sounds like my Werian," Rhianne said, grinning, her cheeks pinking.

"It's no crime to be an entertainer at heart." Eawynn glanced at Aurora, and the Princess of Lore nodded. The fae drew Brielle over to the stool near the hearth and began to braid her hair.

"What happens before the wrestling match?" With a quick touch, Brielle checked that her dress covered the brand. The fire crackled and warmed her legs as Eawynn worked.

Gytha knelt and began rolling a pair of woolen stockings up to Brielle's thighs. "Eating. Loads and loads of eating."

"Drinking as well," Aurora said, her gaze on something outside the window. "Watch out for the fruit brandy. It is stronger than you might realize at first."

An olive branch of peace? Aurora could've kept that information to herself and let Brielle imbibe too heavily and potentially loose her tongue on Wylfen secrets. "Thanks for the tip."

"No problem. I'm going now. Eawynn, do you wish to come, or would you like to stay with Gytha?"

"I'll walk with you, Princess." Eawynn leaned close to Brielle's ear. "Don't worry. She'll come around."

But Brielle didn't really blame Aurora for loathing her. It was honestly more puzzling how quickly the fae ladies and Rhianne had accepted her. "Why do you all trust me already?"

Rhianne raised an eyebrow. "I didn't say I trusted you, but I like to think most people are good, and I know what it's like to be misjudged based on things you can't control." She flexed her left hand, then grabbed her wand and spun it in a slow circle. A weave of blue, orange, and yellow wildflowers appeared in her hand. She placed it on Brielle's head. "Don't disappoint us, please."

"I'll do my best."

Gytha tied one of Brielle's boots while Brielle managed the other, then they were off for the great hall to see if Dorin could fight without unleashing the dragon hiding inside his elven body.

She'd never admit it, but a part of her wanted to see him lose control.

CHAPTER 24
DORIN

Dorin blinked in the haze surrounding him. Hadn't he been in the library? Swirls of white and black clouds held sparking lights of what he assumed was magic.

Up here, Princeling.

He looked above his head to see a towering, indigo dragon. His heart slammed against his ribs, and he fell backward. The dragon caught him with the tip of one massive wing.

Relax. I'm here to help you, not eat you. After all, you are of my kynd.

Kynd?

Fire Kynd.

"What are you... I'm sorry." He rubbed his face harshly. Was he ill? Was he dreaming?

You are visiting me in the Between. That's how I can speak into your mind.

Don't forget the dead part, another voice said into Dorin's very confused mind.

Wait. Who are you? he asked silently.

The second voice belonged to a powerfully built woman with blond hair. She wore a crown of branches and oak leaves and carried a wooden sword.

Oh. His breath left him. He looked from the dragon to the woman. *You're... I can't believe it. You're the goddess Nix and the goddess Vahly.*

Took him a minute. I'm trying not to be offended, Nix said, raising a ridge of scales over her eye.

Ladies, give the fellow time, a third voice echoed through the mists. A male elf equally as tall as Dorin but with black hair and dark eyes walked into view. A crown of churning light and swirling shadows flickered above his head. *I'm Arcturus, Prince Dorin of Balaur. Pleased to make your acquaintance.*

Dorin's mouth wouldn't work. Here were the three greatest deities of legend, speaking to him. This had to be a wild dream the scorchpeppers he'd eaten last night had brought on.

All three deities laughed.

Definitely part dragon, Nix said, grinning. *It's not the meal, golden darling. You need our aid, and we are here to give it.*

Vahly leaned forward and touched his chest with the tip of her wooden sword, the wooden sword that had unearthed the poison of the evil sea queen's flood. He locked his jaw, doing his level best not to keel over. *You must grow into what your fate requires.* She smiled suddenly, her beauty raw and dangerous. *But don't worry. You were born for this.*

Arcturus gazed at Vahly with a burning love in his eyes. *She knows exactly how difficult it is to be born to a challenging fate,* he said. Then the elven god eyed Dorin, and Dorin held completely still. *You will rise up when the time comes.*

Use that dragonfire, Princeling, Nix said, her nostrils smoking. *You can't be nervous about it. That's what gets you into trouble. You've been confident as a dragon your entire life. Don't lose that proper dragon arrogance when you need it most.*

He took a shaky breath. *But I burned Brielle. I could kill Filip. Or my mother or father.*

Nix's wings expanded, and she narrowed her slitted eyes. A chill speared Dorin's chest. *You are a king! Feel that in your blood! A dragon king! Even when we dragons doubt ourselves, we do not give in to such foul thoughts. Rise to your fate, Dorin of Balaur, or die.*

Arcturus stepped forward, angling himself between Nix and Dorin. He tilted his head and smiled kindly. Power emanated from the god, evident in the shimmering air around his limbs and head. Dorin wanted to go to his knees. *Examine your experience objectively. You were born with a power none have possessed in a millennium. You have the ability to interact with your court and army as one of them, but you also wield the magic to shift into a creature of incredible military and strategic strength. Do you believe that is a mistake? That the universe, the Source, the Sacred Oak and its magic blundered in birthing you as you are?*

Of course not. Dorin dipped his head and went to one knee. *I would never suggest such a thing.*

Nix's breath stirred the hair on his head. *But you do suggest this mistake with your actions, with the way you allow your fear to tie you down.*

Vahly was looking at him when he lifted his head. Her arms crossed, and with a braid over her shoulder, she appeared less frightening than the other two. Perhaps she had dimmed her power to comfort him. The side of her mouth twitched like she knew what he was thinking, but she didn't call him out. *Share your challenges with your people.*

Then yet another voice came from the twisting clouds of light and dark. *He isn't the open-up type, if you'll allow me to speak up about the subject in question.* Maren—the witch Brielle had rescued—appeared, dirt on her chin and still as thin as she had been when he'd seen her at the cave. Had she died since they'd last met?

He's stone-hearted, this one is, Maren said.

Nix shook her large head. *He certainly is not if he is a dragon, which he is.*

But he is also an elf, Arcturus added.

Glaring at Arcturus, Nix huffed. *The dragon part of him is stronger.*

Arcturus chuckled good-naturedly like this was an old argument that didn't truly sting him.

Why are you here? Dorin asked Maren, trying to hide his deepening confusion.

The dead speak to me. It's my unique power, and it makes people very uncomfortable, so you're the only one who knows. Please keep it that way. This magic can lead to...shall we say, awkward situations. It's how I found Princess Brielle in the cave. She's touched so many ancient artifacts that the ghosts of those who wish to visit the land of the living tend to gravitate toward her. I wouldn't want her worrying about it.

Maren didn't seem to notice it, but Arcturus, Nix, and Vahly regarded her with heavy looks. He had no idea why, but it was odd they kept so wholly still and quiet while a mere human witch was speaking.

Nix was the first to break the spark-filled silence. *We all have our parts to play in the history of the world. Choose your steps not with the eyes of fear but with the fire of your soul. Only then can you be the great one the Source called you to be.*

Vahly nodded. *It isn't easy.* She clapped a hand on his shoulder, and the scent of earth, new grass, and spring blooms flooded his senses. *I know that well*, she said. *You must risk it all to have it all. The only way to live your fated life is to embrace your full self. All of you must be given a voice.*

Let that dragon out. Nix purred and flicked her tongue, a spark rising between her lips and falling to Dorin's feet.

And then he woke, still seated in the quiet library's green, velvet chair.

CHAPTER 25

BRIELLE

Banners in scarlet, buttercup yellow, and rich blue fluttered from the dark wood beams across the great hall's ceiling. Below, two long tables held platters of steaming food, and unlike the custom in Wylfen, the nobles talked loudly and sat seemingly where they chose. A few were already picking bits of meat from trays and drinking from large horns painted with black lettering. The scent of herbed potatoes, peppers, and sausage filled the air. Furs had been set in two corners along with leather chairs to serve as additional seating away from the tables, and a square of floor was ringed off with iron links at the far end of the hall. Brielle assumed the men would wrestle there.

But as far as Brielle could tell, Dorin wasn't yet here. Most of the elves had darker hair and gray eyes like Prince Filip, Dorin's younger brother. Dorin would stand out here, his mane as gold as a coin and his eyes to match. And of course, there were the dragon wings and scales. She smiled behind a small cough as her stomach fluttered with excitement. His magic was such an impossibility, and here she was, right in the thick of his life to see what came of this development. There was no place she'd rather be even if this adventure did come with a heap of danger.

Rhianne and Gytha and two guards—who remained politely back a few steps—escorted Brielle to a seat directly in the center of the nearest table, on the side of the snapping fire. The carved likeness of a starry sky and a growling bear stretched over the hearth.

"I do hope seating me in front of a mouthful of bear teeth isn't a prophetic statement."

Gytha chuckled, and Rhianne bit her lip, a grin pulling at her mouth. Aurora glared from across the table like she'd somehow heard Brielle over the din of conversation. Not a chance. The Lore princess might have been fully capable of glimpsing Brielle's past or future in the water, but no one could hear a whisper from that far in a raucous crowd like this. They all looked so...happy. This court was infinitely different from the Wylfen's. Her heart cinched tightly, so she looked away from the people and took her seat.

The platter nearest Brielle featured roasted chicken covered in a bright green herb sauce. A bowl of slightly charred red peppers sat beside it, and the whole thing made her mouth water.

Filip strode through the hall doors, the one-eyed Drago at his side. They greeted those who approached them with slaps on the back and half-hugs. Hopefully, their good spirits meant they didn't fear for their friend's life, the friend who had thrown a knife at Brielle. She didn't really hold that attack against the elven knight named Stephan.

Though she firmly believed she wasn't the cause for the elves' pain and suffering over the last decades. She hadn't even been alive when the whole thing started. But she represented the warriors who had cut down the elves' friends, kin, and fellow fighters.

Drago gave her a nod from across the room just as everyone went oddly quiet.

Dorin walked in, black cloak rippling from his broad shoulders and his wings no longer in sight. The light from the high and slender windows touched the scales on his cheek and temple, and his eyes flashed when he locked his gaze on Brielle. Her stomach flipped, and she dug her fingers into the arms of her chair. He'd smoothed his hair away from his face, and the effect made his strong features stand out even more. Her lips parted to say something to him, but he was already turning away to approach his royal parents at the end of the room.

Conversation started up again, though many still glanced in Dorin's direction, their eyes wide in fear or foreheads wrinkled with confusion. Everyone was talking about the heir of Balaur, the dragon prince.

Gytha poured a clear liquid into a small pewter goblet, and the scent of cherries wafted across Brielle's face. "Oh, don't worry, Princess," Gytha said, "it's fully obvious the lord wants to rip that dress right off you, enemy's daughter or not."

Brielle's face went hot. "I didn't...I wasn't thinking about that."

"Of course you weren't." Gytha filled her own cup and drank it down without stopping.

Suffering gods. Was her attraction to Dorin that clear

to everyone here? Cheeks on fire, she twisted left and right, but no one seemed to be paying a bit of attention to her.

In fact, everyone save Aurora, Dorin, and Gytha looked right past her like she wasn't there at all.

"Have they been ordered to ignore me?" she whispered to Gytha as she took a sip of what had to be the famed fruit brandy. The liquid burned its way down her throat, but it was a pleasant sort of burn—a bit like arguing with Dorin.

"Not exactly. They were informed of the importance of your place here, of the possibility of peace in the future and how no one must ruin this opportunity. King Mihai addressed the court."

"Thank you for telling me."

"I've been ordered to treat you as my lady."

"Well, thank you for doing a nice job of it."

Gytha inclined her head. "Would you like some peppers?"

They ate in companionable silence, but as Rhianne grabbed an eating knife, Brielle flinched.

"Sorry," Rhianne said, her eyes filled with sympathy. "I'm sure it's not easy being here."

"To say the least."

"You have the queen and king's protection. No one will strike out against you."

Brielle didn't want to bring up the fact that someone had already done so. She wanted to push that event to the back of her mind as quickly as possible.

Dorin remained at the end of the table for the feasting. Every time Brielle glanced at him, he was staring at nothing, elbow on the arm of his fur-covered chair and his mouth pressed into his fisted hand. Filip and Werian sat beside him, talking up a storm.

Brielle took a serving of berry pudding from a servant with a silver tray. "This court doesn't have couples sit side by side, I guess."

Rhianne licked a bit of pudding from her lip, then wiped her mouth neatly with her cloth napkin. "At more formal events, the seating is arranged more carefully. This is a casual festive affair. Primāvarā Noroc only grows more formal on the last day."

"What happens then?"

Gytha leaned in and wiggled her eyebrows. "The midnight dancing."

Intriguing. "What does that involve?" Brielle asked.

"Here in the great hall," Rhianne said, "everyone gathers dressed in black to dance the dark months away in style. I've never been, but Werian told me about it. He said no one can see a thing until the queen lights the spring torch at the conclusion."

"Honored guests!" Queen Sorina stood at the end of the table, drinking horn raised high. "It is time for the first match! May the sun shine on the mountains!"

"May the sun shine on you!" the crowd answered, but Brielle noticed Rhianne didn't repeat the phrase.

"My accent is still terrible in elvish," she muttered, grimacing. "I've been studying night and day with this horrible fae, one of Werian's numerous cousins."

Aurora's head whipped around. "Please tell me you haven't been subjected to Bathilda's tutoring!"

"That's the one." Rhianne sighed.

Finishing her drink, Aurora shook her head. "My condolences. You'd think as princess, you'd have a choice."

"I do, but she is actually very good at teaching. It's just not pleasant."

"Efficiency and practicality always wins with you, doesn't it?" Aurora grinned at Rhianne.

"Always," Rhianne answered with a self-deprecating shrug and smile.

Dorin wasn't quick to stand, but Filip jogged to the ring, shedding his cloak and tunic. Were all elves built so well? That family seemed to be, at least. Filip grinned with all of his teeth and rubbed his hands together as the room began to chant, "*Barda! Barda!*" It meant hatchet, unless Brielle's translation was wrong. Aurora joined in the shouting too, clapping so hard her silver hair began to slide from its knots. Her eyes shone as she looked at her prince. Another interesting couple—elf and human water mage. So odd. All her life, Brielle had been told such pairings were impossible both physically and emotionally. But that had been a lie, one of many, she was sure, that her tutors had fed her on Father's advice.

"*Magic kills those without it. It controls and feeds. It will drive both those with it and those simply near it absolutely mad.*" She remembered Father's less formal lessons as she and Etienne had played Stone and Hind by the fire.

"*But what of the old witches that still live in the elven mountains?*" Etienne had asked. "*They would throw themselves off the cliffs if they were mad, wouldn't they? And Jean told me he saw one during a raid that had to be one hundred years old.*"

Father hadn't argued that what Jean told Etienne was

false, but Jean had disappeared from the castle shortly after that.

"Come now, Brother!" Filip shouted.

Dorin stormed through the gathering crowd around the ring, tore off his cloak and shirt, then leapt over the ringside to join Filip. His hair fell over one eye, the ends brushing his metallic scales, then he lunged at Filip, his back muscles shifting beneath his skin.

Jostled by the other nobles and their servants, maids, and warriors, Brielle followed Gytha and Rhianne to the ring. A tall woman stood between Brielle and the view of the match, but Rhianne shook her wand, and the woman turned, eyes searching for whatever Rhianne had spelled her to seek. Brielle took the opportunity to step forward, hands clasping the iron links that marked the wrestling match boundaries. Dorin had Filip pinned to the ground, chest to chest, but Filip was grinning, so perhaps it wasn't over yet. Filip bridged his hips up, scooted backward, then shot out and over Dorin, climbing onto his brother's back.

In a movement so fast it blurred, Dorin stood and growled.

Sparks lit the air, and the scent of dragon magic pricked Brielle's nose.

CHAPTER 26
DORIN

Magic burned its way down Dorin's back, and his ribs shuddered. He was shifting into a dragon, and his dear brother was on his back. "Filip! Go!"

But Filip looped an arm around his neck, trying to lock Dorin into a choke that would end the wrestling match as soon as Dorin raised a hand in defeat. Filip was too caught up in the competition to hear the fear in Dorin's voice. The change was coming, the power rippling down his arms, the tingling in his fingers that preceded talons, a bright sensation that wasn't painful but certainly wasn't comfortable sheering across his back and down his spine. Dorin went to his knee and slid Filip off his back with a quick shrugging movement. Filip laughed as he slammed onto the ground, already spinning as Dorin stood. Filip tried to get a foot behind his ankle to sweep him. Dorin lifted his leg, then leapt onto Filip, holding him down with his weight, knees on either side of his brother's body.

Dorin pinned Filip's upper arms to the ground and glared. Magic swamped his senses, and the colors he only saw as a dragon appeared. The shade between emerald and ruby edged the iron links of the wrestling ring and—

A scent took over. Lavender. The pines and dew-dampened moss. He whipped his head around to see Brielle's large, green eyes and the second hue he never saw as an elf, a bright color circling her pupil. Aury, Gytha, and Rhianne stood beside her. They were holding her captive. He trembled. She was his, not theirs. Heat poured across his chest and into his arms as the dragon inside him roared for release and strained to be free to protect what was his.

Fighting the beast, Dorin focused on Filip's face. "I need this to be over, Brother," he pleaded. His fingers morphed into talons. If the crowd saw, they'd fear him, and not in the proper way of kings-in-waiting and their subjects.

Filip's jovial look fled, and his gaze darted across Dorin's face as if taking stock of his level of seriousness. "I give!" Filip shouted.

The crowd roared approval and began shouting, "Fiul Stelelor!" Son of Stars, the title of the heir to the throne of Balaur.

The voices of the god and goddesses who had somehow visited his dream in the library came roaring back inside his head. Their advice to embrace his new magic and discover the possibilities it offered had lifted his heart, but his mind pressed the hope down. They cared for the fate of the world as a whole. They weren't thinking of the individuals he might kill in his efforts to find a way to use this power he held in his blood. No, he would keep this curse restrained as best he could. They would strike a deal with the Wylfen king for his daughter and his pride, then Dorin's beastly side would be rendered an unnecessary risk. He held to his plan. Seal the peace treaty. Leave his family forever.

His chest tightened, and he stopped, grabbing the edge of the second of the feasting tables.

With another wrestling match starting up in the ring—between two nobles who'd been given land in Lore after the last war—Drago ran up and handed Dorin a blunt-edged sword. Father stood beside him, hand on his chest.

"Son, will you compete in the sword for your people?" Mihai coughed, his lips white and his cheeks gray.

"Anything for you, Father." Dorin accepted the sword from Drago as the announcement was made.

But the steward's loud words faded as Brielle approached, Aury and Rhianne at her sides. He gritted his teeth, torn between wanting to lock Brielle in the prisons and longing to free her from this gilded cage and take her to the skies where he could protect her properly. No. He shook his head. He wouldn't protect her. He was the one who had hurt her.

"Don't sprain something, Prince Dorin," Werian said, sliding up beside his wife, Rhianne.

"Perhaps you should wait on the sword fighting." Aury scowled at the weapon Drago had given him. "Filip doesn't care for it anyway."

"I do think our fiery friend here is enjoying the show thus far though." Werian winked at Brielle, who rolled her emerald eyes, which made Dorin grin for the first time in a while.

"I am here by order of Queen Sorina," Brielle said, "and that's it."

"Correct," Dorin said. "Primāvarā Noroc is a political event this year, and Princess Brielle is wise to remember that."

Brielle's lip curled. "And Prince Dorin would be wise to remember that he is not the one running this political event," she said sharply. "I take orders and advice from Queen Sorina and King Mihai only."

"Calm down, you two. Come now, Princess Brielle." Werian waved a servant with a tray of sugared cakes toward Brielle. "You enjoy the good life as much as my ravishing wife." Rhianne leaned over and kissed his cheek, both of them practically glowing. It made Dorin want to punch every wall in the world even though he knew that was an unkind thought. "I can tell you do," Werian said to Brielle. "Eat, drink, and savor the prowess of your scaled savior here."

Dorin's jaw ached from gritting his teeth. Scaled savior indeed.

Rhianne elbowed Werian, and the fae prince chuckled.

Brielle shook her head at Werian and pressed her hands against her skirts like she wished she weren't stuck here in that gown. Her hands were so graceful. She locked gazes with Dorin as if she somehow knew he was staring. With a cruel grin on her sweet-looking lips, she ran her fingers slowly up her bodice, then let them rest at the scalloped neckline. Desire danced down Dorin, and he found himself breathing too quickly. He ripped his gaze away from her, thoughts tumbling one after another, no path of logic in sight.

Did Werian know Brielle from some past event? With his jesting and her eye rolling, they appeared awfully comfortable with one another even if Werian did seem to annoy her as much as he annoyed Dorin.

Filip jogged over and gave Dorin a tentative smile. He led him away from the others. "All right, Brother?" Filip asked.

"Did Mother and Father send the message to the Wylfen king?"

"Aye. Just now. I saw the messengers leave myself. Two of our best riders."

"Where is Stephan now?" Dorin asked.

Filip sighed. "He is in his rooms, under guard."

"Guards he could best, I'm sure."

Anger flared in Filip's eyes. "He won't strike out at her again. I spoke to him."

"I don't blame him for his anger," Dorin said.

"Neither do I," Filip replied, "but we both know that can't be permitted."

"Of course not."

"I can't tell whether you loathe this woman or long to bed her?" Filip squinted. "Or perhaps both. I'm certain Aury feels both of those emotions where I'm concerned."

A sudden, unbidden vision of Brielle with bared shoulders, smooth as cream, her bright hair loose and brushing her—

"Dorin?" Filip nudged him. "Where did you go there, Brother?"

Dorin swallowed roughly. "Nothing. Nowhere. Let's fight."

"All right. I'm always down for a match."

"But you hate the sword."

Eyebrows lifted, Filip said, "Not as much as I hate politics and discussing my brother's pent-up desire for our enemy."

Dorin glanced back to make sure Brielle hadn't heard his stupid brother and his ridiculous comment. Brielle was talking to Rhianne, her hands moving as she spoke and her accent fascinating to his ears. Her gaze slid to his face, then moved to his eyes. Dorin's heart thudded once, as loud as the midnight dance drum.

"Shut up, Filip," he whispered.

Filip held up his hands. "Shutting up."

Fool. Dorin led Filip past the gathered crowds in the corridors of the castle, through the spring banner merchants and the potato pie stalls that lined the inner and outer baileys, and outside to the wide clearings where the weapons sparring arenas had been prepped for Primāvarā Noroc.

Cleaned of rock and scraped to dry earth, the arena held stone seating in a semi-circle. Nobles in bright velvets and silks poured into the stands above the throng of more plainly dressed common folk. All wore smiles, and many had painted their faces to show the stars of Balaur or green leaves to celebrate late springtime. A group of children burst past Dorin and Filip, knocking into their legs and shouting, "Fiul Stelelor!" as their parents scolded and chased them.

Filip laughed, delighted, but Dorin couldn't let the happy mood of the crowd touch his heart. His mind was in chaos. Nothing the deities had told him made any sense.

Doing his best to shake off that memory, he focused on

the sword in his hand. He and Filip bowed to one another, then took their stances. Filip was an expert, but Dorin could best him, and quickly too.

Dorin feigned a low strike, and when Filip went to jump, Dorin whipped the blade backward, then slashed at Filip's chest instead of going for the throat as he would in battle. Filip just barely lunged back to avoid the hit. The spark of competition in his eye, Filip suddenly spun and delivered a backhand strike toward Dorin's middle. Dorin used Filip's momentary weight shift to slip to the side and smack Filip's ribs with the flat of the blunted sword. A breath huffed from Filip, and he bent double. Dorin paused to make certain he didn't have a broken rib, and Filip raised his sword, flipping it to stab at Dorin's groin.

"Oh, it's to be like that today, is it?" Dorin said, smiling, losing the weight of his problems to the thrill of fighting.

He deftly scooted back, then arced his blade over Filip's head, aiming for the back of Filip's neck. Filip rolled, then popped up, striking like a madman, left and right. It was the way he fought with his hatchet and not the wisest style for the length of their current weapons.

Dorin clipped Filip's hilt, and his brother's sword fell to the ground. Filip raised a hand in defeat, grinning and going to hug Dorin. Dorin stiffened. His wings could appear again... Being touched felt dangerous. But Dorin gave in and put an arm around Filip, slapping him on the back.

"Get your hatchet and show off a bit. You know you want to," Dorin whispered.

Filip pressed his forehead against Dorin's. "You are the greatest brother in history. Don't ever doubt it."

Dorin's stomach turned. No, he wasn't. Filip still had no idea what this curse truly did to Dorin, how he could lose his mind, the blood on his hands, the primal mind of a dragon...

"Shall I try another weapon?" Filip asked the crowd.

"Hatchet! Hatchet!" The crowd chanted Filip's nickname as he caught that very weapon, which Drago had tossed his way.

Filip made quick work of Dorin with the hatchet, and Dorin was soon holding up his hand in defeat. The crowd roared approval, chanting both their titles, a tangled mess of honor and history, quite fitting for their past, Dorin thought.

Dorin turned to find his way back to the castle's keep. He wanted to know exactly how the letter to the Wylfen had been worded, and Mother usually kept to her rooms during the outdoor events these days. Father just couldn't handle that much exertion anymore, and she wouldn't leave him for long.

But as Dorin walked through the arena, he was greeted by his mother's attendants, two noblewomen with identically braided, white-blond hair and dark blue gowns. "Queen Sorina has asked that you lead the hike to Suveran Peak and that you grace her guest with the peace blessing."

Anger whipped through him. "Grace the Wylfen with the Balaur peace blessing?! She must be joking."

The attendants curtseyed low, their eyes downturned.

Dorin swore and raged past them, aiming for the trailhead. Why had his normally wise mother lost her senses over this Wylfen princess? The peace blessing was an ancient rite for their people. To bestow this honor on one of them... No. He wouldn't do it. Yes, he'd brought Brielle here. Yes, he felt terrible for hurting her in such a brutal and personal way that had nothing to do with war. But he'd be dead before he set a crown of Balaur mountain flowers on her head, knelt at her feet, and crushed handfuls of Balaur earth into her palms. No. No. No. On the way up, he'd figure a way to get around Mother's order and bestow the blessing on someone else. Maybe Filip. It wasn't customary, but how could she argue with that? Or maybe on a child? If she berated him for blessing a child and the public heard, that would tarnish her reputation.

He stewed silently as the crowds began to cluster at the trailhead around servants who'd brought the chests of shoe coverings for the nobility who only had court slippers. A bevy of serving maids and manservants brought Dorin hot water to wash his face and hands. One had to be purified to bestow the blessing. He'd have to change his clothing here at the mountain's feet before the hike as well.

He lifted his head to see Brielle, eyeing him with far too much interest. Fantastic. This day was just packed full of appropriate spring celebrations. He turned to allow the attendants to begin the process. The sooner this was over, the better.

CHAPTER 27
BRIELLE

Brielle tried not to gawk. The others seemed to think disrobing a prince in front of the whole place was no big deal. Already his boots were off and set neatly beside the stone-lined trail. The royal attendants pulled Dorin's gauntlets from his arms, then he bent so they could pull his vest free. He unlaced the tunic underneath, and they stripped him of that garment as well. Next, they undid his belt, one man holding Dorin's short sword and dagger like they were royal babies. Two women removed his trousers, then his short clothes underneath. And there he stood in all his glory, as naked as he'd been the day he'd landed in her courtyard at Wylfen Castle and exactly as beautiful.

Goddess save her, he was the most handsome male she'd ever seen.

From his tousled, golden hair to the ferocious look in his eye, his broad shoulders, the proud muscles of his chest and chiseled make of his torso. Two scars crossed on his side, evidence of his war-torn past, most likely done by Wylfen blades, Brielle thought miserably. And there were his powerful legs, narrow hips, and...well, the elven prince was certainly finely built. Finely built indeed. She wished he were truly the beast he thought himself to be. It would have been a great deal easier not to want him.

"Wipe the drool from your mouth before we start walking," Gytha said, a laugh in her whisper. "It would be unseemly if anyone else noticed."

Brielle twisted to look at Gytha, who stood at her shoulder. Aurora and Rhianne were whispering to one another, and Brielle was incredibly grateful they hadn't heard Gytha. "If you keep turning up like that," Brielle said to Gytha, "right at my most embarrassing moments, I'm going to think you're the one with the supposed witch blood."

Brielle began to say something else, but then the attendants were washing Dorin, and her words fled her mind. Thankfully, they dressed him quickly, all in that dark midnight blue the elves so loved.

Brielle knew she was staring again, marveling at the way his fingers curled around the edges of the long, thin cloak they tied at his neck, wondering what those fingers would feel like on her body. High in the mountains when she had been injured, she'd learned he could be both fierce and gentle. She cleared her throat, cheeks hot and belly hotter.

His gaze locked onto hers. All she could think about was how he had flown her away from D'Aboville, from her life of fear and hate, how kind he'd been in grinding herbs and holding her head to help her drink what he'd painstakingly concocted.

Suddenly, desire for this prince, for both his body and his heart, flamed high inside her. A sensation akin to pleasant sparks fled from her scalp all the way down her sides, through her stomach and lower, then to the very tips of her toes. It wasn't magic in the true sense of the word, but the power of a blooming emotion.

Her lips parted. "Dorin." No one else was there. It was only them. Their gazes joined. Their bodies wanting. Hearts beating in time.

He exhaled. Wings burst from his back, glittering jade and emerald in the sun, impossibly large, while vicious talons extended from the tips of his fingers. He looked skyward, then closed his eyes. His throat moved in a swallow, and it seemed as though he wanted to weep as the wind stirred his tangled mane. The scent of dragon magic, citrus and charcoal, laced the air.

Shivers traveled the length of her. He was magnificent.

Everyone had stilled and gone silent. The children seemed to freeze as if under a spell of their own fear. She couldn't even hear Werian cracking jokes. A miracle, that. Only the birds kept singing, the bees buzzing.

She had to do something. He'd done everything for her.

With a glance to Aurora and Gytha, who only looked on with wide eyes, she stepped forward, then turned to face the elves, fae, and the one witch, Rhianne.

"I was dying at the hands of my father's Broyeurs," she said quietly. Two elves spat on the ground at the mention of the magic crushers. "And your prince rescued me from their evil hands. He brought me here to heal. Me. An enemy. A Wylfen."

Every set of eyes was on her, pressing her down.

"The Source has blessed Prince Dorin with a great power for some destiny we don't yet understand. As one who has witnessed his fierce mercy, I ask that you hold off judging this new appearance and give him the respect you've always held for him in your hearts. He is Balaur. Everything he does is for you, his people. Every action speaks of the elven soul, of its power and kindness. Of its strength."

She looked at Dorin, who stared, his eyes flashing, the dragon in him barely leashed. The wind buffeted his outstretched wings. He was shaking. What did that gaze mean? Was he angry or pulled to her like she was to him? Or did he simply want her to stop going on about him? She refused to regret speaking up. It was the only thing she could do for him.

"Agreed," a voice said from the crowd. Filip strode forward, the people parting so he could pass. "We are the Balaur elves, and nothing will see us dishonoring our beloved Fiul Stelelor with such a lowly emotion as fear."

The elves shouted approval, and many pounded on their chests with one fist. They looked barbaric. It was fantastic.

Dorin bowed his head, his chest rising in a deep breath beneath his long tunic.

"Thank you," he mouthed to her, then he started up the trail on bare feet, his cloak sweeping the ground behind him. The crowd followed, taking Brielle along as they moved.

CHAPTER 28
DORIN

Dorin tucked his wings as closely as he could manage as they hiked toward the wildflowers and wide vistas of Suveran Peak. The wind teased his new appendages as if it wanted him to join the sweeping movement through the sky, and honestly, a part of him wished for just that. The cowardly part. The stares of his people, and of Brielle, seared his back, and he tried to fist his hands, talons bracing against his palms, halting the action. His lip twitched, and his incisor bit into his lower lip. The tang of blood bloomed on his tongue. Licking the drop of blood away, he climbed faster, his heart pounding not from the incline but from Brielle's actions and words.

She'd spoken up for him. Unless he was simply being foolish due to her creamy skin and that look in her eye... No, she'd spoken from the heart. She truly believed he was a good person, not a beastly nightmare. She viewed him as a rescuer. Even after the burns. He rubbed a hand over his face, careful not to pluck out his eye with the wild talons. Could he avoid bestowing the blessing on her now? After that?

Memories of past battles with the Wylfen warriors and their trained scar wolves littered his mind. A spray of blood across Drago's chest and the fear that he was dead. The leap of a wolf at Filip's throat when he was just a lad, during his first foray into securing the borderlands. An arrow in Father's shoulder during a border skirmish not unlike the one currently raging in the southeast.

He glanced backward. Filip gestured toward Brielle and said something to three children. They ran to Brielle and offered mostly smashed orange wildflowers for her to accept as gifts as Brielle smiled down at them. The sun glowed through her red hair, giving her a haloed appearance, and he blinked at the brightness. Beside her, Aury glared. The Magelord had obviously not yet given in to Brielle's charm. Perhaps he should follow her lead and continue to hold Brielle at arm's length, to refrain from trusting her. Aury was intelligent, but she was also quite good at holding a grudge and being defensive. Truly, he and Aury had a great deal in common there.

If he did bless a Wylfen princess on this sacred mountain, what would warriors like Stephan think? Stephan's loathing of the enemy was so deep that he'd thrown a knife at Brielle right in front of Mother and Father. He had to have known he was destined for the dungeon with that action, righteous or not.

The crowd included many warriors who had seen battle action. Their scarred faces looked on Brielle. Some were missing limbs due to the attacks of her people. Others limped alongside with their families, still strong and capable but having suffered greatly. Was Mother setting the royal house of Balaur down a dangerous path with her order? Even if Brielle was more good than bad, was this the right move? Mother had her reasons, surely. She was a wise one and had ruled alongside Father successfully for years.

The trail ended in a labyrinth of carefully laid stones that shone white among orange flowers that waved like Lore ladies' fans in the breeze. He walked the labyrinth, following the looping circles, the people going quiet as a heavy feeling of reverence enveloped the area. At the center of the labyrinth, Dorin knelt beside the cleared circle of earth. With his talons, he slowly, methodically dug two handfuls of dry, mountain dirt, the grit grating his skin and slipping over his talons.

He had to trust Mother and Father. He wasn't yet king. He just hoped this wasn't the first step toward an uprising.

"Princess Brielle of Wylfen, please come forward for the Primāvarā Noroc blessing from the House of Balaur, descendants of the god Rigel and the goddess Ursae."

Several people gasped, but no one spoke out against his choice.

"But..." Brielle started forward, eyes wide. Then she handed the posies of blooms the children had given her to Gytha.

Pressing his lips together, he nodded, and Brielle came forward, obeying his command. It was most likely the first time she'd followed a request in her life, he thought wryly. She stood before him, her shadow easing the heat of the sun. On his knees, he held out the handfuls of earth.

"With this blessing, you receive the glory of Balaur.

May its flora and fauna be kind to you. May the ground lift to meet your steps upon this kingdom, and may the paths of the creatures here lead you to your heart's desire." He turned each handful over and released the earth into her open palms.

She closed her fingers over the blessed ground. If she said the wrong thing here...

Bringing her fisted hands to her chest, she closed her eyes as if in prayer. "I will love her if she will take me. I have longed for such a home as this."

A tightness in his chest loosened. Most of the crowd murmured approval, though a few abruptly turned to leave. There was trouble here, but the blessing felt right. Mother had been wise in asking this of him.

The crowd broke apart, clusters of younger elves gathering in the wildflowers, children playing Capture, and some families descending the trail.

Dorin touched the center of the labyrinth, the sun winking on the surface of his sigil ring. "Thank you, Arcturus, god of Air. Thank you, Vahly, goddess of Earth. Thank you, Nix, goddess of Fire. I hope you're right."

He stood, and Brielle remained, a smile tugging at the side of her mouth. With careful movements, she set the earth back into the center of the labyrinth. "You hope the goddess Nix is right about what?"

"What do you think?" He expanded his wings.

She laughed, and he couldn't fight the grin stretching his lips. "Did she reveal something of your status to you?"

Brielle was obviously teasing him. She had no idea how close to the truth she was. Could he tell her about his dream?

"Do you remember the witch from the mountains?"

"Do I remember the person I pulled from my father's dungeon? Yes, Dorin. I do remember Maren."

"Maren. Yes. She appeared to me in a dream."

Brielle's lips bunched. "Sounds like you might need to talk this one out with your brother or one of your men."

"It wasn't like that. She can speak to the dead."

"What? Hold on. Did you dream that she can, or can she actually work this magic? In addition to sauntering into your nighttime imaginings..."

"She didn't saunter."

"Sure."

"She appeared along with... You won't believe this. I don't even know why I'm telling you."

"Spill it, dragon elf."

"I saw the gods. Arcturus. Nix. Vahly."

Brielle stopped, and he faced her. "Well, don't stop talking now, Prince. I have to hear the rest of this fascinating dream of yours. I've heard of some interesting predilections, shall we call them, in men, but perhaps elves are even more imaginative than I'd—"

"They spoke to me about this curse."

"Blessing."

"Goddess Nix said..." He could almost hear the words in his memory. *"Choose your steps not with the eyes of fear but with the fire of your soul. Only then can you be the great one the Source called you to be."*

Brielle smacked his shoulder. "See? I told you. Your magic is important for you and for your role here."

"But watch them, how they stare."

The crowd had given them space to speak privately, but

many sets of eyes focused on Dorin's wings, fear widening their gazes and mistrust showing in the way they cocked their heads to study his new silhouette. Every look was a lance to his chest.

"It will take some time, that's all. I was scared of elves. Now, I'm not. Exposure is usually the cure to unfounded fears."

"I nearly burned you alive."

"So maybe not unfounded, but they have to realize your potential. A dragon for a king! That will strike fear in the heart of even *my* cold father. You must believe this is good if the gods and goddesses visited your dream." She walked down the trail, her dirt-stained fingers fiddling with her gown like she might be nervous. "What did Maren say to you?" A pretty blush spread over her cheeks, and the urge to comfort her, to let her know he wasn't thinking of another woman in that way, overwhelmed everything else.

"She told me of her power. Asked me to keep it to myself. I hope she'll forgive this one indiscretion. And she called me stone-hearted."

"Even though you saved me?"

"She is the one who saw me fly off with you in my arms. I'd have been naked in the mountains for the entirety of the journey if not for her magic."

"She magicked you clothing?"

He nodded, feeling awkward but lighthearted for a reason he couldn't quite decipher. "You have seen me unclothed twice now. Seems unfair." Inhaling, he drew to a halt. "I have no idea why I just said that. Apologies." Now, he truly did want to fly away. She must think him a horrible male, speaking out like that. He sounded like a disgusting fae.

Brielle pinched his backside, and he jumped. "Don't tempt me, Fiul Stelelor. I heard there will be more of that fruit brandy going around tonight."

Dorin tried to think of what to say, but no words came to him as he watched her walk away.

CHAPTER 29
D'ABOVILLE

C aptain D'Aboville's black horse rounded the mountain pass. The drop—only one errant hoof away—had to be over five hundred feet high, and that was just to a small outcropping. D'Aboville's stomach turned, so he forced himself to look forward. The group had gone quiet. His Broyeur fellows were ready to camp for the night, but Balaur Castle was so close...

He tapped his vest pocket, where a large flask of Magebane hid, ready to break the foul magic of the elves. A grin pulled at his beard. Soon, Brielle would be safely under his control again. The stupid girl thought she knew best in every scenario despite the fact that she was a mere eighteen years of age. After that abominable dragon elf had attacked, he'd thought Brielle might be dead. The thought had emptied him. He gripped the locket at his neck so tightly that the metal clasp cut into his skin. Brielle was no replacement for Jacqueline. No, she could never be, for Jacqueline had been the kindest woman in the world, gone too soon, taken by an illness he was certain had its roots in foul magic. But Brielle looked so much like her. That red hair, those green eyes. He had to get that girl to follow him, to do as he bid, or she would die, and he'd lose that visual reminder of his lost love.

He had to purge Brielle's evil from her spirit. No matter the cost.

"The scouts, Captain." Theron pointed ahead to a small clearing lined by dark pines. Two men rode out of the trees.

In the clearing, all dismounted, and the scouts attempted to speak between catching their breath and taking much needed swallows of water.

"No sign of any dragons, Captain. But we believe half the Balaur army remains at the southeastern border. We saw old campfires and prints in the mud as well."

They dismounted and arranged their minimal tents, Theron barking orders for the beans to be heated and organizing the handing out of rationed baguettes and dried venison.

A shiver rocked D'Aboville as he lay in his tent after eating and washing. He never slept well on the Balaur side of the Ecailles Mountains. The wind picked up, whistling through the pines and ruffling the edges of the canvas. The sounds melded into what almost sounded like whispers. He blinked and rolled over, but the wind howled, deeper now and gusting through the small openings between the tent's door ties.

"True power is what you seek. True control."

Pulse galloping, he sat up, knocking the cup of water he'd stashed onto his bedroll. "Who is there?"

A dark laugh rode the wind and snaked into his ears. He untied the tent door and threw himself into the dark. Clouds shrouded the moon. The fire had long been tamped down, and there was no movement from the other Broyeurs' tents. Theron slept against a boulder, the idiot.

With a kick to the boot, he jostled the man. "Theron! Wake up."

Theron wiped drool from his mouth and staggered to his feet. "Sorry, Captain. What is it?" He drew his sword and set a hand against his lower vest pocket. Each Broyeur had been issued their own small dose of Magebane with instructions to imbibe the concoction as soon as anything unnatural occurred.

"I heard a voice. Stay here. I will investigate."

The pines swayed in the night wind, and D'Aboville kept his ears perked for any more sounds that didn't belong. An animal path wove into the trees, bare earth illuminated only by the cloud-dimmed moonlight. Among the pines, a great willow danced. Long branches heavy with leaves dragged the forest floor and tangled with vines of dark ivy that in turn embraced the tree's trunk like a lover.

The wind whispered into his ears and ruffled his hair. He smoothed his curls with quick movements. Of course, the wind wasn't speaking. That would be madness. A magic he'd never seen. And he'd seen it all.

"Come. Grasp victory. I would never fail you. You could control me, and with me, you control them. You control her."

He stopped in front of the willow. The tree reached its branches toward him, the leaves brushing his sleeves.

Magic. It had to be. He leapt backward, removed the

Magebane from his pocket, and drank three large swallows. The taste was bitter and sweet too, foul-tasting stuff.

That same deep laugh echoed through the willow as the ivy around its trunk and exposed roots shuffled as if creatures stirred below.

But if this was magic, why wasn't the Magebane working? Was it not strong enough to defeat this voice? Perhaps it was at least keeping the thing from attacking.

He marched back to camp. "Theron! Wake the others and tell them to bring their axes to the tree line. Just there."

After retrieving his own axe, he met the men by the animal path.

They made quick work of the willow, which thankfully didn't speak to him again or anyone else that he could tell.

"What is wrong with this willow?" Theron asked.

"It's fouled by magic."

"Or simply overgrown," Henri muttered, cutting into one of the larger branches, breaking it into two.

D'Aboville whirled and grabbed the man by the throat. "Are you questioning me?" Sputtering, Henri attempted to speak, so D'Aboville squeezed harder. "I hunted magic for years before you were even a spark in your father's eye. Do. Not. Question. Me."

An inner voice—not the one he'd heard on the wind, but the one that plagued his confidence—asked why he had never been successful at ridding Balaur of magic entirely. His life's work had failed. Witches were born. Mages in hiding and breeding. Even the one person he longed most to have securely under his wing had helped a witch escape.

He swallowed the sour taste of Magebane at the back of his mouth and released Henri, who collapsed, coughing. D'Aboville glared at the others, just daring them to come to this idiot's aid, but the men were well-trained.

"The rest of you are a credit to your kingdom. Keep working. Henri, you will return to Wylfenden with a new post on the northern coast."

Henri kept his eyes downcast. Good choice.

They finished ripping up the ivy and chopping the willow into firewood, then they set the tree to light, all thoughts of sleep forgotten in the fervor to clean the area of magic.

At last satisfied, D'Aboville settled into his tent to get what rest he could while the men tended the towering bonfire with its unnatural green and purple flames.

In his sleep, the voice hissed, sounds crisscrossing his thoughts like the ivy was tying itself around him. *Give me your sacrifice, and I will be yours to wield. Absolute power. Complete control...*

If only he could burn his dreams as he had that tree.

CHAPTER 30
BRIELLE

Three days later, Brielle hummed nervously as she stood with Gytha and Rhianne in a corner of the great hall. She was second-guessing her decision to pinch the crown prince's backside after the blessing on the peak. Perhaps that had been a mistake. He'd steered clear of her, playing the spring games at a distance, his gaze touching her briefly, only to flit away. She'd enjoyed the Primāvarā Noroc frivolities despite missing Dorin. They'd had group circle dances where nobles, merchants, craftsman, and farmers came together almost as equals to join hands and stomp feet. Yesterday, Costel had taken her to see the new goats born to the royal farm, all speckled and ready to butt their heads on anything and everything. The elves had even hosted an archery contest that Rhianne just barely lost to her fae husband.

But Brielle longed to see Dorin, to enjoy his kingdom's festivities alongside him. She scanned the room but didn't see him anywhere. Stones, there were so many pointed ears and horns. Elves and fae packed the hall, ready to create some sort of tree decoration, if Brielle had the translation right.

"What tune are you humming, Princess?" Gytha asked, her words flowing together with the speed of her pronunciation.

"Was I? Oh, it was a lullaby my mother used to sing to me. *No matter the blood that runs through your heart, / You are my daughter, and we'll never part...*"

"Is she still in Wylfenden?" Rhianne asked.

"She died when I was young." The first burn of tears heated Brielle's eyes, but she quelled the emotion that threatened to overcome her. Even after all these years, she missed her mother with a grief so heavy it could drag her to the floor.

"She was your true mother?" Gytha asked.

"True?"

"By blood."

Brielle studied Gytha's face. Did Gytha misunderstand? "Of course she was my mother by blood. I am the princess. My father, may he rot in the underworld before this day is done, only married once."

"That is the lullaby for found children, sang to those adopted. One doesn't have to be married to have children," Gytha said.

The world stopped for a breath, and Celeste's tale of Father's affair with the witch drowned every other thought.

"Gytha," Rhianne said, breaking through Brielle's confusion. "That's enough." Her voice was soft but still held the command of someone who had grown used to being obeyed.

Gytha shrugged. "None of my business, Princess Brielle. Forgive me."

"Nothing at all to forgive." She gave the fae a smile, but Gytha's words had hit her heart. Was she not her mother's daughter by blood? Could she be the daughter of the witch who had ensorcelled Father?

Costel, the frizzy-haired elf she'd seen often with Filip and Drago, climbed onto a table and raised his arms. "Five groups! It's not that difficult!"

If she were the witch's child by blood, what did that mean for her? It would certainly explain the humming she sensed in the rune stone and what the fae and Maren had said about her blood and her scent.

Filip and Drago were laughing and looking up at Costel, and Dorin leaned on a stone pillar beside Aurora, Hilda, and Eawynn. Brielle couldn't comprehend what Costel said. Her mind was fully occupied with this possible development. But what did it truly matter? Brielle's mother had been her true mother even if Brielle had been born of another. A breath left her, and she settled herself with this development. No, Mother had been the only mother that mattered. Nothing else was important.

"Poor Costel." Rhianne tapped the end of the wand tucked into her belt with one finger. "He should have been born a human."

"Why do you say that?" Brielle was genuinely curious.

"Because we like organization, don't we? Yes, you know you do. We regard intuition and pleasure as secondary to planning and control. Unlike the elves, who follow their instinct without fail, and the fae—"

"Who would like nothing more than to ravish their mates and let their lands go to waste," Dorin said, his voice stern but sugared with jesting.

Brielle's stomach dipped. He towered over them, golden-eyed and full of coiled tension as he tried to keep his wings from brushing the wall or the many passersby.

Gytha laughed. "It's true, Princess Rhianne. I need to find a new mate. Perhaps I'll find one at the midnight ball."

"I hope you do," Rhianne said. "Want to see what my magic says of your fated match?"

"Not yet. I only want a dalliance for now."

Dorin exhaled. "You see? They are a hedonistic kind."

"What's wrong with that?" Brielle crossed her arms and challenged him with a look.

He began to say something, but then fisted his hand and touched his lips with a knuckle. "Nothing. Especially during the Primāvarā Noroc."

Rhianne and Gytha traded surprised looks. "Your Highness, do you have her side now? Because we'd like to sit and begin our decorations," Gytha asked.

"I do," Dorin said, his tone stirring something deep inside Brielle. "Enjoy yourselves."

"You seem better now." She led him to one of the many seats along the two wooden tables where baskets of red wool, twigs, and dried flowers waited.

Sitting beside her, he reached for a length of spun wool and a hazelnut. "Despite my worries," he said quietly, "I love dragons. I'm trying to focus on the good. At least for today." With his teeth, he cut the wool into two smaller pieces, then began winding the first around the nut to form a ball.

"What do you love about them?" It was amazing to watch the same hands that handled a sword so magnificently carefully craft a tiny decoration.

"Their unabashed pride. They know they are intelligent, faster than anything else in the world, and nigh on indestructible, and they revel in their own glory."

"Talking about me?" Werian nudged Dorin with his elbow as he passed to join Rhianne farther down the table. Werian winked at Brielle. He had yet to speak for her, but then again, perhaps he was behind Queen Sorina accepting her so quickly. She wished he'd say something to Aurora, but it wasn't worth endangering the politics here just to have another friend.

Dorin glared at Werian's back.

"You truly can't stand him, can you?"

Shrugging, Dorin looked at her. "He has a good heart."

"Come on, dragon lord. Tell me what you really think."

"I do think that. I won't speak ill of him. Not on purpose. He has fought by my brother's side with great valor."

"All right. Sometimes it's fun to vent a little steam though, Your Highness. Venting keeps you from exploding."

A ghost of a smile passed over his lips. "Noted. What do you think of mine?" He held up his tree decoration. "Too clumsy?" He'd created a second red sphere, and he attached them with a twig in such a way that they resembled cherries.

"No, they're lovely. Very well done."

A small girl opposite them raised her eyebrows and pursed her lips.

"Oh, no?" Dorin leaned on his elbows and tilted his head.

The girl grinned and held up her own bunch of woolen cherries. She was missing two teeth and was absolutely adorable with her pointed ears and quick, elven movements.

Dorin tossed his decoration onto the table and sighed dramatically. "I'll be embarrassed in front of my entire court. What am I to do now?"

The girl's mouth opened. "Dear Prince Dorin, please don't be sad. You can show them mine. I made them for you!" She handed them over, and he accepted them with a solemn nod.

"Many thanks, young crafter. You do your kingdom a great service by honoring the Primāvarā Noroc and your grateful prince."

Blushing to match her decoration, the girl hid her face in her mother's sleeve, the attention suddenly too much for her to bear.

Brielle's heart softened, and she took Dorin's hand under the table. He jerked in surprise but didn't pull away, instead curling his fingers around hers. Light filled her, shunning the darkness she'd lived with her whole life.

"Now, tell me something I don't know about you. Not about the courts or politics. About Brielle, the woman."

His thumb brushed over her wrist, and her mouth went dry.

"Need some water, Princess?" The small girl's mother handed her a clay cup.

"Thank you so much." She began to drink it, but Dorin snagged the cup from her hand and took a quick sip, his nostrils flaring.

After one more sip, he returned the water to Brielle. "It's fine."

The woman who'd offered the cup stared, then looked away quickly.

Brielle drank it in full then thanked the woman again before turning to Dorin. "She thinks you believe her to be a poisoner," she whispered.

"Not her. But anyone could have touched that water. Let's not speak of it anymore."

"Agreed. Do you know much of the history of dragons? I have spent my entire life digging up their artifacts," Brielle said. "Teeth ringed with gold. Broken crockery. Rings upon rings. Oh, and the coins!"

"I love the old story about Matriarch Amona and her rescue of the goddess Vahly when the Earth Queen was only a babe in swaddling."

"Yes! It's so tragic." Brielle sighed. "That poor mother. And how Amona risked herself."

Dorin ran a hand over the wood grain of the table. "I never did find out what magic threatened the dragons then."

"I think it was something about the ancient oceans."

"Glad that's faded with time," Dorin said. "Have you seen many dragons in your seafaring journeys?"

"Werian told you!"

"He did."

"I'm surprised you two stopped arguing long enough to have a conversation."

"Does that show my dedication to my kingdom? I'm willing to suffer Prince Werian's company to gain information on the Fire of Wylfenden."

She pulled her hand away.

"What? What did I say?"

"Please don't call me that."

"Why?"

"My father uses it. He wants me to be..." This wasn't the perfect time to tell him she'd been branded as a Broyeur, not in front of all these people. Even if he completely understood how she'd been forced into receiving it, the general masses might not be so easy to convince. "Just please call me Brielle."

"As you say, Brielle." The way his tongue touched his teeth as he said her name...

She took a breath. "Is it warm in here?"

"Let's follow Costel's group outside. They appear to be finished with their decorations and will hang them on the trees outside. It will be nice and cool as opposed to the stuffy warmth of the hall."

He took up the cherries the girl had given him, stood, then waited for Brielle to gather her own poorly constructed decorations. She'd given up on cherries altogether and had simply wound wool around a branch and added some dried flowers that kept falling off.

They placed their decorations on the branches of the blooming trees in the courtyard, then the sweetness that had eased the pain etched into Dorin's face faded, and he frowned.

"I need to share something less pleasant with you. That

way you'll understand at least a portion of what those like Stephan have eating at their souls."

"I-I do understand."

"No, you don't." His hand brushed the place on his belt where he would normally wear a sword. "You haven't been in battle."

"You don't have to show me anything." She didn't want to see whatever he wanted to show her, but that was fear talking. "But I'll go where you lead."

CHAPTER 31
DORIN

Dorin and Brielle walked through the inner and outer gates, Drago and two other castle guards following at a discreet distance.

A merchant hawking sweet potato pies called out, "My prince! Buy a pie for your friend!" He wiped his hands on his orange apron and held up the finest-looking of today's selection.

"That's not his friend," a woman snapped behind him. Realizing her rudeness, she covered her mouth, then curtseyed.

Heat pulsed through Dorin's head, but he reined in his anger and his fierce need to protect Brielle. He'd judged Brielle in the same way when he'd first learned she was Wylfen. Perhaps once her declaration about him at the base of Suveran Peak got around, more of the common folk would see her with new eyes as he was beginning to.

She wasn't just an enemy anymore. Brielle had become the one he looked for in a crowd, the face he desired most to see. He wasn't ready to admit it aloud, but she had proved herself a good person, a brave royal, and he longed to learn everything about her. She understood parts of him that he hid from others, saw the devotion that hid behind his stern exterior. His foul temper didn't shove her away as it had the others he'd courted in the past. And none of those ladies had drawn his attention like Brielle. Truly, she was the center of his thoughts now, and he didn't think he had much choice in the matter of growing to like her very, very much.

"Hold on," Dorin said to Brielle as he dug a few coins from the small pouch at his belt. He handed two golds to the merchant.

"That's three times their cost, Your Highness." The merchant bowed low. "Please forgive my sister's outburst."

"There's nothing to forgive." Dorin accepted the pie, then walked on with Brielle, handing the steaming treat to her.

She glanced back at the merchant and his sister. "I wish they could view me as I view them."

"And how is that?"

"I don't blame them for at first hating me, but I now see them as simply caught up in the wars of their leaders. I don't blame them for killing Celeste's nephew in battle or anything."

"Who is Celeste?"

"She was my nurse and maidservant. I helped her slip away before I escaped with Maren."

Brielle's thinking was off. Hopefully, this visit to the destroyed village of Stejari would help her see what his people experienced at the hands of her kingdom.

"This is astounding!" Brielle spoke over a mouthful of sweet potato and crumbling crust.

He chuckled. "Simple fare on a sunny day is always the best feast."

She raised the remainder of the little pie like she was toasting him with a drinking horn, then she gobbled the rest down.

"Couldn't save me a bite, hmm?"

"Oh! I'm so sorry. Stones, I'm a horse's arse."

A full-bellied laugh erupted from him. "No, you're not. I was just teasing you."

Her grin told him she didn't mind. The streets of Balaur central gave way to dirt paths as he took them northeast of the castle town, leaving the sounds of merchants, children, and singing behind for the soughing of the wind in the oaks and the scent of the river, fed by the snowfields, as it rippled down the mountain.

The path dwindled to nothing that anyone save a true Balaur native would be able to discern, and then the ruins of Stejari appeared like a ghost from another life.

Time-worn walls sat in a crescent shape around what had once been a market with over twenty-five stone and wattle shops, two-story homes with freshly thatched roofs, and the fierce faces of a community used to defending themselves against Wylfen attacks and surviving in the harsh climate of these mountains. Now, piles of broken rock lay sadly along the cobblestone pathways, and large oaks grew through the homes and guild house. A sense of hollowness sapped Dorin's strength, and he let the grief wash over him.

Brielle stood, her hand on the back of her neck and her

breath coming slowly and in uneven patterns. "My people did this." She began to walk the ghostly streets, and her gaze snagged on a blood stain. One of many.

"They did."

She bent to pick up a crumbling basket and a weather-cracked spindle. Turning, she looked at him with tears shimmering in her emerald eyes. "I've never seen something like this." Her words tripped over one another. "This destruction."

"Because Wylfenden are the invaders. The aggressors. They come here to make war. We have never once pressed into Wylfenden's boundaries and have not once destroyed a town in our efforts to remain an independent kingdom."

Nodding, she wiped a hand across her eyes. She had set the remains of the basket down, but she tucked the spindle in her cloak's inner pocket. "I don't know what to say."

"You don't need to say anything. I only wanted you to see this for yourself so you could further understand what it means when my mother and father invite you to be their guest. I want you to know why I have struggled and why I struggle still. I knew these people. Some of them, anyway. The master blacksmith made my sword and my brother's too. He had the wildest laugh." Dorin smiled, remembering the man's penchant for crafting metal flowers for his wife. "The smith told the worst jokes, but he'd laugh so high and loud at his own jests that everyone ended up joining in."

Brielle sniffed, grinning, her hand in the pocket with the spindle.

"I heard the scar wolves got to him first. Before the Wylfen warriors were even past the town gate. They leapt through a hole in the wall near his forge..." A lump blocked

Dorin's telling of the rest of the story. He sighed and let it go.

"May I say something here? Offer something?"

"I don't see why not." What was she planning?

"Just for a moment, may I borrow your eating knife?"

It was the only weapon he was wearing at the moment. He looked back at Drago and the other two, making eye contact so they wouldn't move against Brielle for some imagined plot, then he set the small knife into her outstretched hand. She knelt, drew her hair over her shoulder, then braided and tied it with a length of twine she must have kept from the activities in the hall. She began to cut off the lower third of her hair.

"Brielle, you don't have to—"

She held up a hand, then went back to her grim chore. Once a thick sheaf of her flame-bright hair was cut free, she set the braid in the rubble.

"Pardonnez-nous. Je suis tellement désolée du tord que vous ont causé ceux de mon sang."

Dorin's Wylfen wasn't as strong as Brielle's elvish, but he could translate this well enough. *Forgive us. I am so sorry for the wrong those of my blood have done to you.*

She cut into her forearm, just a small injury, but the sight of her blood dripping onto her hair riled the dragon in Dorin. He fought to keep his breath steady as magic sparked down his spine and the wings that were apparently there to stay. He couldn't shift now. This was too important.

Sealing his eyes shut, he asked for help from the goddess Nix. Peace stole over him, and the magic abated. Had she aided him? Or was it coincidence?

Brielle cut a strip from her cloak, then stood. "Help me bandage it?"

He wrapped the cloth over her wound, careful not to tie the knot too tightly. As he sheathed the knife, a surge of warmth pushed at his chest, and he found himself turning and grasping her hands. "I never thought I'd see the enemy bless an elven town."

"I hope my ransom will do more to mend the errors of the past and the horrors that might still come. The least I could do is the Esprit et Sang sacrifice."

"Spirit and blood?"

"It's the sincerest ceremony we have. And the closest thing to magic aside from the Magebane, if you ask me."

What was Magebane?

A flash of movement showed on the distant slopes, and Dorin rushed past Brielle to scale a ruined wall.

"What is it?" she whispered as she climbed up after him.

"A group is moving. Just there." He pointed, the dragon in him stilling like it was preparing to pounce. Wylfen soldiers—and a couple Broyeurs too—walked along the Graytooth pass. A large canyon separated the enemy from Balaur Castle.

"I can't see anything. I wish I had your elven eyesight."

He couldn't believe what he was seeing. Broyeurs backed by a small army. "It's D'Aboville. I'd bet all. And he's brought a score of warriors with him."

Brielle's face drained of color. "How long until they reach the castle?"

"I'm not sure. They're taking a route I haven't seen them try before."

"You should shift into your dragon form now, Dorin. Go, reduce them to ash. Use what the Source has given you."

All Dorin could think of were the burns on her skin, her bubbled flesh. He winced at the memory. "No. I have no control when I shift." He'd had control during that one shift, but that had been a fluke. "I can't risk it. I might lose myself and turn my fire on Balaur."

"You won't learn control if you don't try. This is certainly worth the risk, isn't it?"

"Our forces can come up with a wiser plan than working off a cursed prince and his fiery temper."

He leapt down to meet Drago and the guards, informing them of what he'd seen, while Brielle stewed.

"You're being an idiot," Brielle hissed as they hurried back to the castle. "Have you even tried to shift at will? How do you know you'll fail at being what you were born to be if you haven't even attempted what the gods have set on your shoulders?"

"Brielle! Please, stop!" He glanced over his shoulder to see her lip curling and her eyes shooting arrows directly into his soul.

"Stop telling you the truth? I won't. I'm not a pretty liar like the rest of my father's court. I'll tell you the rough truth or nothing at all."

"This is a matter for the king and queen to decide."

Brielle harrumphed and swore in Wylfen, but he did his best not to let her rankle him. He wasn't ready to try out the dragon in him. He would never be ready. She didn't understand that part of him. Yes, she was learning what it was to be of Balaur, but the rest of this new life of his...

"We'll see what Mother has to say." His hands itched to wield a sword, to cut down those who dared to cross into his land, to hunt him and his kinsmen. He had to work up a plan of action as soon as possible. The dragon inside him wouldn't permit inaction and was raring to go.

CHAPTER 32
BRIELLE

In a matter of hours, Brielle stood near the armory outside the castle walls. On a cluster of boulders, Dorin had been addressing what was left of the Balaur army and its leaders. Most of the elven forces were unfortunately in the southeast on the border. Queen Sorina, the Magelord Aurora, Filip, Werian, Rhianne, and the fae ladies were in attendance, scattered at the front of the forces near Brielle, their concern evident, though Rhianne's face was turned toward a willow tree growing near the wall. The tree was similar in size and development to the one Maren hadn't liked, the willow near the cave where Dorin had held Brielle.

"We have had no word from the Wylfen king," Dorin's mother, Sorina, said loudly. "I want to hear your advice on the developments Prince Dorin has detailed."

"They will have Magebane," Brielle said, curtseying quickly. "They take a dose, and for a time, I don't know how long, any magic within a mile or so of their bodies will be deadened. Those with magic in their blood will feel sick."

"Do you know how many doses they will have on them?" Sorina asked. "Will the warriors be dosed as well? I suppose there is no antidote to this new poison."

"The rune stone!" Brielle bowed her head briefly to apologize for the outburst. "Forgive me, but I unearthed an ancient rune stone, and when I gave it to a witch my father had imprisoned, she was able to work her spells and escape with me."

"Where is this stone?" Rhianne asked.

"I don't know where it ended up. I should have paid more attention. It was in my pocket when I arrived."

Dorin opened his mouth like he wanted to say something. She'd never told him that she managed to steal it back during their time in the cave.

Aurora gestured to the fae ladies, and they hurried off. They had been the ones to treat Brielle the night of her arrival, so perhaps they knew the whereabouts of her belongings.

"The rune stone only works when the magic-blooded individual holds it," Brielle added, hoping this wasn't a waste of everyone's time.

Sorina looked around the field. "Magelord Aurora should hold it, then. She is the most powerful of us all."

"Agreed," Dorin and Filip said in unison.

Rhianne lifted her wand for attention. "Your Majesties, I have the amulet of Apep." From her gown, she withdrew a circular piece of jewelry that hung on a long necklace. "The Defenders of Lilia will come if I call them with the amulet."

"And they are..." Brielle said to Drago.

"Gryphon riders."

"Oh."

"They need no magic to fight," Rhianne added. "Their mounts will be handy in a battle involving Magebane."

"Call them, if you would," Dorin said.

Rhianne curtseyed and began speaking low over the amulet, drawing her wand in a loop. Pale smoke billowed around the amulet, then a wind rushed across the area.

"Do you know when they'll arrive?" Sorina asked.

"No, my queen," Rhianne said. "They are somewhat of an enigma." She stepped back to join Werian, who put an arm around her and whispered something in her ear.

Dorin tapped the long sword he now wore alongside his short sword and dagger. He was dressed for battle already though the fight wouldn't come for days most likely. "We have a third of our forces. Potential aid from the gryphon riders. And we're prepared for them. We can catch them as they approach, surprise them."

Aurora gave a quick curtsey, then tucked her mage staff under her arm. "If our dragon, Jewel, can be found, we can send her to Darkfleot and have her fly a unit of our best Lore foot soldiers here." She looked to Filip, who nodded.

"She was hunting a mate so I'm not sure we can find her. I will try," Filip said.

"Please do so," Dorin said.

Filip immediately began issuing commands to a messenger dressed in Lore livery with its red stag on a field of dark blue fashioned to look like water.

Sorina addressed Rhianne. "Could we possibly make

duplicates of the rune stone so all with magic could have one to wear about the neck?"

"I'd have to study the stone," Rhianne said, "but I doubt it. I have never heard of such magic and would guess the rune stone's power rests in the fact that it was crafted in ages past when the goddesses walked the earth."

"I suppose we couldn't break the rune stone into pieces to share?" Werian asked.

"That would most likely destroy its ability to function," Rhianne said.

Werian and Sorina nodded as murmuring spread through the gathered warriors, generals, and nobles.

"Noting the distance the Broyeurs and the Wylfen units were spotted, we likely have another four days before they strike," Sorina said.

"We won't go to meet them?" Filip asked.

"We will, but only a short distance from here." Sorina went on to detail the plan of attack, listing paths and names of places that Brielle had never heard. "Today, we will rest and enjoy one another with simple games. Tomorrow night, we will have our Primāvarā Noroc midnight ball. Balaur continues to thrive in the midst of strife."

She raised her fist, and the crowd mimicked the movement, everyone shouting, "Stars blaze in the dark!"

How would they relax enough to enjoy a ball? Impossible, Brielle thought as she walked with Rhianne to the great hall.

"Why didn't you show me the stone when you first arrived?" Rhianne asked.

Brielle clutched handfuls of her gown with her damp hands. "I forgot about it. I swear."

Hilda walked up, rune stone in hand. "My ladies," she said, holding it out.

Rhianne accepted the stone and raised it up to study it in the light streaming from the windows. "Thank you, Lady Hilda," she said before facing Brielle. "I might be busy for a while with this magic. I'll see you at the midnight ball. Well, rather I won't because all will be dark. But if you get antsy to be near someone you know, watch for me near the right side door to the great hall. I'll pop over there time and again and make the end of my wand glow so you can find me."

"Isn't that against the ball rules?" Brielle asked. She'd heard a great deal about the event from conversations in the corridors and during meals.

"Werian's naughtiness has rubbed off on me, I guess." Rhianne waved to her fae husband, who had somehow made it into the hall before them and was setting out a game board. He winked at them.

Brielle laughed. "Rebels reign."

"They do! Now, go keep him busy, will you? I have to take a good look at this stone in a place where I won't be distracted."

"Will do."

"Oh, I meant to tell you... Werian is the reason Queen Sorina and King Mihai gave you a chance when you first arrived. He had to keep his influence quiet because of politics at the Fae Court, but I trust you now in full. I wanted you to know. He can be a braggart, but in this he has been too humble."

"I figured as much," Brielle said, smiling.

"He started to speak to Aury for you, but I told him she must be the one to figure you out, all on her own. Only then will she really accept you. She was deceived a great deal during her early life, so it's a difficult thing, getting to know her."

"I can handle that." She gave Rhianne a quick hug and set off to play a game with the most powerful fae in the world, or so the others claimed.

CHAPTER 33
BRIELLE

The next day, Brielle once again sat across from Werian playing a dice and board game. The goal of the game was to trap your opponent in his or her corner of the small, octagonal arena.

"So it's fair to use a decoy, yes?" She rolled the carved bone cubes and managed a three, a five, and two sevens to move her six free pieces as she saw fit. Werian had only four pieces remaining free.

Hearth light flickering across his features, Werian leaned back in his high-backed chair and smoothed his hair behind his horns. "You act so ignorant of the rules, and yet here you are destroying me."

"This was your idea, Prince Werian."

"My lovely Rhianne did warn me of your intelligence."

"As did Princess Aurora, I'm sure," she said tightly. The Magelord loathed her still.

Werian chuckled. "She is a warrior first and a person

second. Anything that attempts to hinder her people's freedom will earn her ire for eternity."

"But she knows I had no part in my father's wars."

"She doesn't trust easily."

"I am the same about my freedom," Brielle said quietly as she pushed the dice toward him.

"Father a bit overprotective, aye?"

"Very. And D'Aboville..."

"The Broyeur captain?"

"Yes. He takes a special interest in me."

Werian paused in rolling the dice, his eyes going sharp. "You never...hunted, did you?" Fae power rolled off of him along with the scent of clean water and the woods. He could rip her heart out with a bare hand most likely, and the brand on the back of her neck burned as if she'd just received it.

"No." The tremble in her voice was unmistakable, but perhaps he'd think she was nervous because the Broyeurs were horrible. Not because she had been branded as one. Rubbing her sweating hands on her ruby red gown, she forced herself to look him in the eye. "I helped a witch escape after they caught her. Dorin told you that."

"Prince Dorin, you mean." Werian grinned, showing a dimple, his arms and the muscles around his jaw relaxing.

"Prince. Yes. Of course." Heat flickered across her face. He was teasing her, but there was danger in this too. She had to show respect for the authority in this kingdom, to display her willingness to remain here as an ally, a subject, a friend to magic and those who wielded its ancient powers.

The dice clattered across the wood grain of the lemon-polished table. "Don't fret, dear," Werian said. "I'm cheering for you two."

"We aren't—"

He touched his nose. "Royal fae noses are well known for their ability to pick up the scent of chemicals in the body. Including the ones that tend to signify attraction and a willingness to mate."

Her flush deepened as a wild image of Dorin washed over her mind—his uplifted face, strong elven cheekbones and chin, his throat moving... "That isn't known in Wylfen."

"Well, now that you have even more information on this side of the world, we will definitely need to keep you here."

He smiled, and a mix of both hope and worry threaded through her. She had seen little of Dorin and was dying of curiosity. What did he think of her now? Did they have any hope for a future together? Or had his interest in her faded? She looked to the door, wishing to see him, but only the fae ladies—Gytha, Hilda, and Eawynn—stood there, waiting on Aurora, most likely.

And then suddenly Dorin was there, as if her imaginings and their words had beckoned him like the rune stone. He bowed his head to the fae ladies, and they moved to allow him to pass, Eawynn whispering behind her hand to Gytha, who nodded vigorously while Hilda shook her head. Brielle stood to greet him, her heart smacking the back of her teeth. She was such a fool for this dragon lord. No hope for her at all. Her memory of him on his knees before her during the blessing filled her with a sizzling heat. She could very easily imagine him in such a position and envision pulling him close, his large arms wrapping around her, and his lips parted for a kiss. Her breath hitched.

"Ah, speak of the fellow and he appears, stormy as always." Werian pushed away from the table at Dorin's approach, then bowed from the waist. "Prince Lightning, how are you this fine afternoon? We have missed your scowls."

Dressed in his usual black leathers with a dark blue cloak tied over one shoulder, Dorin bared his teeth slightly, and his wings—they never had disappeared again like the talons had—flexed outward past the drape of his cloak. "I have been in meetings with King Mihai, if you must know."

All the humor left Werian's gaze. "I am sorry for his struggle, Your Highness." He bowed once more, this time deeper and more reverently. "If you need us to see him again, the ladies and I are fully at your disposal."

Brielle assumed Werian meant that he and the other fae could attempt a healing on the elven king. She'd heard that Mihai was too far gone for healing, unfortunately.

Dorin's features relaxed, and the corners of his lips turned down. He fidgeted with the sigil ring on the smallest finger of his left hand. "I would appreciate it if you could ease his discomfort. But please discuss your ministrations with the queen. She can sense what he needs."

"Your Highness." Werian bowed yet again, then looked to Brielle. "We can resume our match at a later time if you like?"

"I would enjoy grinding you into a full defeat, yes. Perhaps tomorrow after breakfast?"

Dorin and Werian both grinned, and it was disturbing how nice that felt. She was growing too comfortable here; she had to stay on her toes. They'd heard nothing from Father yet. Soon, this situation would come to a head either by treaty or war, and she had to be ready to defend herself or flee if things went awry.

Werian walked away, tossing an eyebrow wiggle over his shoulder.

"Princess," Dorin said, his voice low and rough. Her body warmed, and she clutched her gown tightly to keep from reaching out to touch the scales on his face. "Will you walk with me?"

"Oh. Absolutely."

She pushed her chair back into place, then took his offered arm, looping her hand around the muscles of his forearm. His wrist showed beyond the tight sleeve of his tunic, and she let one finger shift to touch his flesh. A shot of fire bolted up her arm, and his step shortened briefly like he'd felt it too. She glanced sideways at him as they exited the hall and began walking the busy corridor. He stared straight ahead, stoic as ever. Courtiers moved aside to allow them through, and soon they stood on a balcony overlooking the inner bailey and the stone-walled courtyard of the keep.

Below and beyond the balcony, people streamed through the bailey, stopping at merchant stalls, singing in groups where drinking horns were lifted in celebration, and even some were tucked into the spots where the buildings came together, stealing a moment for a tryst.

Brielle pulled at the green ribbon Eawynn had tied around her neck this morning. "Have you heard back from...from the Wylfen court?"

"Not yet."

"Have you seen Maren or the gods in your dreams again?"

"No."

This conversation was really flying. "So..."

"The king has released Sir Stephan."

The knight who had thrown the knife at her. "He won't try anything again."

"We don't know that."

"But he was punished and seemed repentant."

Dorin turned and took her hands in his, but then he dropped them like she was made of fire. "It's not just that." He licked his lips. "I have word of a plot against you. It's vague. A guard who usually watches the eastern courtyard entrance was discovered writing some sort of message. The man devoured the slip of parchment before it could be read."

"I'm sure there are a few plots. Their golden prince returns not only with dragon wings but with a Wylfen she-wolf, hmm? If there weren't plots against me, I'd think elves weren't nearly as smart as I'd given them credit for being."

He almost smiled, looking toward the bailey. Then he seemed to notice the couple nearest to them, the two growing rather heated in their embrace. He cleared his throat and turned his back to the view, but he didn't blush like she surely was. She hated blushing.

"I've done my best to keep my distance from you in

hopes of deflating the few who oppose your presence here," he said quietly.

That was why he'd been absent. Not only his sick father, but also he'd been doing his best to protect her.

She stepped closer, pressing against him lightly. His gaze flicked to her face, down her neck like a quick touch of fingers, then he focused on her eyes. "Thank you, Dorin."

He leaned in, gaze on her lips now, his eyes going liquid. Blood rushed to her ears, and her heart crashed against the sides of her chest.

"I've not been fair to you," he whispered, his mouth only a breath from hers. "I should have listened to you when you had information about my magic. I'm learning to control it. I feel more myself again. Perhaps a new self, but..." He swallowed.

She inched upward on her toes.

"I find myself rather tangled up over you, Princess."

"I would apologize, but I quite enjoying ruffling your feathers," she said.

"You mean my scales."

She began to laugh, but he cut off the sound with his lips. His mouth covered hers in a soft kiss. Grasping at his vest, she pulled him closer, and a sound like a fire popping emanated from his throat. He deepened the kiss, drawing his tongue over hers and twisting her into delicious knots that begged to be untied. His hand smoothed across her side, giving her glorious shivers, then that hand found her lower back. With a gentle but firm tug, he urged her body to form against his, a command in his movements that brought a moan from her.

"You're not afraid?" His voice was raspy and close to her ear.

"Never," she whispered back.

His fingers dragged through her hair, and he cupped her head, drawing her mouth to his and teasing her lower lip with his teeth. His grip on her was unrelenting, and she squirmed, wanting to have her go at him, to somehow get them closer, to be done with this foolish clothing that barred them from further pleasure. But he would not release her.

"Mine," he rasped, his voice darker now. What did he mean?

His lips caressed her chin, then he set his teeth against her throat as the blazing heat of desire thrummed through her.

"Yours," she proclaimed, feeling the truth of it. For good or bad, she was his in every way he wanted to have her.

He drew back suddenly, and she blinked at him. His eyes had gone slitted and bright, the dragon in him hiding just below the surface.

She eased him with a smile and touched his cheek. "I think your dragon has claimed me."

Frowning, he shook his head. "I think so." His gaze snapped to hers, and he searched her face. "I can find a way to break it if you don't wish for this. I didn't intend to do this. Whatever this is."

"I like it. Don't stop now."

He pulled her into the shadow of the castle wall where no prying eyes could see, and a thrill ran down her spine. Every muscle of his body, all the shapes of his form, leaned into her, the cold wall at her back. His hands slid lower on her back, then to her thighs, and he kissed her hard and without hesitation.

"Prince Dorin?" A voice came from the doorway to the balcony and shattered the haze of desire clouding her thoughts.

Dorin stepped back, chest rising and falling like he'd run a course up Suveran Peak just moments before. His breathlessness pleased her. "Yes?" he said gruffly.

A young lad in Balaur livery bowed and muttered, "It is time to ready you for the midnight ball."

Flaming stones of the underworld, what timing.

"This early?" Dorin whirled on the servant. He looked like retribution made into elven flesh.

The lad cowered, covering his chest with a hand. "I...I was told you must be fitted for a new...a new costume considering your...your developments." His wide eyes went to Dorin's wings.

"Right." Dorin pinched the bridge of his nose.

A laugh tumbled from Brielle. "Go on, then. I'll see you tonight."

"No, Princess. You won't," the lad said. "It'll be pure dark in the hall."

Dorin cuffed him on the back of the head and urged him through the door and back into the castle. "I will see you tonight, Brielle. Count on it."

She inhaled sharply, her every muscle tensing. Trailing him inside, she found Gytha waiting for her.

"Looks like you're already enjoying this special day," Gytha said.

"As Hilda said, *hush*," Brielle warned, making certain no one had heard, but grinning like she was cracked. She resisted the desire to rub her hands together like some maniacal overlord. The dragon would be hers, and she'd live out her days surrounded by magic, far, far from Father, D'Aboville, and his Broyeurs. All was going according to plan. At some point, she had to show Dorin the brand and explain, but there was time for that. He'd understand. Surely.

GYTHA AND EAWYNN DREW BRIELLE A BATH. AS WAS now the norm, Brielle asked for privacy, and they gave it. The brand was almost fully healed now. Her fingers ached to claw it from her flesh. The edges were still rough on the side where D'Aboville had first pressed the brand, where the metal had sunk deeper. She traced the lines of the fist. Someday, she would set her own mark across this one, maybe a knife. Yes, that sounded perfect.

Brielle ate and rested until night fell on Balaur Castle. Gytha and Eawynn dressed her in a sweeping gown of midnight blue. Gray fox fur lined the edges of the low neckline and the even lower back.

"I can't wear this."

"It'll be so dark. Even a modest lady such as yourself has nothing to worry about," Eawynn said.

But it wasn't modesty bothering her. It was the fact that her brand would be fully on display. "Then my hair must be kept loose. To cover my back."

Gytha nodded. "As you wish it, Princess."

It wasn't ideal. She'd still have to make certain not to pull her hair too tightly over her shoulder or allow anyone to touch the spot just below the back of her neck. But the gown was incredibly lovely and the softest garment she'd ever worn. Fitted but flexible along the arms, and plenty of room to move her legs. The Balaur sigil marked the waistline, a constellation she saw in a whole new light now.

"You like it, don't you?" Eawynn asked, her voice tight.

"I usually loathe gowns, but this one is just about perfect." She'd prefer trousers and a night of digging up bits in the mountains, but heading to a ball where a handsome, dragon-blooded, elven prince awaited wasn't so bad.

"What's that sudden grin for, my lady?" Eawynn tied the front of the gown tightly, and Brielle thought her breasts might pop out of the top.

"Not so tight, all right?" Brielle asked, and Eawynn nodded, easing the laces.

"I'll take a guess on the grin," Gytha said.

"Will you be able to find Prince Dorin?" Eawynn said, clearly realizing what Gytha was referring to.

Brielle ignored them and took up the brush before they could see her upper back.

Gytha crossed her arms and studied Brielle. "He'll find her."

"You look glorious!" Beaming, Eawynn clapped her hands. Her enthusiasm was catching, and Brielle couldn't help but smile.

"Thank you. Should I take a knife tonight? Am I permitted?"

The fae traded a look. "You won't need it," Gytha said,

tapping the short sword at her belt. "We will be within arm's reach of you the entire night."

"Unless the prince orders otherwise." Eawynn tied a mask onto Brielle's face.

"Indeed." Brielle bit her lip, hoping exactly for that moment.

CHAPTER 34
DORIN

Dorin walked toward the great hall, and Drago nearly ran straight into him. "What are you doing here? I ordered you to protect Princess Brielle. You volunteered for the position. What has happened?" Dorin worked hard to keep his anger in check, but if he had left her on her own, Drago was doomed.

"I'm on my way to escort her now. Gytha and Eawynn are with her too. Princess Aurora ordered them to remain by her side, despite the rules of the ball."

"Good. Take her through the main entrance."

Drago bowed, and Dorin nodded before continuing onward and shaking his wings free of the edge of his cloak.

In the great hall, starlight drifted through the high, slitted windows. The moonless night only allowed the view of silhouettes, but his sense of smell had grown incredibly reliable of late. Part of being dragon-blooded, he guessed. He probably still couldn't scent as well as a royal fae, but he could find Brielle if she were close enough. His skin tingled at the thought of her hands on him, the memory of their moment on the balcony. He would stay near the main entrance so she would be easier to locate.

Drawing his cloak aside, he passed a cluster of nobles whispering. They grew quiet at his appearance. The light must have been at least enough for them to see his wings and know who he was. The music from the stringed liras on the far side of the hall floated above the increasing crowd, the tune haunting, dark, and low.

Adjusting his pointless mask—the same dark blue mask that everyone wore tonight—he wondered what Rhianne had thought of the rune stone and what Brielle had discussed with the witch. There would need to be a meeting about the power of that artifact as soon as possible. It was ridiculous that Mother had ordered this ball to carry on with Wylfen on their way. The only thing that made it tolerable was the thought of having Brielle in his arms again. Dancing was a frivolous, silly thing, but if it meant she would be close, then dancing was exactly what he would do.

The dragon in him stirred. *Mate*, his mind said, reminding him of how he'd set his teeth against her throat.

What did that mean for them? If the enemy weren't on their way here, he'd be researching again. He knew so little about shifting dragons aside from what Werian had told him last night, of how they'd had matriarchal societies— not a surprise there—and that they'd gained power from lightning storms and proximity to earthblood. Had they mated for life like the dragons he had studied here in

Balaur? Most likely. It felt true. It was as if his and Brielle's moment on the balcony had solidified what the dragon in him already knew. It was unbelievable, but Brielle, the enemy's daughter, was his heart, his soul, his reason to face the day. That would never change, no matter what happened. It had all happened so suddenly, but it was no less true. Could he stay here with her though? He might still lose control...

A scent wafted toward him. Brielle. His heart surged, and he turned, watching what had to be her entering the hall flanked by two horned fae and a silhouette he assumed was Drago.

He was at her side in a breath. "My lady, care for a dance?"

Her smile hid in the dark shadows, but it lightened her voice. "You sound more like we're heading into battle."

Drago snorted behind them.

"Go away," Dorin hissed. "Thank you."

The fae and Drago nodded respectfully and disappeared into the crowd as Dorin took Brielle's hand. Her fingers were cool and soft. He lifted her hand and kissed the back of her knuckles.

"You smell divine."

"Is that how you found me?"

"It is."

"Everyone will know who we are. Your wings are obvious even in this darkness. The starlight clings to them."

"I hope you find me...that my appearance doesn't disgust you."

"Did I seem disgusted on the balcony?"

242

The dragon in him preened and stretched, and suddenly he was pulling her to him, pressing himself against her softness, heat coiling in his abdomen and lower. His hands sought and claimed her bare back, and desire shot through his blood. Her flesh was like a strong drink to him, making him insensible. He wanted to take her to the floor right now; the dragon in him roared for that very thing, and he struggled to maintain his composure, his breathing too quick as he braced his forehead on hers.

"Are you unwell?" Brielle's hand slid around his shoulder, and the neckline of her dress showed far too much skin.

"No. I am not." He was shaking, dying to lose himself in her, to touch her as much as he wanted, to make her gasp against his lips.

The music rose, loud and deep, and she took his hand and lifted it to take a dancing pose. "Let's dance awhile, Prince. Then we can perhaps find a quieter spot to talk."

Talking was not what he had in mind.

He lifted his chin, swallowed, and forced his body to behave. Taking up the steps, he led her in a circle around the room, their hips dangerously close and every brush of her fingers at the nape of his neck an exquisite torture. She just seemed like so much...more than anyone else. Her scent filled his mind...

"...and I told her what the stone did for Maren," she was saying.

"I'm sorry," he said. "I missed your last sentence. The dragon in me doesn't wish to behave with you dressed like this."

She huffed a laugh and eased herself against him as they

spun, molding her back against his chest and torso. He dragged his nose along her exposed shoulder and began to draw her hair away from her neck. She spun away.

"I was talking about the rune stone. Rhianne took it to her chambers to study it."

"Aurora doesn't have it? It should be on her at all times with the filthy Broyeurs so close."

"I'm sure she'll hand it over as soon as she is certain it can't be copied or broken into amulets for everyone. That would be a game changer."

"It would indeed. How many more dances until we talk?" He was an idiot. He could hardly think straight with her here in the darkness.

She laughed. "Although I enjoy torturing you and testing that new restraint, let's meander to a shadowy corner."

He couldn't comply fast enough to suit himself. He verily dragged her through the crowd until they were ensconced in a corner of the hall, deep in the shadow of the walls where no prying eyes could see, not even elven or dragon ones.

Without waiting for a proper invitation, he gripped her loose hair and twined it around his fist. He wrapped his other arm around her and held her as tightly as possible. His flesh sparked hotly as he kissed her, devouring her petal-soft lips and brushing his tongue over hers. Her hips jutted into his, and he sighed her name. "Brielle."

"Shh." Her words dusted across his chin and gave him chills. "Exciting secret tryst during the midnight ball, remember?"

He simply growled against her throat, then nipped her round, human ear. Her chest lifted against his leather vest, and he hated all of this clothing. "I don't give a whit what anyone thinks. You are mine, and I will have you." And he meant every word.

CHAPTER 35
BRIELLE

"Not in the middle of a great hall," she said, pretty much hating that her dignity decided to show up right now when his mouth felt like unadulterated joy made tangible, and his hands were moving in all the right ways.

She ignored said dignity for a few more minutes as he gripped her hair, pulled her head back, and used the tip of his tongue to draw a line from her chin to her collarbone. Something about being in this darkness with him, only sounds and touch to go on—pleasure thrilled her blood, her heart straining to keep up with the reckless desire and new emotions flooding her from head to toe, soul to heart.

"Dorin..." Her voice sounded muffled, and his wings blocked the faint starlight. He had cocooned them, shielding her from everyone. A clicking, growling noise reverberated through his chest to hers, and she smelled the magic of dragonfire.

Her skin flamed in the wake of his hand on her bare

back, and she dug her nails into the leather of his vest. The muscles beneath her grasp tightened, and his finger came up under her ear, his thumb skimming her jawline and making her shiver wildly. He sucked her bottom lip lightly before grazing her cheek and temple with his sharp teeth. She straddled his leg, and he exhaled roughly against her chest.

Suddenly, Dorin lurched backward and bent double, his silhouette one of pain and torment. The scent of his magic disappeared entirely, and the room was filled with cries of surprise and anguish. Nausea swamped Brielle, and she clutched at her stomach.

A hand seized her throat, and the pinch of a blade pricked the skin just beneath her jawline.

"Brielle!" Dorin was drawn away from her, his voice echoing as he called her name again, shapes tumbling into what had to be a fight. There was a smack of flesh on stone, then a crack.

"You've done well," a slippery voice said into her ear. "Your father will be so proud of you catching that abomination of a prince."

Ice hardened her veins. "D'Aboville. Get your gods-cursed hands off me." Magebane, that was what was making her stomach turn.

She slammed her foot on his instep and gripped his forearm, pulling the knife away from her neck. Keeping a hold on his arm, she turned inward and jammed her shoulder into his torso, trying to pierce his side. He huffed a breath but wrestled his arm free. He took hold of her and dug his fingers into the flesh her gown exposed. Pain lanced through her, and she released what little control she had on his other arm only to make him stop gripping her skin.

A torch blazed to life in the center of the hall, illuminating the wretched scene. Sweat dripped from Dorin's face as his captor—a man Brielle thought was named Theron—pressed a blade against his throat. Blood trickled down Dorin's neck, the tendons standing out as he strained against the pain he must feel with the Magebane in his captor's body.

He met her gaze, and her heart quaked, unshed tears blurring her vision. Seeing him like this, his proud struggle, the ferocious love in his eyes... One truth rang through her bones and blood. He belonged to her. Forget the consequences, the outcome, the fact that they had been born enemies. Her heart and soul had claimed the dragon prince.

A wave of nausea hit her. She slumped. Perhaps Maren and the fae ladies had been right about Brielle having magic in her blood. The Magebane was definitely making her feel sick. The concoction hadn't affected her at the castle when Father had used it on Maren, so something about being here with Dorin had increased her minimal power. He had more magic in him than anyone she'd ever heard of, except for the goddesses and gods. He had to be near to death with the agony of the Magebane.

Filip was on the ground, shouting unintelligible commands as Drago and several guards surrounded him protectively, swords drawn. She could no longer see Dorin. They'd pulled him into the mass of dark-cloaked and masked nobles.

"As you can see, we hold your eldest prince, Queen

Sorina!" D'Aboville shouted, his grip on Brielle switching, crushing her ribs and making it hard to breathe. The dagger now bit into her side, through her gown. Warm blood pooled under the fabric of her gown. "Let us leave, and we will consider keeping him alive to form the peace you are so set on. Yes, we saw the message you sent. But we knew Princess Brielle was only doing her duty as a Broyeur."

Gytha, Hilda, and Eawynn leaned against the wall not far away, their faces gone gray, their bodies shuddering. Werian lay at their feet, only his slack mouth visible amid the feet of the panicking revelers. Where was Rhianne? Aurora? If they brought the rune stone, this would be over in moments, and D'Aboville would die.

Sorina ripped off her mask, and the crowd cleared to give her a view of D'Aboville. "Princess Brielle is my subject now, courted by my son and heir. She is not, and never was, a Broyeur." Sorina spat onto the hall's stone floor. "I would never believe it of her. She is a victim of your kingdom's wretchedness just as the rest of us."

Laughing, D'Aboville somehow grabbed Brielle's hair, spun her, and exposed the small brand at the base of her neck. "Not a Broyeur, eh? You're mistaken, Highness."

The room went quiet, then whispers rose.

"The brand..."

"She bears their mark."

"If you kill my heir," Sorina said, her voice a sword, "there will be no end to the violence I send to your door, Wylfen. We will never stop taking our revenge. Even if it sees every last one of us bleeding out in the snow and rocks of our kingdom or yours."

Brielle sagged, the wound aching, burning, and her stomach rolling. "I didn't want the brand—"

She tried to speak, but D'Aboville held her mouth against his shoulder so tightly that she couldn't get anything out. Heat pierced her lip, and she knew it had split. Raising a knee, she rammed D'Aboville's groin. He grunted, but she'd missed hitting the mark squarely, and he continued dragging her toward the main doors of the great hall.

Dorin was there, held tightly by Theron and the third Broyeur. Brielle's chest snapped at the sight of him. He was as gray as a corpse.

"You won't live..." Dorin, hair wet with perspiration and lips white, rasped out threats as he and Brielle were stolen from the hall. "You won't live to see another day. Get your hands off her. Now."

D'Aboville just laughed as they hurried down the corridors and out of the castle's keep. "You're the one staring down the Shadow King and his realm, dragon elf. You will die a slow and miserable death, your traitorous whore learning exactly what it means to go against my will."

Brielle had gone numb and cold. It wasn't blood loss. She didn't feel too much warmth around her knife wound, and the bruises that were rising where D'Aboville had gripped her weren't serious. It was a strange calm and a silent fury.

She smiled, making Theron blink.

This evil creature might kill her and her love by the end, but he would suffer, and she would make sure of that. No doubt about it.

All she needed was for him to make one tiny mistake. And then she'd be on him like a true scar wolf—one untainted by mind-tampering training—a beast who fought righteously for her mate, using tooth and claw to rip apart the creature who dared to hurt him.

BY THE TIME THE GROUP LEFT THE OUTER BAILEY, DORIN was basically unconscious, his feet just barely moving across the ground. Ten more Broyeurs met them at a meadow beyond the city, and with a knife to both Brielle's throat and side, they tied her and Dorin, stomach-down, onto horses that snorted and stamped. The one holding Dorin tossed his head, eyes rolling. D'Aboville hit the horse across the face, and the animal jerked, nearly losing Dorin before settling under the hand of his foul master. Four Broyeurs, including Theron, mounted their own horses and led Dorin down a trail, only the stars showing the pale outline of horses and men.

Then D'Aboville and the rest took to their mounts.

"You should rest, Princess." D'Aboville grinned, then hit her with the hilt of his sword, and everything disappeared.

CHAPTER 36
DORIN

orin dreamt of dark hallways and fire. His head spun until he couldn't hold the contents of his stomach any longer. In this nightmare, he was sick on the floor where he lay forgotten, shuddering with fever. Gone were the wings he'd been growing used to. Gone was his magic. Even his elven abilities had faded into memory. He was a shell of a creature. Lost. Approaching death. Too weak to rise. And the pain stalking him, hitting him with every beat of his heart...His eyes burned as the dream went on and on.

DORIN WOKE IN A CAVE, TIED, LYING ON A LARGE, FLAT stone, and feeling as if he'd been repeatedly dropped from a cliff and run over by ten carts filled with stone. "This isn't a trend I wanted to continue," he growled out, thoughts whirling.

Then the image of a redheaded artifact hunter flashed across his memory.

"Where is she? Tell me!" He fought the chains that held his arms and legs to the stone as a cool wind made several oil lamps flicker above him. "What have you done with her?"

"Quiet yourself, now, Princeling." A lean man with gray hair and eyes like a hungry wolf leaned over him and shoved a cloth into his mouth, gagging him. "Or I'll have to use the last of the Magebane to reduce you to tears again."

The nightmare had been real. His wings were gone. His magic crushed into nothingness.

He snagged the cloth with his tongue and forced the gag from his mouth. "Brielle!"

The man who had to be D'Aboville struck him hard, banging Dorin's head against the stone. Spots flitted across his vision.

"You were so easily fooled," the Broyeur captain crooned. "I posted some of our forces on that hill just for you to spot and believe we were farther away than we were. Genius move on my part, if I do say so myself. In the hall, you could've overtaken us, I think, even with the Magebane at our disposal. Sadly, lust distracted you." He sneered, his face doubling due to Dorin's injuries and the Magebane's effects. "Of course, we killed your scouts, your messenger, and a unit of patrolling soldiers as well, so I suppose you were a bit shorthanded at the time." His quiet laugh raised the hair on Dorin's arms.

"Brielle!" His chest ached, and the scent of illness clouded the smell of the damp cave where the Broyeurs must have set up a camp. But where were they exactly?

How long had he been in and out of consciousness? Was Brielle already dead? Had they mistreated her? His hands shook as he fisted them. "Brielle!"

The dragon in him reeled and thrashed, weak and infuriated. Then his wings shot from his back, dragging against the rock and freeing themselves from the tight space between him and the stone.

"Hmm." D'Aboville tapped the end of a dagger and regarded the ends of Dorin's outstretched wings.

"...King Raoul comes," another voice whispered somewhere in the cave. "He and the rest of the army are beyond the—"

"Enough. I know," D'Aboville said.

So the entire Wylfen army was once again marching on Balaur. And now the elves, fae, and witches had no magic on their side. Dorin's bones were made of lead, heavy and impossible to move. This would be the end of his kingdom.

CHAPTER 37
BRIELLE

Brielle's mind had lost the ability to judge how much time had passed. Though she'd paid as much attention as possible between bouts of being sick from the Magebane, she had no idea whether she'd been held for a day or three. The Broyeurs had tied her atop a horse once again.

A disembodied voice whispered in her ear. *Rhianne and I managed to get the stone in your pocket there.*

It was Maren!

Brielle tried to sit up, her heart lifting with hope. What was this spell Maren was using to speak to her?

It wasn't easy, Princess, Maren said. *Use it wisely. I'd ask where you are, but we can't hear you. Magelord Aurora can see you in her scry bowl, but we can't tell where you both were taken. They are searching though. And the gryphons are flying over the mountains now, or so the Magelord says. I can't wait to see those wild beauties! Sadly, Filip's dragon, Jewel, is off laying dragon eggs so she's off the roster for the battle. Rhianne is telling me to wrap it up. Remember, stone in your pocket. Get out of there, and we will finish cleaning the muck from our kingdom, all right?*

Mouth gasping like a fish thrown from the river, Brielle struggled to feel the rune stone in her pocket. She still wore the gown, though it was torn at the sleeve and up the side. The folds were so thick... Her fingers cramped with the effort of trying to reach the stone. No, she couldn't get to the pocket tied like this.

"Settle yourself. We're here." Theron pulled her from the horse and cut the ties on her ankles. He and another took her by the arms and began marching her into a cave shrouded by yellow lichen and cascading ivy. A willow leaned on the rock beside the entrance, its leafy hands brushing their legs as they moved forward.

Glancing at Theron, Brielle eased her arm down slowly to keep the man from tightening his grip. She finally slid one hand into her pocket. The rune stone's carvings warmed her fingertips and hummed against her skin. Rhianne, Maren, and Aurora were goddesses in the making.

Now it was time to escape.

She lurched sideways and bit Theron's hand. He shouted as she stomped on the arch of her other jailer's foot, and he jerked to a stop. Using the change of direction and the men's loosened grip, she yanked an arm free and slammed a palm into Theron's face. Blood exploded from his nose as she turned to run.

A shouted phrase in the Balaur tongue made her stumble.

Dorin.

"Filthy demons! Do what you will. My people are too

wise to break for such a small thing as my life." He sounded horrible, but his deep, accented voice still echoed off the crevices, ledges, and cracks of the tunnel walls. The sound wrapped Brielle and held her still. "They know where my heart lives."

His love for his family and his kingdom rang through his words.

Her heart shuddered, and she couldn't leave. Not without him.

"This is all your fault, you amazing, mythical creature," she muttered, running into the cave and leaving her jailers to chase her down. "If you'd listened to my plan and torched them while you were able, as I suggested, neither of us would be here"—the cave opened up to show Dorin chained and lying on a flat rock, oil lamps lighting rough walls, Broyeur bed rolls, water skins, sacks of supplies, and an array of weaponry propped against saddles—"in Monsieur Maniac's torture dungeon..."

Hands grabbed her once more, this time more tightly, their fingers digging into her skin. She shouted with impotent rage, furious with herself. If she'd have kept on, maybe she could have escaped and helped Dorin by bringing help. Foolish. But leaving him under the evil control of D'Aboville for even one moment was too long.

The sweet scent of the spring breeze should have been too innocent to touch this place. It tousled Dorin's golden hair as he lay tied on a stone slab, his wings pinned with iron nails, the scales on his cheek and arm reflecting the light. They'd gagged him with a black strip of linen. His body quaked, and his eyelids moved as if he were dreaming —no, experiencing the worst of nightmares. Brielle had seen that sort of shaking once before—in Maren, deep in the dungeons of Wylfen Castle.

"Ah, our newest recruit is here. Wonderful." D'Aboville's voice twisted Brielle's stomach harshly. "I have your dose of the Magebane. Swallow it down quickly, Princess. We don't want this abhorrent thing to transform and burn us all alive." He laughed darkly, and the other Broyeurs joined in.

He didn't need her to take the Magebane. He was just enjoying his hold on her, his ability to force her to do his will. "Best begin forcing it down my gullet, maggot, because I'm not bowing to any authority you claim to hold. We are in Balaur. You are nothing here."

"What makes you think we are in the land of the elves?" He cocked his head, genuine curiosity in the pinch of his eyes.

She had no clue, but he didn't need to know that. Maybe he'd reveal more if she pretended to have some knowledge of their whereabouts. "We haven't crossed the boundary. We're only an hour's ride from Balaur Castle. I wasn't quite as unconscious as you might have been led to believe."

His eyes narrowed for a heartbeat before he relaxed and turned away with a sick grin, giving her no information on their location at all, curse it.

"Did you hear how your beast fought us?" He faced her. "How the abomination suffered when we took the Magebane?"

He wanted to see the hurt in her features, to feed on her pain and wallow in the control he had over her and Dorin, so she smoothed away the curl in her lip and let her eyes show only calm. "You will lose in the end. That's all that matters."

"And what will become of you if I do, in fact, lose?" He stalked her, walking a circle. "You are in enemy territory. These elves may pretend to accept you, but..." He came close, his mouth near her ear. She readied to headbutt him. "They will run you through the moment they are satisfied you are no longer useful. Especially since their queen saw that brand you wear."

She rammed her head sideways, banging into his lips. He grunted and rocked back, then spit blood at her feet. Anger blackened his gaze.

"Tie her down next to the elf."

Brielle fought to keep the triumphant grin from her face. The rune stone's warmth spread through the tattered layers of her gown. The Broyeurs forced her to lie flat on a boulder near Dorin.

D'Aboville leaned over Dorin, their foreheads nearly touching. "Try to become the mad beast that you truly are, Prince. Come now. Try your very best."

Face graying and wings trembling, Dorin struggled against his chains and cursed against the cloth tied across his mouth.

Tears burned their way down Brielle's cheeks. Why hadn't he listened to her? She should've pushed him more to shift and use his magic earlier, to surprise them. There were a thousand things she should have tried.

"I'm here, Dorin."

"You disgust me," D'Aboville hissed at her. "A traitor to your family. To your kingdom. To your blood. That you would choose not only an elf but one with such foul magic darkening his soul... If I weren't seeing it with my own eyes, I wouldn't believe it." He touched her hair, a wistful look pulling at his eyes. "You look so much like her, but your heart..."

What was this madman blathering on about?

Dorin's hand was just out of reach. If she could only brush his fingertips, perhaps the runestone's power would travel through her and into him? It wasn't a safe bet, definitely not a sure one, but it was all they had.

They lashed her wrists above her head and tied her ankles together as they had when she'd been set over the horse. They didn't bind her with chains as they had Dorin, but with twine. The rough stuff bit into her skin.

"You're a true piece of donkey shite, D'Aboville. You know that, right?" She managed to call him several colorful names before Theron—still bleeding from both nostrils, she was pleased to note—gagged her like they had Dorin.

D'Aboville and his cronies gathered near the entrance, plotting away, while Brielle touched her thumb to her smallest finger. She worked one hand out of its twine circle, slowly, carefully removed the stone from her pocket, and stretched toward Dorin's arm. She didn't want to risk not having the magic travel through her. He needed the stone, and the stone he would have. Then he could destroy these idiots.

The rune stone slid from her grasp.

She froze. No. That hadn't just happened.

Footsteps approached, and she opened her eyes to see Theron bending to see what had fallen to the cave floor. Brielle gripped his hair with her free hand, smashed his nose into the boulder, then released his hair to grab the dagger at his belt. She stabbed him in the gut. He crumpled, and she quickly cut her ankle ties as the others ran toward her. Clambering off the boulder, she snatched up the rune stone and pressed it to Dorin's hand.

He shivered and opened his eyes wide.

"Shift, you magnificent beast, you!" she hissed. "Shift!"

But he only swallowed and gasped for air, the color coming back into his face. He was too weak.

"Hold this." She curled his fingers around the stone, then turned and threw the dagger at D'Aboville's chest.

The blade struck its mark and sank deeply, spreading the dark stain of death over his clothing. He met her gaze, then dropped to his knees, one hand gripping the dagger's hilt. The other Broyeurs crowded D'Aboville, their voices rising with questions.

Brielle kicked Theron backward and drew his short sword from his belt. She sliced Dorin's ties and helped him to stand.

"I'm well now. Not perfect, but well enough." He showed her the stone in his hand, then he shoved it inside his vest, under his shirt.

They tore through the room, the Broyeurs coming to their senses and chasing them. A knife flew past Brielle's side and clanged against the cave wall. Another was surely coming. They probably didn't know how to throw as well as Brielle did—knife-throwing wasn't a part of Broyeur training—but at this distance, she and Dorin would be overcome soon.

"Some dragonfire would be lovely right about now," she said.

"Trying." Dorin put a hand to her back as they cleared the entrance of the cave.

The Broyeurs were just behind them, but they shouted in alarm as they ran out of the cave. Running, Brielle twisted. The willow's high and gnarled roots had tripped the men. They shouted and wrestled to untangle themselves and the short bow one man had raised.

Another strange willow—similar to the one she'd seen with Maren. There had to be something going on here...

Dorin handed her the reins of a horse, then in moments they were galloping away, arrows following them.

"Now to face the rest of Wylfen," Dorin shouted over the wind.

The horses covered the ground quickly.

"Do you know where we are?"

Dorin nodded and took the lead as storm clouds gathered above the peaks.

They had the stone. They could face Father and his forces now. At least D'Aboville was dead. Small mercies.

CHAPTER 38

D'ABOVILLE

"**N**o," he whispered as the men pressed cloth after cloth onto his chest wound. "I won't succumb to your darkness."

"That's right, Captain. Keep fighting," a young Broyeur said as they carted Theron's corpse from the cave.

But D'Aboville wasn't talking to the man. He was replying to the female voice slithering through his head, the same voice that had been snaking around his thoughts day in and day out.

I will give you life. My power will make that wound but a scratch. Show me you are willing, and my power will be all yours. Victory. Control. Everything you want. The girl under your command. The elves crushed beneath your strength. Together, we will turn it all to your desires.

A vine, dressed in dark leaves, and a gnarled root slipped across the floor and circled his boot. He gasped.

I am here, the voice said. *All you need to do is give of yourself truly, and I will rise for you.*

The oil lamps went dark, and the man nursing him left to speak to the others. D'Aboville was losing the battle to live. His sight blurred.

Esprit et Sang, he thought. That was how the Wylfen made sacrifice.

Yes, the voice answered.

I tried to defeat magic, he said. *But they always win.*

They do. The voice sounded pleased. *Why not embrace it? It's the only way...*

If he didn't, this would be the day of his death. He knew it. A chill spread its hands over his back. Shaking like a colt, he unsheathed his dagger, cut a lock of hair from his head, then sliced his forearm. He set the hair in the puddle of blood beneath his leg.

"Given freely," he croaked. So cold. He would die before he finished. "I freely give you my essence. Rise, witch, for that is surely what you are. If I cannot win against magic, I will turn their darkness against them."

The ground trembled, and the distant voices of his men rose in alarm. The root and vine at his boot crawled into the pool of his sacrifice, then a cloud of dark green unspooled from the blood. A tug in his chest moved with the cloud, helping him to stand. He touched his chest. The wound had closed. His pain was receding.

"I will need sustenance," the cloud said, spinning toward the men and their gaping mouths.

"Take what you need to save me for I am your master."

A dark laugh issued from the thing he had brought from the earth, then the cloud grew larger, and the men dropped to the ground.

D'Aboville ran to them. Withered husks of who they

had once been lay on the ground. Their corpses looked hundreds of years old, dry and utterly lifeless. He couldn't breathe.

The cloud morphed into the shape of a woman made of black ivy with willow leaves running down her back like a mass of thick and tangled hair, and her eyes...

"What is this?" the shape whispered, its horrible eyes flashing dark and light and back again.

The stores of Magebane sat in bottles that had been tied into leather bags designed specifically for the concoction.

"It's a mixture th-that deadens magic. Be c-careful."

"I will make it a gift to the Source's Sacred Oak." A tendril of smoke extended from her form and covered the bags of Magebane. "May your roots soak in this blessing," she murmured as the entire store faded slowly from view. Her laugh made him shudder. She turned, leaf hair undulating. "I am the winding abyss. I am chaos. I am the one who will change everything. To war, we go," the witch said.

For the first time in his life, D'Aboville was truly frightened.

CHAPTER 39
DORIN

All Dorin wanted was to tear Brielle from that horse, wrap her in his arms, and kiss her until they both forgot everything they'd been through. But the Wylfen were coming, her evil father leading the way, and survival had to remain the priority of the day.

With the guards calling out their arrival, Dorin and Brielle rode into the castle's inner bailey and dismounted to find Filip, Aury, Rhianne, Werian, and Maren running out the keep's doors.

"They are here, my lords and ladies!" a guard on the wall shouted again.

Filip hugged Dorin tightly. "Brother."

"I'm happier to see you than I've been all my life," Dorin said.

"I bet." Werian touched Dorin's arm and sent healing warmth into him. The wounds in his wings began to mend.

"Thank you. Can you tend to Brielle?"

Brielle handed her horse's reins to a stable girl, then

strode over, her red hair wild around her pale face and her lips bright red from exertion. She hugged the petite witch, Maren, and the two had a quick conversation in Wylfen. "I'm fine," Brielle said to Werian. "But the Wylfen army is coming," she said, saying the name of her people like she was no longer one of them.

Dorin flexed his wings and studied her features. Was she firm in her decision to stay here? Had she even truly made that decision?

"All of them," she said. They spoke about what bits of information they'd overheard during their captivity. "We killed D'Aboville, the Broyeur captain, but a few of the Broyeurs will surely join the main army. They might still have Magebane. We don't know. Listen, about the brand..."

"You didn't choose to have that mark put on you," Dorin barked, taking her right side and glaring at Aury, who stood with her arms crossed.

"I certainly did not. I should have told you earlier," she said more quietly, her words directed at him.

He took her hand and kissed it quickly. "Did any of our scouts get through? Have you seen anything in your scrying bowl, Aury?"

"I saw her."

"I want to hear all about how you managed to get the rune stone into my pocket," Brielle said. "That is amazing."

"After we figure out whether we are living or dying today, I'll tell you everything. It was difficult." Rhianne wiped her hair away from her eyes. She touched Brielle's arm and smiled warmly. "I'm glad you were able to escape. I wasn't sure I could manage it even with Maren's help."

Werian put an arm around her shoulders. "My astounding witch."

"She is," Aury said, relaxing her arms. Then she looked at Brielle. "I saw how they treated you. I won't apologize for not trusting you, but know that I consider you one of us now and for as long as you choose." She grasped Brielle and pulled her into a hug.

Brielle's eyes about popped from her head. "Umm, thank you. Thank you very much, Magelord Princess."

Aury planted a kiss on Brielle's head, then stepped back as Mother strode from the keep's main doors.

"Dorin!"

Dorin gathered her into his arms, and for a moment they were just mother and son, not queen and heir. She kissed his cheek. "I thought I had lost you." Tears silvered the edges of her tired eyes. She turned away and waved to a servant standing by. "Tell the king his son is returned to him and we are off to win the day."

The servant dipped a quick bow, extending his leg, then hurried away.

"To the battlefield, my loves," Mother said, one hand still on Dorin's shoulder. "We must do what we can to save Balaur. Brielle. Dorin. Tell me what you experienced as we walk."

They spoke to her and the others about D'Aboville, including details about the stone's inability to help Dorin shift when he was so injured, but how the artifact increased his energy level the longer he held it against his skin. The group ate a simple meal of bread and watered wine before donning what armor they could and mounting fresh horses. The rune stone was now in Aury's possession, her incredible water mage powers secured in case the Wylfen had more Magebane for the upcoming fight.

Dorin spoke to everyone and made certain all was planned carefully, then they were riding toward the Wylfen army to do battle.

SEVERAL UNITS RODE NORTHERLY WHILE THE MAIN FORCE —what little there was of it since the bulk of the Balaur army was still on its way home from the far-off border skirmish—traveled the same route as many had during the last war, toward Dragon Wing Pass. It was the only way through to the castle for more than a handful of warriors, so the Wylfen would have to take that path. Thankfully, several units of the Lore army had arrived and more were on their way, delayed only because of a camp sickness.

On the twisting rise before the descent into the pass began, a voice called out, and everyone was pulled to a halt.

"Attack!" someone shouted.

The back of the main force was moving then, the fighting already started.

Wings catching the wind, Dorin wheeled his horse around. A crack of lightning blasted a nearby oak, and shouts went up as the madness of battle ensued.

How had the Wylfen slipped around this way? Dorin slashed at a leaping scar wolf while Brielle, riding beside him, threw knives into her former kingdom's warriors, dropping them with expert strikes to the throat, eyes, and groins.

"Is there Magebane? I don't feel it," Dorin said to Filip, who had forgone his mount to fight on foot with Stephan, Drago, and Costel at his side.

"I haven't sensed it." Braided hair flying and lips pulled back into a vicious grimace, Filip moved in a haze of impressive speed, his hatchet at last felling one of the scar wolves while Dorin fought off five Wylfen warriors.

They fought and fought. Time lost meaning. Dorin's mind buzzed and whirred, his fear for those he loved pouring power into every sword strike.

A stone's throw away, Werian shot arrow after arrow, aim true. Running over the fallen, black hair stuck to his forehead and his horns, he plucked the arrows from the bodies to use again.

Dorin's horse lurched as a wolf sank teeth into its throat. The horse kicked at the wolf, and Dorin leapt away before he could be trapped beneath the losing animal. He threw his dagger at the wolf, but though it hit the beast, the wolf kept tearing at the horse's flesh. Three arrows found the wolf, courtesy of another warrior, but still the wolf lived. Dorin wheeled his sword around and slammed the edge into the wolf's head. Finally, the wolf dropped, the horse dropping beside its attacker.

They were fighting well, but the Wylfen forces vastly outnumbered the Balaur and Lore warriors. Dorin killed two more of the enemy as Aury shouted something and sent a blast of fiercely cold water across the steeply sloped field of battle. Most of the Wylfen were caught in her ice, and the Balaur warriors, Dorin and Brielle included, cheered.

"No!" Filip shouted and ran in Aury's direction.

Dorin couldn't see what had alarmed Filip. "Brielle! What is it? What's happened?"

"I don't know... I—the Magelord has been taken down."

"Go. I'll be right behind you."

She nodded but yelled over her shoulder as she rode into the fray. "Shift, Dorin! You know there are more Wylfen on their way!"

But he couldn't. He could as easily become his people's greatest enemy as their savior.

A whirring sound drowned the clang of steel and disjointed shouting. A swirling mass of darkness, edged in leaves, cascaded down an escarpment toward Filip and Brielle. A figure in Wylfen colors rode on horseback behind the bizarre mass.

"D'Aboville!" Dorin ran faster, dodging frozen warriors and free ones too. The tip of a sword caught his wing, and he whirled to slice his blade through a Wylfen who had to be at least seven feet tall. The man went down all the same.

"Brielle! It's D'Aboville!"

The bright hue of her hair showed between moving groups of fighters. She remained firmly on her horse, now beside Maren and Rhianne, who had their wands out and were doing whatever magic they could to cut down Wylfen and tame the mind-altered wolves.

How was the Broyeur captain alive? From what Brielle had said and what little he remembered, the man had been stabbed in the heart. A fatal wound to anyone no matter what magical power they had up their sleeves. And D'Aboville had no magic. How was this possible?

Brielle's horse reared as the churning, dark cloud spun toward the remainder of the Balaur warriors. She bared her teeth as she rode toward D'Aboville, who was grinning like he'd fully lost his senses. Or like he knew something she didn't.

"It's the old Matchweaver!" Rhianne shouted over the din, her gaze locked onto the dark and spinning cloud, its ruffling willow leaves and spinning, snaking ivy. "I feel her magic!"

Dorin grabbed for a riderless horse. He had to get through this crowd and make it to Brielle's side, but the reins of the horse were slippery with blood, and the horse panicked and leaped away from his attempts to mount. Swearing, he pushed through the fighting, sweat salting his tongue and his muscles quaking. Magic sparked its way down his spine, and he pushed the dragon down, down, down. No. He couldn't use his power. Especially not in this chaos.

Talons sprouted from his fingers, and he shouted, shoving his magic into the depths of his soul, suppressing it. A sick feeling—similar to the sensation Magebane brought on—flooded him, and he bent double. Forcing himself to rise, he broke through the fighting.

D'Aboville raised a hand and pointed at Brielle, who was grasping for a knife and not finding one. She was unarmed.

"With my order, you will be mine to control," the captain said, his loud, grating voice speaking the Wylfen words like a spell.

What in the name of the gods did he think to do? He had no wand. He had no magic. The man was against all things magical. If he thought he could control or even point at Brielle, he was mistaken. The dragon inside Dorin roared, and Dorin echoed the sound, his vision shimmering into new and brighter focus.

"Abyss! Take her mind." D'Aboville's face lit up as the mass of leaves and cloud spun toward them.

Brielle threw a knife at D'Aboville. It hit his stomach, but he didn't flinch at the strike. He laughed, the sound echoing through the air unnaturally.

Magic surged through Dorin, and he erupted into the air, talons flashing long and deadly, wings beating the air, and dragonfire burning his throat. He flew at D'Aboville and knocked the man from his horse, then unleashed his fire in full.

Flames engulfed the place where D'Aboville had been. Dorin flew higher and halted his firestorm, and Brielle squinted, shaking. Had he done the wrong thing? Ridding her of that man?

A pile of ash lay on the scorched ground. Hair flickering around her like she too held the power of dragonfire, Brielle turned away from D'Aboville's remains. She looked to Dorin, her hands pressed over her heart and her eyes filled with gratitude.

In the air, vision clear and focused, Dorin whipped around and readied to destroy anyone who dared get close to her.

The churn of cloud and leaf wheeled over Brielle, and a laugh similar to the one that had echoed through D'Aboville filled the air, making everyone, including the Wylfen and their wolves, shrink from the noise.

Rhianne and Maren shot bolts of light and raucous

winds at the whirling black cloud, but nothing slowed its descent onto Brielle. Dorin flew into the cloud. He lost his vision as the foul magic gripped his wings and thrust him backward.

A scream issued from Brielle as Dorin hit the muddy ground. He rose up again, ready to fight.

CHAPTER 40
BRIELLE

Brielle shrieked, fear stripping her confidence as the winding darkness cloaked her view of the battlefield and Dorin. The crackle of dragonfire heated the air above Brielle's head, and screaming sounded outside the spinning mass. An invisible strength gripped her and she fell silent, immobile. The unseen hand of power lifted her from the horse, then squeezed her chest. The cloud whirred with a high-pitched sound like a slow shriek of pain. But no pain touched Brielle.

The memory of Mother's voice drifted through her mind. Her heart beat loudly in her ears, her blood surging as if in answer to a question she didn't realize she had asked.

Daughter. The voice in her ears was dark and horrible, straining and hissing. *Daughter of mine.*

Why was this foul being calling her daughter? The memory of Maren's story blinked through Brielle's mind, about how D'Aboville had tried to force Maren to use her magic against her parents, how a witch's power couldn't work against one's close kin. But this being wasn't Brielle's kin, of course. Unless...

Her mother's lullaby echoed in her thoughts, the lullaby Gytha had said was for adopted children...

The voice gasped then hissed, *Daughter of Raoul, the one I ensorcelled...*

Brielle's chest contracted. Cold sweat beaded across her back. Celeste's tale about Father's affair with a witch sliced through Brielle's thoughts. Of course. This foul, magical being was her blood mother.

Thunder hammered the air as the witch's power rebounded against Brielle's blood, the same blood that had once flowed through this foul being's corporeal form. Blinding white light streaked the dark green cloud. There was a flash, then there was nothing but willow and ivy leaves showering Brielle as she tumbled to the ground. The high-pitched whirring of the abyss faded, and the voice in her ears disappeared.

The dark magic was gone.

She blinked and there was Dorin, eyes slitted, tight with concern. His wings sheltered them, the wind buffeting their leathery surface. He helped her stand, his grip warm, strong—perfect. The magical creature that D'Aboville had called the Abyss, the witch that had borne Brielle, was no more.

The Balaur warriors faced Father's incoming army.

Thousands of Wylfen and their twisted scar wolves marched down the slopes, Father's white steed leading the charge. It was too far to know for sure, but Brielle could almost feel Father's gaze on her, cutting her with its hatred. A shiver shook her bones, but she kept staring at him.

"I will never again bow to you," she whispered, heart shaking. "I have no father."

Dorin held her tightly, his presence making her stronger.

Only fifty or so elves remained, scattered around Queen Sorina, who held her sword at the ready. The fae ladies encircled the inert form of Aurora while Filip, with his blood-painted hatchet in hand, stood watch. Werian and Rhianne held one another while Maren glared at the Wylfen army, her wand loosely gripped in one hand.

This was the end of them all.

Brielle's muscles uncoiled, and her mind shed every question about the dark magic. She took Dorin's face in her hands and pressed a kiss on his full lips, then another on the scales of his cheekbone. She met his ferocious gaze. "I love you."

He kissed her with tooth and tongue and fury.

When they broke apart, the Wylfen were nearly upon them.

Dark shapes filled the sky above King Raoul's warriors. She would never call him Father again.

"It's them! The riders from Khem!" Rhianne shouted, her face lighting and cheeks flushing.

"Dramatic timing. I approve," Werian said loudly.

Three great creatures with lion bodies and gray-feathered eagle heads ripped into the Wylfen army with their bright yellow beaks, then they veered through the sunlight lancing through the storm-cloud sky. Brielle couldn't help but hope, her mouth gaping open at the sight of the creatures. Rhianne's gryphon riders had arrived indeed; her amulet's magic had worked.

"Where are they going?" Maren shielded her eyes with a hand. "The battle's here! Don't take off now!"

The gryphons and their riders gathered above a glacier on one of the slopes above the approaching Wylfen. They began to strike at the ice.

They were trying to shake the glacier free, to cause an avalanche. "Go, Dorin!" Brielle shook his arm. "Use your fire! Bring that ice sheet down on them!"

He squeezed her hand, then took off into the sky like the most majestic being she'd ever seen. His wings blocked the sun for a moment, and then he was there with the gryphons.

With Hilda's and Filip's assistance, Aurora stood. Blood covered the right side of her face. Thank the goddess she wasn't dead!

The ground shook, and ice shunted across the rocks and wildflowers of the mountain. The Wylfen shouted in alarm, scrambling to escape the glacier's path. Standing in the center of the chaos, King Raoul turned his face toward Brielle. The ice was faster than any creature, and it shot into the army and covered them, Raoul too, until all was silent.

The gryphons and Dorin flew toward Brielle and the others as the Balaur warriors shouted, "Biruintă!" Victory!

A brief sensation of grief traveled through Brielle. The man who helped give her life was dead under that ice. It was good he was gone from this world, but she didn't feel as triumphant as she should have. She looked down at her hand. Her fingers faded from view, her body too. Panic hit her, but she reappeared, solid and normal again.

Dorin landed and held her. "It's your magic. You disappeared like that when you were first suffering from the burns I gave you. Pain, this time in the heart, brings your power to the surface. I'm so sorry for the loss of your father. I hope you won't hold it against me, against us."

He understood. He was right, and she felt it in her heart. Somehow, he knew. Everything had happened so quickly, but this was right, being here with him. She wiped unwanted tears off her cheeks, then let him hold her as her new family rejoiced, the Wylfen in her faded into memory, and the Balaur she had become rose to life.

CHAPTER 41
DORIN

One Month Later

"Not funny, Filip. Not at all funny." Dorin stormed through his chambers, soaking wet with no bath sheet on hand nor any clothing anywhere in his armoire. His attendants were also mysteriously missing. "Filip! It's nearly time!"

Filip burst through the chamber doors grinning with Drago, who was laughing so hard he could hardly walk.

"Oh, but it is funny, Your Highness," Drago choked out.

Tossing Dorin a sheet and a stack of underclothes, Filip flopped onto the bed. "We had to do something. It's tradition."

"Tradition to steal the groom's clothing?" Dorin dried himself quickly and threw on the underclothes.

"No, just to tease you until your left eyebrow begins twitching." Filip put a boot on the chest sitting at the end of Dorin's bed. It held every scroll and bit of parchment they had been able to find from the library about early dragons.

Costel hurried in and gave Dorin a bow. "Congratulations on your big day, Prince Dorin." Then his face screwed into a frown. "My prince," he said to Filip, "please get your boot off my perfectly organized collection of research."

Filip removed his foot from the chest. "Apologies, Costel. I hate when I upset you." He glanced at Dorin, mischief in his eyes.

"Under the warrior, you're still the same little arseling I chased about the market, aren't you?" Smiling, Dorin shook his head. "Where are my attendants? Tell me you didn't get them drunk with plans to have me style and shave my own hair. Brielle doesn't deserve a blood-spotted and wild-maned groom."

"I bet she'd like you that way." Drago grinned, and Dorin hit him in the stomach.

"Oh by the way," Costel started, "the gold you sent to the two farms who loaned you items during your adventures..."

"Yes?" Dorin eyed the knight.

"It's been delivered. But the lad on the second farm you listed requested a position in the army."

"Granted." Dorin studied his visage in the window glazing's reflection. He needed sleep, but mending eons of strife between two kingdoms was not a leisurely pursuit.

Stephan entered the room and Dorin's hands fisted.

The man had the decency to lower his gaze. Dorin hadn't spoken to him at the ball or even after. It wasn't that he hated Stephan, but he wasn't sure how to resume a friendship with someone who had tried to murder the love of his life.

Stephan went to his knees. "Prince Dorin, I beg forgiveness for turning my hand against your intended."

Dorin had never thought he'd see this man humble himself like this. Excuses, explanations—those he expected. The memory of Brielle's ceremony at the town of Stejari, of her sincere sadness at what had happened between their two peoples simmered in his mind.

Offering Stephan a hand up, Dorin clapped him on the shoulder. "This isn't a time for grudges. We are moving toward peace. I must believe that. I know for certain that Princess Brielle holds no ill will toward you. Not anymore. I took her to Stejari and...well, it moved her."

"I can imagine," Filip murmured.

"Tragedy," Costel said as Drago agreed.

Stephan's lips pulled in, and he nodded. "Thank you very much for your mercy, Fiel Stelelor. I will give up my life for her from this day forward unless my lord refuses my vow."

Filip held out his sigil ring, and Stephan kissed it. "I approve your vow, Stephan."

Heart swelling, Dorin said a silent prayer to Arcturus, Nix, and Vahly, to those benevolent spirits who had bolstered him in his time of need. *Please bless these warriors and steel their souls against pain in the future.*

Filip let the attendants in, and soon they were applying the dark cosmetics to Dorin's eyes, shaving the sides of his head, and dressing him for the ceremony. Drago and Stephan offered wine, and he took it with thanks.

Tonight, Brielle would be his in every way.

He swallowed down the rest of wine. "More."

"Not too much, Prince," Costel warned. "You must be able to perform your husbandly duties this evening."

"I wouldn't worry too much about our hero here," Werian said, knocking as he walked in as if that somehow gave him permission. "I saw the bride, and let's just say, there isn't enough wine in the world to douse a male's fully alert interest in that beauty."

Dorin fisted his hands in the furred cloak Costel tied around his neck. "I'll thank you to refrain from talking about my bride in that manner."

Dressed in a delicate style of finery that seemed out of place among mountain elves, Werian bowed in the fae style, all flourish and no gravitas. He'd painted gold runes on his horns. "I brought you a gift to make up for my presence and the ire I cause you so often, Prince of the Stars and Peaks."

The fae prince held out a box. Dorin flipped the lid open to see two golden rings etched with black phrases. He lifted the larger one carefully.

The etchings on one side read, *To the ends.* Dorin smiled at the traditional writing on the wedding ring. On the opposite side, he read, *To take your heart in your teeth.* It was an old saying, something Filip was known to use now and again.

"You think us brave?"

"Braver than any of us," Werian answered, his voice grave. The others murmured agreement. "She risks losing everything she has ever known by marrying you. You risk being gutted in your sleep by the enemy."

A dark laugh bubbled from Dorin's throat. "Thank you, Werian. They're lovely, well made."

"Fae blessed, too."

"You can do that?"

Werian shrugged. "It's debatable, but Hilda, Rhianne, and I endeavored to thread healing into the writing. Our hope is that when you wear the rings, you'll have a nice dose of energy."

Dorin grasped Werian's forearm and squeezed it. "Thank you, friend."

The fae's eyes widened for a second, then he gripped Dorin's arm in return. "You're welcome, friend."

Drago leaned in, wiping his eye. "That was beautiful."

Dorin and Werian both shoved him backward, and Filip and Stephan caught him, laughing.

CHAPTER 42
BRIELLE

"There was a very large part of me that hoped princessing was over when I took off into the mountains to chase a dragon elf." Brielle tucked away the letter from Celeste, an answer to the message she'd sent her old nurse as soon as the battle was won. Celeste was doing just fine, helping out at her sister's farm in the midlands of Wylfenden. Blowing out a breath, Brielle extended her arms as Eawynn and Gytha dressed her in gold-trimmed underclothes and an almost transparent shift that had a slit for each thigh to peek through.

Rhianne set a crown fashioned to look like golden branches and wildflowers into Brielle's loose braids. "Are you uncomfortable in this clothing? We can dress you in something else if you prefer."

"I don't mind showing some flesh for Dorin." Her cheeks went hot, and she chuckled at herself. "After all, it's tradition, right?"

Eawynn nodded. "The elves have their primal ways."

"Anyway, I was only pretending at being shy to hide my Broyeur brand." Brielle hated to bring it up, but they'd been so kind. They deserved another truth from her.

"Understandable." Gytha applied gold cosmetics to Brielle's eyelids, her touch quick and gentle.

Exhaling, Brielle adjusted the neckline of the shift. Thank the goddess they believed her. "I just look forward to days of exploring these mountains in trousers and boots," she said.

"I'm with you on the clothing choices." Rhianne took the cosmetics from Gytha and began drawing runes along Brielle's arms. A shiver—magic, she supposed—warmed her skin. "When Werian and I sail, I never dress as a fae princess. A gown on a ship is a nightmare."

"It is! What are you magicking into me right now?"

Rhianne chuckled. "Fertility runes." She wiggled her eyebrows. "Unless you'd rather me not? I can keep them from working."

A child? The thought turned her lips up at the edges. "I'm up for what fate holds."

Once Rhianne, Gytha, and Eawynn finished the runes and cosmetics, Brielle carefully hugged Rhianne. "Thank you for sticking around. Seeing a familiar face saved my sanity during my first days here."

"Of course. My pleasure." She secured a fox fur cloak onto Brielle's shoulders. "I still can hardly believe the old Matchweaver was your blood mother. Thank the Source you were raised by the Wylfen queen. She must have been a wonderful woman."

"I remember so little, but I think she was. I recall her

gentleness, but also her strength. She gave me throwing knives, so she had to be a tough one."

"Definitely," Rhianne said, laughing.

Gytha straightened Brielle's crown. "I wish we could have met her."

"I hate that Raoul must have broken her heart with his affair."

"I had no love for the man, apologies," Gytha said, "but the old Matchweaver certainly ensorcelled him into that act. Her true form was far from seductive."

The way the Abyss—the old Matchweaver—had spun into that cloud of magic and leaves, the way she'd spoken into Brielle's ear... Brielle shuddered. "It's better for the world that both of them are gone. My father and the old witch."

Rhianne hugged her again. "I mourn the childhood you didn't have. I lost my parents early too, so I comprehend at least a portion of what you experienced."

She and Rhianne had spoken about Rhianne's uncle and his neglect during Rhianne's younger years. Perhaps it truly was fate that had called Brielle to this place where people understood her challenges.

"If you keep Prince Dorin waiting much longer, he might burn this room down," Gytha said, swinging the chamber doors open to show the contingent of castle guards ready to escort them. Their livery was bright and fresh, newly tailored for the ceremony.

Brielle walked through the doors. Her heart was light, and her insides fluttered. "Time to marry a dragon."

. . .

THE WEDDING CHAMBER TURNED OUT TO BE THE PLACE where the elves held all their important ceremonies. It was not a joyous spot, but one with an alluring severity to it with its black walls and flickering oil lamps in the pattern of a constellation. Countless tall candles separated the clusters of nobles that lined the narrow room. They nodded as she passed. She kept her steps slow and reverent.

Beside a smiling Aurora and Filip, Brielle's brother, Etienne, lifted a hand in greeting, and her heart warmed. She grinned at him, the new king of Wylfenden. They'd had countless meetings about what the future held. Etienne had truly stepped up for this new role of his. His airy and hedonistic nature remained under the surface, sneaking out for a joke or two, or when he was ten minutes late for a meeting with Queen Sorina, King Mihai, and Dorin, but he was solidly decisive, logical when necessary. Wylfen and Balaur still had much to discuss, but the two kingdoms appeared to be on their way to a long-lasting peace.

Dorin stood inside a tight circle of standing stones. His eyes locked on her, and she stopped walking, her breath stuttering. Here was the one she adored above all others. His bravery on the battlefield had inspired her to keep fighting though she had been surrounded by trained warriors and magic-wielding foes. The way he'd slain D'Aboville for her, how his wings had shielded her when she'd fallen. He had the strength of spirit to stand firm when she pushed him, not backing away anymore or hiding his feelings and opinions. He had the humility and intelligence to admit when he was wrong. They would argue, yes. But their relationship was all the more powerful for it. They were both made of fire, in a way. Like calls to like, as Rhianne said.

It didn't hurt that he was a beautiful creature either. His bare chest and stomach were smooth but muscled from a life of war, training, and climbing these mountains. His golden hair shimmered in the candlelight and his kohl-ringed, light eyes lit her with want. His tongue touched his lower lip, and she swallowed. Soon that mouth would be on her.

She entered the stone circle and stood barefoot only inches from him. His thighs, clad in tight black leather, brushed hers, and his chest touched hers. The air between them seemed to sizzle, and Dorin spread both of his hands, holding them up. Brielle splayed her fingers and set her palms against his. Sparks danced across the places where their bodies met. A breath shuddered from Dorin's mouth. She loved her ability to affect this powerful dragon lord.

Dorin bent to take up a bowl and knife someone had set at the stone circle's boundary. He handed her the blade. The hilt was cold, and she prayed she wouldn't drop it as she set the sharp edge against his throat. Remembering her instructions, she nicked his skin until blood welled. He raised his chin a fraction, and his nostrils flared. The scent of his dragon magic swirled through the aroma of beeswax candles and leather. She ran her thumb through the blood and rubbed it onto the bottom of the crockery bowl. Then it was his turn to perform this wild part of the binding ceremony, what they called a wedding. It was far more sensual than any Wylfen wedding. Far less boring, that was certain. He cut her, but she hardly felt the sting even as he wiped her blood away and set it against his in the bowl.

Filip placed a branch on the circle's boundary. This had to be indigostar, the plant the elves could use for both destroying objects in a blast of fire and to relax a person in the way of some herbs. Dorin snapped the stem and poured the indigostar sap into the bowl. There was far more sap than she would've guessed, and it flowed easily, looking like thick water. She dipped her finger into the mix.

Suffering stones and fires of the underworld! She was supposed to use her thumb.

The side of Dorin's mouth lifted like he thought it was funny, so she simply touched her finger to her thumb, hoping that would serve tradition well enough. She drew a circle below his cloak's clasp, his bare skin moving beneath her thumb. A row of golden scales shone faintly near her markings, the glimmer beautiful against his smooth, elven skin. Warmth slid down her chest to her navel, then lower, and she fought to keep her breathing steady.

And now he was drawing the marriage symbols on her, every trail of his touch hot and tingling. His thumb traveled slow and sure across the base of her collarbone where her shift and cloak exposed her skin. When his gaze flicked to her eyes, a bolt of desire shot through her. When was this thing over? She was ready to move on. Now. She shook herself. This was important. Dorin was her mate for life, not simply for a roll in the hay. If her body would calm down a bit, she'd enjoy this moment.

Dorin almost chuckled, tucking his lips in tightly as he

handed Drago the bowl and knife. Etienne brought a drinking bowl filled with the ceremonial liquor.

The gathered nobles and knights spoke the joining words. "*Doi devin unul. Doua inimi. Un suflet.*" Two become one. Two hearts. One soul.

Dorin held the drinking bowl to her lips, his gaze lowered and piercing. The drink went down like a flame, and she loved every burning moment of it. She covered his hands with hers and tipped the bowl so he could drink too. The liquid made the room a little hazy. She was glad she'd only sipped once.

She blinked, and he was uncurling his palm to show their rings. He slid one onto her finger, and a rush of magic sizzled across her chest. She placed the other on his finger and watched him respond to the binding magic, his eyelids fluttering and his chest rising.

He held out a hand for her to leave the stone circle, and soon they were hand in hand, accepting wildflower posies from Aurora and Gytha as well as braids of brightly colored ribbons from all the children bumping their way through the crowd.

Dorin pulled her against his side and set his lips on her ear. "Are you hungry?"

"Not for food, my love."

He laughed quietly, then lifted her into his arms. She gasped as he broke through the wedding chaos and carried her quickly to his bedchamber.

"Out!" Dorin shouted to the attendants stoking the fire and pouring wine.

He threw Brielle onto the bed. The sheer, gray bed

hangings fluttered around her as the servants scurried away.

"And shut the door soundly!" he added, voice rough and eyes smoldering.

Wings tucked, he tore his cloak free and climbed slowly onto the bed, his gaze ravaging her face, chest, and bare legs. He lifted her hand and kissed his way from wrist to elbow, his mouth so light on her skin that he was hardly touching her. It was a sublime torture.

"What would you have me do, my ruby, my rose, my light?" His wings spread wide, blocking the moonlight from the window and the flicker of the fire.

She kissed him, tasting the strong ceremony drink on his lips and tongue and delighting in the feel of his hand grasping the back of her neck like she was a wild horse he had to gentle. He returned the kiss with blazing heat, his touch no longer sweet and slow but untethered and dangerous. His eyes flashed with bright color and went slitted, the dragon he was taking hold.

"Are you afraid?" he asked, his voice soft and tentative.

"My answer hasn't changed. Never. You are my protector, not my predator. Besides, a little danger only makes it all the better." She shoved him onto his back and straddled him, the slits in her shift tearing, lengthening. Of course, with his strength, she knew well he'd allowed her to push him about, but that only had her smiling. His wings spread out beneath him, the ends tipped in sharp claws. "That doesn't hurt, does it?" She didn't want to crush his wings.

His hands went to her waist, his fingers warm and his thumbs sketching circles over the fabric of her shift, which sent chills down her back. "In all the proper ways, my ruby," he purred.

Trembling and blazing with heat, she drew the slip of a dress over her head and flung it onto the floor. He moved under her, and her mouth went dry.

"I've waited a long time for this." She ran her fingers down his chest and stomach. His skin was like velvet and so very warm.

"You think I haven't been pining away for you?" His hips lurched upward.

She bit her lip and fell onto his chest. Her arms wrapped around his neck, pulling his face to her chest. He nipped her collarbone. He was shaking all over.

"I love that I can bring a dragon lord to his knees."

"Is that what you want?" In a graceful flurry of movement, he had her at the end of the bed. He was on his knees at her feet, his belt loose and trousers slipping beneath his hipbones. He kissed the arch of her foot, and desire tingled up her leg and thigh.

Laughing, she fell back as he crawled over her, dragging his lips over her calf, then her hip, then stomach, where he whispered in her native language, in Wylfen, his rough accent clipping his words and curling her toes.

"You are my only desire, Brielle. I would tear the world apart if you asked it."

He was on her now, his weight supported on his elbows and his wings above them. She melted into a blissful state she had never known was possible as he kissed her achingly slowly. She put her hands in his hair and lifted herself to press against him, wanting more of everything about him—his rumbling voice against her neck, his intoxicating scent, his strong arms shielding her from the world...

They moved together, her heart bursting with joy at their union. The night would never last long enough to suit her. Their kingdoms still had much work to do, but this bond would see them through anything.

Fabulous Reader,

Thank you so much for reading about Brielle and Dorin! I hope you enjoyed their story as much as I loved writing it. I wish we could all spend a day digging up dragon artifacts and then dance at a midnight ball. Le sigh. Please consider writing a review for ETDL if you loved it!

Next up in the Kingdoms of Lore world is a story about the King of Shadows and Maren, the witch Brielle saved from her father. This next story takes place in the underworld and will be a bit of a medieval Pride and Prejudice/Hades and Persephone mashup. It will be a book one in a new series.

When I taught fourth grade (years ago), I had my class perform a Hades and Persephone play to learn their state standards in a fun way. It's still one of my fondest memories, and the girl who played the lead role went on to act in her adulthood. I am so proud. Though my book won't be a retelling—not even a little bit—it will harken back to the elements that drew me to that myth in the first place. As for Pride and Prejudice, well, that is just my all time favorite romance.

Anyway, I hope you'll buy STOLEN BY THE KING OF SHADOWS (early 2022) and help me get this book in the hands of fantasy romance readers everywhere!

Thank you!

Alisha

P.S. *I will be returning to the regular Kingdoms of Lore series next year with a book four (release probably spring of 2022) which will most likely feature Zahra of Khem and her male siren (the one they saw in book two). Sign up for my newsletter at https://www. alishaklapheke.com/free-prequel-1 to see the covers of the next books first, for updates, and for exclusive, behind-the-scenes freebies!*